Praise for The De

All Scot an

"Hot romance and tantalizing intrigue . . . Readers will be delighted."
—*Publishers Weekly* (starred review)

"Will ensnare readers with its soul-searing, richly sensual love story, expertly spiced with just the right dash of dry wit and generous measure of thrilling danger."
—*Booklist* (starred review)

"Byrne crafts a smoldering romance that combines an enticing, well-matched couple with an original storyline about the underbelly of Victorian society that keeps the readers guessing."
—*Library Journal*

How to Love a Duke in Ten Days

"Tantalizes readers with the couple's teasing and building passion."
—*Publishers Weekly*

"An un-put-down-able story that combines sensuality, tenderness . . . and memorable characters."
—*Kirkus Reviews*

"In this brilliantly conceived start to her captivating new series, Byrne once again delivers the beautifully nuanced characters and seductive storytelling her readers have come to expect, while at the same time deftly conjuring up the spirit of Victoria Holt's classic gothic romances."
—*Booklist*

"An amazing story of how two broken people find a way to heal each other . . . A beautifully written historical romance that was impossible to put down."
—*Affaire de Coeur* on *How to Love a Duke in Ten Days*

. . . and her Victorian Rebels series

"Byrne's writing comes to vivid life on the page."

—*Entertainment Weekly* on *The Duke with the Dragon Tattoo*

"Another winner in a stellar series."

—*Library Journal* (starred review) on *The Duke with the Dragon Tattoo*

"The dark, violent side of the Victorian era blazes to life . . . in this exceptional and compelling, vengeance-driven romantic adventure."

—*Library Journal* (starred review) on *The Highwayman*

"The romance is raw, edgy, and explosive. . . . The path they take through adversity makes the triumph of love deeply satisfying."

—*Publishers Weekly* on *The Highwayman*

"A truly mesmerizing series that highlights dangerous heroes who flout the law and the women who love them."

—*Library Journal* (starred review) on *The Hunter*

"Romantic, lush, and suspenseful."

—Suzanne Enoch, *New York Times* bestselling author

"A passionate, lyrical romance that takes your breath away."

—Elizabeth Boyle, *New York Times* bestselling author

"Beautifully written, intensely suspenseful, and deliciously sensual."

—Amelia Grey, *New York Times* bestselling author

Also by
Kerrigan Byrne

The Highwayman
The Hunter
The Highlander
The Duke
The Scot Beds His Wife
The Duke with the Dragon Tattoo
How to Love a Duke in Ten Days
All Scot and Bothered

The Devil in Her Bed

KERRIGAN BYRNE

St. Martin's Paperbacks

First published in the United States by St. Martin's Paperbacks, an imprint of St. Martin's Publishing Group

THE DEVIL IN HER BED

For information, address St. Martin's Publishing Group, 120 Broadway, New York, NY 10271.

www.stmartins.com

ISBN: 978-1-250-31888-6

Our books may be purchased in bulk for promotional, educational, or business use. Please contact your local bookseller or the Macmillan Corporate and Premium Sales Department at 1-800-221-7945, ext. 5442, or by email at MacmillanSpecialMarkets@macmillan.com.

Printed in the United States of America

St. Martin's Paperbacks edition 2021

10 9 8 7 6 5 4 3 2 1

Chapter One

Mont Claire Estate, Hampshire, 1872

Pippa Hargrave was about to have her heart broken.

When she heard the Cavendish twins were turned out of the schoolroom so early on this particular afternoon, she tore through the Mont Claire estate knowing they'd spill out onto the lawn and head for their hedge maze.

Her father, Charles Hargrave, looked up from the counter where he stood and snacked on a repast of cold chicken and greens as she burst through the door to the kitchens.

"What ho, little'un?" His eyes wrinkled kindly at the edges, and he hinged at the hip to tweak her fondly on her nose with a gloved finger. "Where are you off to in such a hurry?"

An elegant Romani woman stood by her mother, Hattie, and added a few more herbs to the pot. "You were in a rush to come into this world, Pip." Serana warmly used the household's nickname for her, and it sounded strange in what Hattie said was her Carpathian accent. "It is no surprise you want to hasten your way through it."

Pippa had been told that she owed her very existence to Serana, as her mama and papa had endeavored to conceive a child for decades to no avail. Serana had given Hattie a tonic, and she'd become pregnant with Pippa right away.

Pippa's father, the butler of the Mont Claire estate and already eleven years Hattie's senior, was the age of most children's grandfathers. He treated his daughter with a kind of mystified but devoted indulgence.

"I'm going to find Declan Chandler." Pippa squirmed to get outside.

"I think I saw him cleaning out the fountain as I came in," Serana supplied helpfully with a little wink.

"Oh no, I must go help him," Pip lamented dramatically. "He hates cleaning the fountain, it terrifies him. Though he's too brave to say so." She sighed for his courage, closing her eyes to properly give it the knightly due it deserved.

"My daughter's besotted." Hattie palmed Pippa's cheek with a warm hand before passing an implement to Serana.

Pippa wrinkled her nose. *Be-what?*

"That Declan Chandler has the soul of a tiger," Serana said. "And you, Pip, have that of a dragon."

"Dragons aren't real," Pippa informed her with a giggle.

"Aren't they?" Serana asked, winking cheerfully. "I've been many places where they would disagree with you."

"Do you have any peppermints in your pockets?" Pippa turned to her father, already searching his coat. Peppermints were Declan's favorite. She always found him pale after dredging the fountain, and a bit irate. Peppermints cheered him up and made him smile the smile that produced scores of rampant butterflies in her belly.

"Gads, I must do somewhere." Charles slapped every pocket he could find more than once before producing a handful of treats for the children.

Pippa seized them, divvying them up. One each for Ferdinand, Francesca, and herself. She saved the remaining two for Declan. He deserved extra.

She kissed her father's smooth cheek and leapt toward the door. Sprinting down the stretch of lawn lined with resplendent arborvitae, she ate up the distance between her and the boy who owned her heart.

Declan Chandler had once been short, like her, and devastatingly underweight when he'd landed on the steps of Mont Claire some years ago. He'd been grimy and freezing, starving half to death.

But his frame had stretched out over a long, thickening skeleton, and even though he ate enough to feed a horse, he remained curiously lean.

Lately, instead of focusing on the primers Francesca allowed her to study on her own, Pippa would make up ridiculous fancies about Declan Chandler. Today, for example, she spent a good deal of the early afternoon chomping on her pencil, leaving crunchy indentations as she pondered the perfection of the word *thunderstruck*.

After all this time wondering how to properly

encompass the effect the houseboy had on her, Pippa could finally claim a description.

Once she'd scampered past the stately gardens dripping with an embarrassment of blossoms, she ran through the hedge maze she'd memorized with the loping speed of a fleet-footed bunny.

She broke into the clearing bedecked by the fountain just in time for her heart to break.

Declan stood to his knees in the fountain while droplets from the spray gathered on his skin and sluiced down the indentations of lean muscle that had never been there until recently.

He was like the progeny of the powerful-bodied ancient gods cast from marble behind him.

And Francesca Cavendish was slipping a peppermint past his lips.

The smile he bestowed upon her—the smile that *should* have been Pippa's—nearly outshone the noonday sun. He said something Pippa could not hear and tucked a shining wisp of scarlet hair behind the lovely Francesca's ear before placing a kiss on her knuckles with a deference that went beyond her station as the young mistress of the house. A reverence that was no longer innocent . . .

But interested.

The fountain still spewed water out of the horns of satyrs and the mouths and baskets of various gods and goddesses. The spray refracted the sun into delicate rainbows and glittering gems in the air around them.

Pippa's heart squeezed so hard she didn't think it beat for a full minute. Her hands were cold and wet. Her throat dry and her stomach full of lead. At thirteen, Declan was the epitome of beauty to Pippa. Now she looked at Francesca to see in her friend what Declan might. A slight and perfect nose and heart-shaped features. Slim, even for a girl on the cusp of womanhood, and more elegant than a child ought to be. Vibrant red hair and shy eyes the color of the sea on an overcast day. Perhaps blue or green, but mostly grey.

Pippa had dull fairish locks and retained a face round with youth and a penchant for seconds at dinner. Her beauty, her mother said, was in her rare green eyes. Eyes that now stung and a throat that ached with such fervent pain she couldn't swallow, let alone breathe.

Did Declan—*her* Declan—fancy Francesca Cavendish, her best friend in the world?

Could the fates be so entirely cruel? Was there anything worse than this searing pain?

No, she realized. No, there was no agony more excruciating than this.

How could he not know she was his perfect match?

Francesca wouldn't dip her dainty shoes into the fountain, but Pippa had often waded in beside him, plunging her elbows deep in the muck if only to make his work go faster so they could play. When the water seemed to churn with his melancholy, they'd toss soggy clumps of moss at each other, giggling and squealing with a side-splitting mirth until her jaw ached from constant smiles and so much brilliant love.

Francesca wouldn't deign to dirty her frocks. She couldn't; she was going to be a lady someday.

Pippa had no need to be a lady. She would be a *woman*. Declan's woman. She'd decided that long ago.

Regardless of what her parents said, no one could love someone this deeply unrequited.

The gods of the fountain wouldn't allow it.

And yet, there they were . . . Declan and Francesca, with eyes for no one but each other.

"There are men on horseback coming up the way," Ferdinand, Francesca's twin, called down from his perch in the ancient ash tree on the other side of the maze.

Mama had told her once, Ferdinand had been born without enough breath, and he struggled with something called asthma. It was why the veins beneath his skin were so iridescent, and his lips often tinged with blue.

Despite that, he was a striking boy, and since she'd never had a brother, Ferdinand was one of her very favorite people with whom to have an adventure. He'd told her once he'd make her a countess when he was old enough.

She hoped that didn't mean marriage.

She would marry Declan Chandler, of course, she knew this with her entire heart. She'd be Mrs. Chandler. Indeed, she'd already perfected her signature.

"Are we expecting callers?" Francesca asked.

"There are entirely too many men for callers." Ferdinand curled his fingers to resemble a spyglass, and put it to his eye. "Maybe twenty."

"It's unseemly to show up with twenty people and not send a note." Francesca's mouth drooped into a pretty pout. "Mrs. Hargrave won't know to make that many sandwiches at this hour."

Pippa looked from Francesca to Declan, noting the

troubled thoughts wrinkling his smooth, angular good looks. "Perhaps you and Pip should go inform Mr. and Mrs. Hargrave," he said, helping Francesca from the ledge. "They'll know what to do."

"I'll go and meet the riders," Ferdinand declared, having climbed down from his spot and set off out the opposite side of the maze.

"My lord, you really shouldn't." Declan released Francesca and winked at Pippa before trotting after the future Earl of Mont Claire. "Not until we know who they are."

Despite her pain, Pippa locked hands with her friend and skipped toward the estate. Francesca really was such a dear. So sweet and agreeable. Proper and ladylike. All the things Pippa was not.

All the things she'd try to be for Declan if that's what he wanted.

They jogged for several minutes of silence before Pippa couldn't keep herself from asking, "Do you fancy Mr. Chandler?"

"What?" Francesca laughed, a merry sound that bubbled into the spring air.

"He loves you, I think," Pippa grumped.

"I fancy him a little. He's rather handsome, isn't he?" Francesca squeezed her hand. "But never you worry, I'd not bother with him in a hundred years."

Suddenly Pippa felt a ridiculous spurt of protectiveness for him. "And whyever not? He's more than good enough."

Francesca tugged her to slow down and turned to her, so they were facing each other. "Because I love *you*, Pip, and I'd never betray you."

Pippa surged forward and enfolded the girl in her arms. "I love you, too," she said upon a sigh of relief.

"Besides, Father would never allow me to marry below a viscount," Francesca bemoaned. George Cavendish, the Earl of Mont Claire, was nothing if not a snob.

Pippa looked over Francesca's shoulder. She could see the men in the distance now from her vantage on the open lawn, which gently sloped upward toward the manor house. They rode low over the necks of their horses as they galloped closer, all dressed in dark colors, their faces indistinguishable.

Or covered?

Ferdinand had almost reached them, his arms waving an energetic greeting. He stopped some yards away to cough, apparently deciding he'd exerted himself enough for a throng of men who would eventually be upon him.

The riders didn't slow as they approached. The merciless, pounding hooves churned up clumps of earth and tossed them in their wake.

No. Surely they weren't . . . she was seeing things . . .

Dumbfounded, she waited for the riders to stop.

Why weren't they stopping? Ferdinand was right there. He was *right in front of them.*

With a scream, she turned around, closing her eyes against what she'd already witnessed.

They killed him! Some of her numb disbelief surged into paralyzing terror. They'd killed him, *and they didn't slow down.*

Which meant the men were coming for them next.

"Run," Pippa breathed, clutching Francesca's hand and bolting for the house. "Don't look back." She didn't want her friend to see the nightmare of her twin's mangled body.

It was an anguish Pippa would never forget.

They streaked across the grass toward the kitchen entrance and dove inside just as the marauders broke into four clusters of masked nightmares to encircle the manor.

"Ferdinand!" Pippa screamed as her mother gathered her and Francesca up into her arms. "They . . . they . . . the horses!" Her throat closed over, sobs threatening to choke the life out of her. It was unthinkable. Unspeakable. What was happening? Who would do something so monstrous?

"Take a breath and tell me what's done," Hattie soothed. "Serana's gone outside, and your father went to see what this is about. He took all the footmen and—"

The door to the kitchen crashed open, the glass of the window breaking against the wall as huge, sinister men swarmed inside.

"No one here but women and children," a dark-clad monster with a red bandanna over his face reported in a Cockney accent.

A thicker man in a distinctly American hat seemed to be in charge.

"They said no witnesses." He kicked a table out of the way to get to them as he pulled a knife larger than any in their butcher block from his belt.

Hattie thrust the two girls behind her, snatching her cleaver from the counter. "You leave these little'uns alone." She brandished the blade at them, wagging it as she would a scolding finger. "We didn't see a thing. We can leave quietly, and you'll never hear from us again. Just don't hurt the girls."

"Problem is," the American drawled from behind his linen mask, "we can't leave that there girl alive." He pointed his blade at Francesca, who whimpered before her terror piddled down her leg and spread beneath both of their shoes.

With a burst of strength, Hattie thrust Francesca and Pippa backward through the door to the servants' hall. "Whatever you do, just live. Live! Get out of this house." She slammed the door and locked it behind them.

Pippa didn't just run from the men this time, she ran from the primal sounds her mother made as she fought for their lives, and the screams that pealed from her as she failed.

Tears blurred the lines of the servants' stairs, causing Pippa to trip as she scrambled upward. A door on the main floor led to a small cellarlike room where a furnace warmed the house. Declan had showed her a coal depository that led outside, which would possibly be unguarded. If they could make it there, they might be able to attempt the short dash to the forest undetected.

She could lose them in the forest. The children of Mont Claire spent their entire childhood slithering through warrens, exploring primordial root systems, or climbing trees on imaginary adventures.

Pippa breached the main floor to the sound of violence and chaos. Even though their hands were slippery with sweat, she and Francesca kept a tight, painful grip on each other as they ran.

Her mother's words became a mantra, a throb in her head, an agony in her heart, and the strength in her legs.

Live. Live. Get out of this house. Live. Live. Get out of this house.

The force with which Francesca was ripped from Pippa's grasp nearly pulled her off her own feet. She whirled around to see the American with the white cowboy hat put a knife to her best friend's neck.

Francesca Cavendish, her grey eyes wide with terror, was the last person alive to say Pippa's name . . .

And her last word before the blade moved was an admonishment to run.

An irritating siren pierced the air at a terrible pitch, ceaseless and grating. It drowned out the sounds of fear and death filtering to Pippa through the tremendous halls of Mont Claire.

Could no one stop these men? Would they simply swarm the manor like an army of ants, and dismantle every living thing inside?

Pippa had to escape it. It would deafen her, surely. Turning on her heel, she fled down the hall, but was intersected by another masked man before she could reach the furnace room.

"Grab the little bitch!" the American ordered.

Pippa leapt to the side, scrambling down a narrow service corridor that dumped her into a main marbled hallway.

The siren scream haunted her as she sped down halls, blindly crashed through doors, and leapt around and over the bodies of those she'd known her entire life. She was grateful for her tears. For the way they softened and blurred the sights of gore, blood, and the dead-eyed features of her beloved. She left a trail of her tears as she ran.

A man seized her braid and yanked with such force, she lost her balance.

It wasn't the American, but a smaller foe with a blade no less fearsome. He lifted it over his head, his intention unmistakable as it arced toward her chest.

A battle cry cracked on a high note as Declan Chandler leapt from the study and drove a fire poker into the man's head. He didn't stop swinging, even after the man crashed to the ground like a felled tree. Declan's movements remained tight and frenzied, his eyes black with a rage Pippa didn't understand. After the fifth blow, Declan tossed the instrument at the man's misshapen skull and seized Pippa.

The wail that had been aggravating her miraculously ceased when he clamped a hand over her mouth. Yanking her forward, Declan half dragged, half carried her through the study and into the Mont Claire library, a two-story phenomenon with more books than could be counted.

Before she could struggle or stop crying long enough to ask what he was doing, Declan took them to the fireplace, which was large enough to have housed a small tenant family.

Declan held a rough finger to his smooth lips. "If you're not quiet, they'll kill us both, do you understand?"

Upon her nod, he took his hand off her mouth. Turning to her, he seized both her wrists, then stared down in horror at the drops and smears of blood marring her flesh and white sleeves.

"Pip, are you hurt?"

She shook her head, unable to form words for the horror of it.

"What is this?" he demanded. "Whose blood?"

Francesca's blood.

"Not mine," was all she could say.

Loud boots and bloodthirsty calls filtered down the grand marble halls as a cadre of men threatened to discover them.

"Here," he whispered, and shoved her up the chimney before following her.

Soot and grime coated them both as they shimmied up the wide, cylindrical flue, their bodies wedged so tightly, Pippa worried that they wouldn't be able to get out again. Rough walls abraded her arms and back, and tore at the coarse wool of her dress and stockings.

Declan braced his legs beneath her so she'd have something of a perch and used his long arm to stabilize them, wrapping the other around her.

Pippa's chest burned from exertion, and ached with a well of grief so intense, she worried it would crush her lungs. She could see nothing in the dark of the chimney. She could only feel.

And hear.

The timbre of masculine voices changed from excited to outraged when they came upon the dead body in the hall. Their angry, clipped conversations ebbed and waned as they searched the study and the library for the culprit.

As they neared the fireplace, terror weakened Pippa's limbs.

Seeming to intuit this, Declan pulled her close,

settling her ear against the bones of his ribs. He trembled, as well, whether with fear or the exertion of keeping them aloft, Pippa couldn't tell.

His heart became a staccato metronome against her ear, driving all other thoughts and sounds away. She held her breath when Declan did.

And shut out every sound in the world but the thrumming beneath her ear.

If she'd lost everything, she had this. This boy. This heartbeat of time. She'd always known he was possessed of the strength and goodness of a mythical hero.

Now everyone else would know it, too.

Because he'd saved her.

Pippa didn't know how long they stayed like that. Perhaps minutes, perhaps hours. But when all fell eerily silent and the men moved on, Declan lowered his mouth to her ear.

"Ferdinand . . ." he said, his voice breaking with sorrow. "Did you see them? Did you see what they did?"

Pippa nodded, wishing she didn't still see the tiny body bouncing and contorting in the darkness of her mind's eye.

"What about Francesca, did she . . . did she make it?"

Despair choked off her breath once more, and Pippa swallowed several ragged sobs before deciding she was unable to answer.

She didn't have to. The tension in his trembling muscles and the hitches in his breath as he fought his own sobs told her Declan understood.

"Where . . . where is my papa?" Somehow, Pippa knew her hope was ridiculous. Because her father never would have left them behind. Even to save his own life.

Declan didn't answer for a long moment, and when he finally did, his voice was husky with shadows and pain. "Your father . . . they . . . they stabbed him first. It was quick. I-I'm sorry. He sent me to find you."

A sharp blade of grief slid through her ribs and into her heart, this one finding purchase next to where her mother's wound belonged.

"Am I an orphan now?" she whispered as her tears trickled from her chin and onto the still-bare skin of his abdomen.

"Yes."

"How do you bear it?"

His arm tightened around her, and his face pressed into her hair. "I can't tell you that. It was different for me."

"How?"

"Because—because I didn't lose good parents, Pip . . . not like yours."

She lifted her head, swiping at her tears with the back of her hand. "I never thought your parents were good."

His features shifted as he peered down at her. "I've never said a word about them."

"But you were already sad when you came here. A kind of sad that isn't gone . . . and now it might never be."

His eyes fluttered closed as a gathering of tears dispersed beneath the fan of his dark lashes. "Pip . . . this kind of sad will never go away. But—" He stopped. Stiffened. Tested the air with sharp inhales. "Do you smell that?"

She gave the air a delicate whiff. Something was burning.

They both looked down to the dry fireplace beneath them. Little tendrils of smoke curled into the shafts of light.

"Bloody hell," he cursed. "They've set fire to the manor."

"What?" she cried. "Why?"

"To cover their crimes, I suspect. To burn the bodies." He nudged her back. "Can you climb down on your own, Pip? We have to get out of here."

Seized by anxiety now that he was pulling away, she clung to him with desperate arms. "Don't leave me," she cried. Could they not stay here in the stillness forever? Could she not simply listen to his heartbeat until the rhythm drowned out her loss? "Why did this happen?" she whimpered.

"I don't know, Pip," he said gently. "I just know we have to get out of here. Now. Come with me. And whatever happens, just don't let go, all right?"

"I won't," she vowed. "Not ever."

She clutched at him as he led them through rooms with treasures she'd coveted and memories she'd stored away as they filled with smoke that seemed to billow in from every direction. He led her down the back hall toward the furnace room, the choking air forcing them lower and lower.

Francesca's little body had disappeared from the hall, but Pippa fell to her knees atop the bloodstains, no longer able to contain her sobs.

"Come on, Pip." Declan seized her. "I know. I know, but we must go. There will be time for that later. A lifetime for that."

Pippa allowed him to drag her up, and she stumbled

after him. They navigated the furnace room, muting their racking coughs with cloths Pippa snatched from a shelf. She bounced from foot to foot as Declan scrambled through the coal door, checked to see that the coast was clear, and then reached back in to pull her out.

The smoke was a blessing in that it shielded them from view as they raced for the forest.

At least she thought it had, until a shout of their discovery sounded the alarm.

Declan used a string of curses Pippa was yet unfamiliar with as he yanked her into the tree line as the first shot rang out, showering them with chunks of bark.

She ran with all her strength. Her lungs burned and her legs felt as though they would tear open, but still she ran.

Another shot scattered the birds and creatures of the Mont Claire woods. A burning sting buckled her leg and she crashed down hard enough to scrape both her knees and the palms of her hands.

She didn't even have the breath left to cry out.

Declan dropped beside her, calling her name.

"My leg," she wheezed.

He checked frantically and she was comforted by his breath of relief. "Pip, it's a graze," he reassured her. "Can you walk?"

Pippa nodded, swiping at the tears burning hot tracks of pain down her cheeks. If he could be brave, she would be valiant.

Her calf buckled as soon as she put her weight on it, and she dropped with a devastating moan of pain.

Declan glanced around, his eyes going wide and wild as he heard the men crashing through the underbrush.

"Here." He dragged her down a ravine and stashed her beneath the roots of one of her favorite trees, covering the system with fallen branches and other detritus. "You put this leaf on your leg and press down so it doesn't bleed too much."

"Come in with me." Pippa scooted over, making room for him.

"No." He shook his head, perking to a distressingly close sound. "You stay here. I'll lead them away."

"You can't!" She reached for him. "They'll find you!"

He leaned down very close, thrusting her deeper beneath the tree, his eyes more serious and frightening than any she'd ever seen. "You'll be safe here. And I always survive best if I'm alone. Just trust me."

She'd never trusted anyone more.

She kissed him then, full on the mouth. A desperate mashing of lips salted with tears and ash.

"I love you," she said fiercely.

He blinked several times and opened his mouth before a crash to their right stole his attention.

And he was gone.

Footsteps followed too closely on his heels, and Pippa shrank into the depths of the tree, both hands clasped over her mouth.

Several gunshots caused her to jump in the dark, then a victorious shout rang through the forest. The American calling for his comrades.

Several times, Pippa thought about going out there to throw herself over his body, but her pain and terror paralyzed her to the ground, so she simply curled up in the root of the tree and silently sobbed.

Eventually a rustle of branches revealed a dark and beloved face.

Serana.

With a soul-ragged sound, Pippa surged into her arms, burying her face against the wiry Romani woman as her anguish overcame her.

"I know." Serana smoothed a hand over her hair. "We must flee. Now."

"But Declan!" she wailed.

"Darling, they ran him down. They . . . shot him in the back." Serana's brown eyes shone soft in the muted light the flames reflected onto the overcast sky.

Devastated, Pippa allowed herself to be carried by the woman to a nearby horse. Her lungs ached and her leg throbbed, but the pain was nothing compared with the pain in her soul.

She sat limply where the strong woman had settled her on the horse before joining her there, riding with a leg over each flank, like a man.

They stood on the restless beast and briefly watched the flames breach the night through the cracks in the boughs as her childhood was reduced to ashes. Everyone she knew and loved was in that house. She thought of them all burning, of the various beasts her mother had roasted and what happened to the meat when the flames would lick at it. Of the sizzle of the juices and the curling of the skin.

She wanted to be sick.

"Why?" she whispered once again through a fog of pain and rage. "Why did I live and no one else?"

Serana's hold tightened. "Perhaps you did not." A soft wind picked through the trees as gently as a tentative doe before picking up speed. The air smelled of decisions and destiny.

"Perhaps . . . Pippa Hargrave perished with her parents in the flames, and only Francesca survived. The heir to the Cavendish title and fortune. The one who can escape this tragedy with enough fortune to do something about it."

Pippa strained to turn and look at Serana, wondering if she'd heard the woman correctly. "I am nothing like Francesca. She was . . . delicate."

"*Delicate* is another word for 'fragile.' *You* are not weak. I knew from the moment I brought you into this world that, like the dragon, you would have fire nourishing your heart. I simply didn't see that the fire would be ignited here, with such tragedy." A strange light flashed from Serana's eyes as she looked down at Pippa, flames licking at the depths of her pupils. "You lived because the dark deeds of this night needed a witness. Because your destiny is to bring justice to your fallen loved ones."

"But . . . I'm just a girl."

Serana's sigh contained all the yawning sadness of several lifetimes lived in only a handful of decades. "You are no longer just a girl, I think. And if you decide, I will find those who will teach you to become a woman who can reap justice."

"I don't know what *justice* means," Pippa whispered through her tears.

"What about *revenge*, do you understand the meaning of that?"

Pippa thought about the word. *Revenge.* It thundered through her with a new meaning, igniting in her breast a spark that was fanned into an inferno by loss and grief and pain.

Vengeance. It meant every person responsible for tonight would burn.

She'd save the worst of her wrath for whomever had taken Declan Chandler from her.

CHAPTER TWO

London, 1892; Twenty Years Later

Lady Francesca Cavendish glared at the naked man draped across the bed with disgust.

She would never live down *this* tryst. The ton would be in an uproar. *Why would a woman as young, rich, and titled as she, bother with a creature as old and odious as Lord Colfax?* they would ask. *Can she really be so craven?*

Was she being too obvious? Would her enemies guess what she was about?

Frowning, Francesca rolled her eyes and pulled a few more pins from her hair as she assessed her appearance in the gilded mirror of Lord Colfax's bedchamber.

She just might look like a loose-moraled spinster who'd enjoyed a rollicking night of unbridled sex. Not, however, the kind of night other unfortunate women had reported to have had with Lord Colfax.

He was a famously passionate rake. A ruiner of clothing and reputations. A user of women and worse.

A man who deserved what he was about to get.

Pursing her lips, she let out a breath of exasperation. What could she change about her appearance to make the ruse more believable? Her gold bodice drooped in tatters, the lace mangled and torn. Her skirt was a puddle of silk on the carpets, and one of the ribbons on her garters had disappeared. Her scarlet coiffeur hung limply to the left, half the pins scattered or missing. She'd never really been able to hold a curl, so her locks appeared more garbled than tousled.

Still . . . it didn't look right. *She* didn't look right.

Puffing a bit of fringe away from her forehead, she shrugged a slim, pale shoulder. Old Colfax likely wouldn't notice. Men were so extraordinarily oblivious. They'd believe just about any sort of hogwash if it fed their largely undeserved egos.

And yet . . . how could they not suspect her deception?

A woman's skin glowed with dewy luminescence if she'd been well and truly ridden. Her eyes would laze at only half-mast, glistening with a dreamy satisfaction. Her lips were often swollen and the skin about her mouth a little pinkened as though scrubbed with something abrasive. Like a man's stubble or beard.

Sometimes those marks were elsewhere. Her neck, her clavicles.

Lower.

Francesca did her best to soften the gem-hard green of her eyes, to blink them with a slothful sort of decadence. There, that almost seemed like—

A loud snore shook the crystals twinkling from the wall sconces next to the stately bed.

She whirled, studying her so-called lover for signs of consciousness. Her heart gave a few kicks, threatening not to remain as steady as she'd trained it to be.

Lord Colfax was larger than most of the men with whom she played this sort of sport. Not tall, exactly. But wide and sturdy, strong despite his aging status. Not many men retained such strength into their fifties, but then again, he was part of a powerful and corrupt society.

One with many enemies.

It wouldn't do to be seen as weak.

His mouth dropped open to reveal revolting, uneven teeth stained by every imaginable sort of vice. Francesca swallowed her revulsion and crept back toward the bed.

Her reflection would never truly seem right. No matter how much she scrubbed at her skin and bit at her lips. She never quite adopted that appearance of pleasure. She'd never *been* pleasured. Pleasure wasn't something she had the time or inclination for, all told.

She supposed, in Lord Colfax's case, she didn't have to exactly seem as though he'd done well. Because men such as he only ever thought of their own pleasure.

She had to convince him that their night was one of sexual abandon he was too drunk to remember.

Her concoction of belladonna, senna, and a few other exotic herbs Serana could only procure from the Chinese tent city would wear off within the hour. A few drops rendered a person drowsy, susceptible to suggestion. She only had to whisper something in their ear to make it a memory before they sank into the nether.

And then, while her lovers slept, she discovered their secrets.

She already had Lord Colfax's fate locked beneath her corset and in the trap of her brain. Her suspicion had been right. He was a toad, one who croaked for the Crimson Council, a secretive occult society only whispered about in the darkest corners. Their purpose was to use as much of their power, money, and influence as possible to spin the world to their whims.

Those whims had become increasingly sadistic. Sexual.

And possibly treasonous.

Evil enough to massacre everyone she'd ever loved. To slit the throats of children.

Her entire life, every decision she'd made, had brought her closer to finding them.

An old hatred rose within her, and Francesca had to swallow three times as it splashed the back of her throat with acid.

Lord Colfax had nothing to do with the Mont Claire Massacre, but he was guilty of other crimes. And was climbing the council ranks, adding to their influence with his political contacts. Feeding their corruption with his respected name and estates dripping with money.

While he'd been under the influence of her serum, Francesca slid into his library, his study, his escritoire, and anywhere else she could think of.

She found the documents indicting him for fixing the London mayoral elections in his study.

But another envelope burned against her skin, this one so much more valuable, pilfered from a lockbox beneath his bed.

An invitation to an event a few weeks hence. One signed personally by the Lord Chancellor, himself, and stamped with the seal of a three-headed serpent. This seal, she'd gleaned, was only used by the Triad. The three men at the lead of the Crimson Council.

She now had proof of this three-headed serpent. And Lord Cassius Gerard Ramsay—the man her best friend, Cecelia, was about to marry—had unwittingly taken one of the serpent's heads when he'd arrested the Lord Chancellor.

Which left two. Unless she didn't work quickly enough, and a third head grew to replace the one they'd lost.

Next to her, Lord Colfax stirred.

Francesca turned toward him, draping herself on her side in a pose she'd dubbed *the relaxed temptress.* One knee bent, showing her slim, creamy thigh. Her left leg, the one with the bullet scar, remained tucked under her skirts. Her head rested on her hand as she twinkled sleepy eyes at him.

Another loud snort choked Lord Colfax awake, and he lifted a squat hand to wipe at a dribble of drool from his greying beard at the same moment he looked over and noticed her.

"By Jove, Lady Francesca," he rasped before clearing the sleep out of his throat with a disgusting wet sound. "You're still here."

His breath was rank and dry, even though he'd only been sleeping for a handful of hours.

"Where would I go, darling?" she flirted, flashing him a lazy smile. "You've quite worn me out. I doubt I should be able to walk."

Befuddlement dragged his chops down as he ran a hand across his forehead, unable to clear away what she knew was a monster of a headache.

Senna dehydrated men worse than red wine. And she made sure they drank plenty with their alcohol, so they'd be too weak to want more of her once they woke.

"Usually, they leave," he muttered as though to himself. "They run crying and carrying on so. Are you certain we . . . ?" He lifted his sheet and looked down at his body. A body she'd undressed. A body that was now more lumpy than molded, with drapes of skin that sagged in unflattering ways.

She suppressed a shudder.

"Who is usually crying, my lord?" she cooed with enough syrup to give herself a toothache. "The women who are not lucky enough to share your bed?"

"No." He drew out the word, regarding her strangely from eyes clouded with misery and confusion. "No, the women unlucky enough to catch my particular attentions." He took in the state of her gown, her hair, and the marks he supposedly made on her neck.

"I'm not so easily frightened," she said boldly. "I can take what most women cannot."

It was the truth, after a fashion. She took so much.

"I—didn't frighten you?" he asked. "I didn't hurt you?"

"No." She drew a finger down his chest.

"What a shame." Disappointment flared behind the dull pain in his murky blue eyes. "I'm surprised I was able to perform for you."

His cock had been stiff with excitement at the thought of hurting her. He'd grabbed her arms and dragged her upstairs, and had barely made it to the bed before her tincture had taken hold.

Francesca's cold heart froze another degree. *Hard.* Harder than stone. Than steel. Perhaps diamonds. A bit more innocence and goodness slipped away, but her mask never did.

"Well, my lord. You didn't get what you wanted from me," she said icily, "but I got what I came for." She rolled away as he made a halfhearted swipe at her.

"What nonsense are you speaking?" he demanded.

Wordlessly, Francesca swept out of his bedroom.

Colfax's bellows followed her down the grand stairs and out into the night as she navigated his gardens and used the wan moonlight to open the back gate where Serana's man, Ivan, waited with the carriage.

He tipped his hat at her and she offered him a salute.

Once secured inside, she pulled the documents away from her breast and stared down at them, her breath quickening with excitement.

She knew where the other leaders of the Crimson Council would be. She might touch one of them . . . dance with him.

Seduce and destroy him.

Her hands trembled. She was in this game now. She had some decisions to make. Some secrets to keep, even from those who loved her most. Especially them. Because there may be a point of no return, and if that was the case, she couldn't get them involved.

Those who went after the Crimson Council didn't tend to survive.

Chapter Three

Obsession.

It was something the Devil of Dorset often used as a weapon, but never succumbed to. He'd seen it bring the most powerful of men to their knees, because it distracted them from what they should be doing.

As a spy for the Secret Services who'd already sold his soul for secrets and blood, he *should* be doing any number of things.

But he remained crouched on a St. James balcony, observing through a window as Francesca Cavendish, the Countess of Mont Claire, undid the buttons of her bodice. Her every deft and decisive motion exposed one more inch of her décolletage and stole that much more of his composure. His pulse quickened, and then his cock as she shucked her blouse down slim, creamy shoulders.

She didn't wear a corset. How scandalous. Not that

she required one, he noted as his eyes greedily traced the expanse of her lightly freckled chest before a silk chemise frustrated the visual exploration. She was but a scrap of nothing. So slim as to be androgynous. Small, pert breasts puckered in the chill beneath the thin fabric; he could make out the slight protrusion of her nipple even from here, as her underthings were simple and without adornment.

The way his body reacted, one would think he'd never before watched a woman disrobe.

And he had. So many in his lifetime. Some had been allies. Others, enemies. A few had even been lovers. Most of the women he'd seduced, however, had been little more than marks.

None had been as dangerous as the Countess of Mont Claire.

The Devil of Dorset had been following the Lady Francesca since Swifton Street, and found himself quite uncharacteristically short of breath. Generally, he wouldn't even work up a sweat when breaking into a shop, sprinting up four stories, sliding out the top window, and lifting himself onto the roof with nothing more than the strength of his arms, only to leap across several rooftops in the noonday sun. But as he made the one-story drop onto the balcony into a crouch, his chest fought a strange difficulty drawing in the requisite air.

The balcony afforded him an unrestricted view of the countess through the large window of the modiste's top-floor dressing room. She stood amid her two roguish cohorts, improbably outshining them both.

And, brazen thief that she was, she'd taken his breath away.

The self-named Red Rogue Society consisted of three uncommonly lovely redheads with a penchant for mischief and all pastimes generally agreed to be masculine.

Lady Alexandra Atherton, archeologist, bluestocking, and the recent Duchess of Redmayne might have widely been considered the beauty of the infamous trio, but to call her dark-mahogany hair "red" was rather generous, and her features were much too perfect to be interesting.

The voluptuous Miss Cecelia Teague was about to marry the fierce and uncompromising Lord Chief Justice, Cassius Gerard Ramsay. So, though she might be as sweet and decadent as her strawberry lips suggested, a brilliant mathematician, and now the wealthiest businesswoman in London, her intelligence was forever in question. Ramsay, the surly Scot, wasn't the cold, impeachable character he presented to the world.

At least not where Miss Teague was concerned.

Despite their distressing connections to recent investigations of his, the Ladies Alexandra and Cecelia were no longer of any interest to the Crown nor to the Secret Services. He had no reason to be following them anymore.

But he had to see *her* again.

The Countess of Mont Claire.

If only to prove to himself that she was real.

A gentleman would have looked away as the lady continued to undress, slipping her skirt and bustle from her lean hips to pool at her feet. He wouldn't salivate at the sight of her long legs and curse the shapeless drawers that covered her backside as she bent to help the seamstress gather her discarded clothes.

The Devil of Dorset was no gentleman. Indeed, he was a voyeur by trade, lethal in both the back alley and the bedroom. He could steal the spotlight at any soiree and hold an entire audience in the palm of his hand, manipulating their every emotion and whim. He could assassinate in a room full of people, and no one would remember what he looked like.

He was a ghost. A chameleon. A shade of a man whose sole vocation in life was to be both notorious and invisible.

He pulled that ability about him now and stood against the summer sun blazing over the rooftops with only an alleyway between them. If the women looked in his direction, they'd be blinded.

Francesca was as much of a ghost as he. The world had presumed her dead after Mont Claire had been razed to the ground. But she'd risen from the ashes somewhere on the Continent, claiming to have suffered days of unconsciousness due to smoke inhalation. The story went that a Romani woman had spirited her out of Mont Claire in time, and the child had regained consciousness at a country hospital some counties away.

The Devil of Dorset had learned along with the rest of London about her impossible survival. She'd attended some finishing school on Lake Geneva and subsequently gallivanted with her fellow spinster friends across half the globe by the age of twenty-five.

He squinted through the window as Francesca apparently refused tea, punch, or champagne in favor of a strong scotch. Her gold hat lay upside down on a settee where she'd tossed it. Uncovered, her coiffed hair glinted with a ruby sheen, upswept to uncover the long, graceful curve of her swanlike neck.

The Red Rogues, indeed.

In a few short months, the Countess of Mont Claire had become the most notorious of them all. She'd famously fucked her way through half the available men in the ton and twice again the married ones.

His fingertips twitched. Fists curled. An indulgent outward showing of a growing inner turmoil.

He wanted to break every finger that profaned her. Rip out every tongue that'd tasted her. Unman every sod who'd taken his pleasure inside of her.

And that was why obsession was dangerous. Wrong.

This had to stop.

And he knew it wouldn't.

The Countess of Mont Claire's return to England had been quiet, at first. The engagement soiree and subsequent wedding of the Duke and Duchess of Redmayne, a few other intimate dinner parties and social gatherings. Just enough to cause a stir, and rarely far from the sides of her two compatriots.

How she collected so many lovers was a miracle and *why*, a mystery.

The stories of her exploits were as varied as the men, themselves. Some reported that she'd been as gentle as a dove, cooing at their masterful touch. Others claimed her a kitten, pouncing and playful, purring as they drove her to heaven. Yet more lovers swore she was a lioness. Fierce and passionate, a huntress and a heathen. Her hunger insatiable and her roar mighty.

Which was it? Could her tastes and talents be as vast and varied as his own?

Gods, but he yearned to find out.

He squinted through the window, drinking in the vision of her like a man about to lose his sight.

What did she desire? Why had she become such a wicked woman? Had loss and pain driven her into dark corners where throbbing, straining, damp sins momentarily filled the void left by violence? Did she strive to fill the emptiness with penetrations of hard flesh and yielding lips?

Were they that much alike?

He had to know.

Because her return had stirred not only the bright stars of the ton but the shadows, as well. Her name was whispered in curses and chants.

What did she know about what happened to her family? What, if anything, did she have to do with it now?

Was she truly a seductive spinster? Or a serpent siren?

The Devil of Dorset vowed to find out, if only to rid himself of this obsession.

Chapter Four

Francesca felt a gaze upon her the way one might feel the presence of a ghost. Or demon. The fine hairs of her body lifted and tuned toward the window. She fought the instinct to turn and look. Her neck tensed until it ached. But finally she gave in, her head whipping around to find the glowing eye of Ra that was the sun.

Blinking away the black shadow left upon her vision, she turned back to her friends, who were both undressing for the final fitting of the gowns they'd wear that evening to Cecelia Teague's engagement soiree.

"Do you know what a woman's worst enemy is?" Francesca spoke the question that would start the conversation she'd been burning to have all day.

Cecelia's fingers paused, her stocking only halfway rolled down her shapely calf. "According to you, it's a man, isn't it?"

"It's submission," Francesca corrected, her brow wrinkling in concern. "Cecil." She used the masculine moniker they'd coined at the Chardonne Institute for Girls in Lake Geneva, where they'd met and forged their years-long friendship. "You are the kindest soul in the known universe, and I worry that Scotsman of yours is going to trample your tender heart under his ambitions. Are you absolutely certain such a prompt marriage is advisable?"

Cecelia slipped her stocking off the rest of the way and methodically arranged it before unhooking the other one. "I hear what you're saying, Frank, and your concern touches me, but Ramsay is not so demanding as you think. He doesn't require submission from me, only understanding, and I give that gladly."

"Yes, but—"

"I'm no shrinking violet." Cecelia stood to her full height, appearing, even in her corset and drawers, a broad-shouldered Valkyrie. Beautiful, strong, and devastating to any man who would cross her. Her lashes, however, swept down over shy cheeks. "Not anymore, at least."

Her argument might have meant more if she weren't wearing violet, which happened to be her favorite color. But no, nothing about Cecelia was shrinking; in fact, her figure had become fuller than ever now that she'd been applying herself to enjoying life with her Lord Chief Justice fiancé, a monstrous large man with determination and appetite to match.

"Not all men are the grotesque goblins you consort with, Frank," Alexandra, the Duchess of Redmayne, teased from where she selected an assortment of chocolates from a dish.

Francesca's mouth twisted wryly. "You know, I'm no great hater of men. I just . . ."

"Detest them?" Cecelia proffered helpfully.

"Despise them?" Alexandra chimed in.

She rolled her eyes at them both. "Distrust them."

"As you well should, of course." Alexandra bustled over to Francesca to pluck at a ribbon that had become tangled in her chemise. "However, it's interesting to note that all of us have been betrayed by women, as well as men, and have learned they can be twice as vicious if need be."

"An excellent point," Cecelia agreed. "Women make just as fine heroes as men, but I daresay the inverse is true as well. They are fantastic villains." She turned to the mirror, smoothing hands over her curves. "I'll take this moment to remind you both that many women gossip and talk about frivolous things whilst being fitted for an engagement ball, rather than secret societies, villains, and suspicion."

Alexandra, her wealth of dark curls shining auburn in the spectacular sunlight, squeezed Francesca's arm with gentle reproof. "We are sorry, aren't we, Frank?"

"Yes," she muttered as the modiste swept in with a few of her assistants, pouring a confection of cream silk and lace over Cecelia and molding it to her curves.

"You do look like a goddess," Francesca marveled. "I'm an utter ass."

Cecelia's sapphire eyes crinkled at the corners with a fond smile. "You're a dear to worry for me." She turned to Alexandra. "Ramsay's your brother-in-law, Alexander. You don't share Francesca's worries about him, do you?"

"It's not that I worry about the man," Francesca cut in before Alexandra could reply. "It's only . . . are you certain you want to marry so soon? That you can keep both your husband and the business he so detests without him forcing you to choose between them?"

Alexandra twisted her perfectly formed lips into a contemplative posture, guiltily glancing down at the floor. "Not to be a hypocrite, Cecil, but you *do* have the luxury of a long engagement if you need it."

Cecelia glanced back and forth from Alexandra, who'd had all but a daylong engagement to her duke, and then to Francesca, who never slept in the same bed twice. "Do you two doubt me?"

"Of course not!" Alexandra reached for her.

"I do not doubt your ability, your brilliance, or your heart, dear," Francesca clarified, "only I—*we* worry that your expectation to both live in marital bliss and maintain your personal sovereignty is a bit . . . optimistic, that's all."

Cecelia pouted, an unintentionally sultry gesture. "Naive, you mean?"

"I didn't say that."

"She didn't say that out loud," Alexandra corrected helpfully.

"When did *optimistic* and *naive* become synonymous?" Cecelia huffed. "Can a woman not hope for happiness, fulfillment, and love without being made to feel that she isn't cynical enough for the trends of the day?"

"I don't want you to be cynical," Francesca argued. "Just . . . careful. In the span of a few months, you found out you had a wealthy aunt who owned the most successful gambling hell in London and half of the ton's darkest secrets. You've been shot at, kidnapped, betrayed by a close friend, and your business burned to the ground." She ticked these recent events off on her fingers. "You made an enemy, and then a fiancé, of one of the surliest, most unyielding, ill-tempered Scots in the empire—"

"Let us not forget handsome, loyal, rich, and generous—" Cecelia cut in, defending her lover.

"And then you've agreed to marry him even though he still does not want you to rebuild the establishment—"

"—as well as a school and employment placement program for displaced women—" Cecelia corrected.

"Also, the investigation into who imprisoned those girls in your cellar isn't exactly tied up, if you'll pardon the expression. I mean we've found the procurer of the children, but not who intended to buy them. Don't you think a wedding on top of all that is too much too soon?"

Cecelia shook her head vehemently. "It's too little, too late, if I'm honest."

"How do you figure?"

"I love Ramsay." Cecelia's voice quieted, as one did when conveying a simple truth. "I want to be his wife, and if our lives are still dangerous, isn't it best that I marry as soon as I can? That I live the life I want because I'm so aware that tomorrow is not guaranteed? We're almost thirty, Francesca. If we're going to marry and have children, now is the time."

"But . . ." Francesca almost bit back the argument burning a hole in her chest. "We vowed not to marry."

They were supposed to be the Red Rogues for life. The Three Musketeers. Going on adventures, making mischief, and leading one another through the mire that was life.

Now she'd have to do that all on her own.

Alexandra rested her head on Francesca's shoulder, all empathy and understanding. "We were young, impulsive, traumatized girls when we made that promise. Things have changed a great deal, haven't they?"

For them, perhaps. Alexandra had found her duke, and he'd slain her dragons both real and remembered. Cecelia apparently felt as though Ramsay was her match, a Scot every bit as hard as she was soft. Powerful where she was pleasant, and disgustingly besotted with her.

What did Francesca have? Her revenge. She could sense that she drew closer to it, but it remained so frustratingly out of reach.

It consumed her every moment. What time did she have for true affection when she was so busy making false love to anyone she could get her hands on?

What if she survived her quest for vengeance? What then? Of course she and her Red Rogues were all still friends—the best of—but now loyalties were split. Love and family came before friendship. And no matter who had buried the bodies of their enemies, she could tell that her friends' hearts had a little less room for her.

The thought made her nearly mad with melancholy, though she'd die before she admitted it.

Cecelia turned on her dais, smoothing the dress over her hips with a look of happiness that was almost painful to behold. "Frank," she asked. "After this is all over . . . do you think you'll ever marry?"

Francesca thought about it. Tried to picture any sort of domestic bliss and grimaced. She'd desired to marry once upon a time, but . . . that was before. Before she'd lost Declan Chandler.

"I think it's impossible for me to be happy with a man," she answered.

"Why?"

"Because I could not endure the rule of a husband, and yet would not respect or desire a man who would be ruled by me." She shrugged at her conundrum.

Cecelia laughed. "You'll need to find a man with the bravery to stand up to you."

"And the wisdom to stand down," Alexandra added sagely.

"Show me such a man, I dare you." Francesca allowed herself to share their amusement until the modiste and the small army of assistants returned with their gowns for the engagement and wedding week's revelries.

This evening's ball gown, a sage-green confection with dramatic black cording and lace at the low bodice, made her appear to have curves where there might be none. This was why she used Madame Jaqueline Dupris, that and because she had made a few alterations specific to her, including extra pockets for weapons, tonics, and whatever else she might need to conceal.

Last-minute alteration notes were made for the subsequent gowns, which would be delivered the next morning.

A restless awareness plagued her as she signed papers, handed hat and dress boxes to footmen, and tossed her scotch back with more relish than usual, glancing toward the tastefully draped window.

The sunlight was . . . was what? Watchful? Expectant? Or was she being dramatic? A heat skittered across her skin that had nothing to do with the unseasonable late-summer warmth. It was as though a foreign gaze touched her. It peered past the art and artifice she'd tucked around herself, through the skin and sinew of her, to the cold and lonely darkness beneath.

She felt, in that moment, like a diary opened to a stranger, and yet she had no reason to do so.

Unsettled, she scanned the busy street from the corner of the Strand to the bright, cloudless horizon. Nothing seemed out of the ordinary. No strange fellows lurked down below or peered from windows across the way. People were everywhere, and she was just one of the throng of Londoners going about her rather pedestrian day.

So why did the heat of the sun call her to strip away the layers of her clothing, exposing her flesh to its warmth?

Perhaps this city was driving her mad.

Again the reflection blinded her, and she turned back to face Cecelia's disturbingly observant assessment, as her friend had drifted closer. A worried wrinkle appeared between Cecelia's brows as she opened her parasol to protect her skin from the rare sunlight. "You're not going to . . . that is to say . . . you're not going home with Lord Brendan, are you? On the night of my engagement party?"

"Of course I will. I'm getting close. I can feel it. My

next bedfellow might just spill the information I've been looking for."

Alexandra drew up to her other side, adjusting her hastily donned hat. Regardless of their fortunes and status, the Red Rogues often served as one another's ladies' maids at such outings, so they might talk freely. "Frank . . . what you're doing with these men is not safe. What if someone hurts you, or worse?"

"You well know anyone with nefarious plans should fear me rather than the other way around." Francesca winked and patted her pocket where a small pistol rested inside. She needn't remind them of the knife in her boot, another up her sleeve.

"Of course we know you're trained in combat." Cecelia spoke more conspiratorially in public. "But . . . oh, I don't know . . . I can't even say it."

"Say what?"

Alexandra and Cecelia exchanged glances before the Duchess of Redmayne forged ahead. "Word is spreading faster than predicted that . . ."

"That I'm an undiscriminating spinster starving for sex?"

Alexandra's peachy cheeks darkened as she glanced up and down the busy street. "Well . . . yes."

Francesca gave a nonchalant shrug. "What care have I what they all say? They can take neither my title nor my fortune from me. Their acceptance means nothing, and my reputation is useless next to my revenge."

Before her friends could reply, a blur of heavy rags and faded wool crashed into the porter's bevy of boxes, sending gowns, millinery, and haberdashery scattering in a fountain of wrapping paper and ribbons.

A portly older man with bad teeth and frizzy grey hair peeking from beneath a weathered cap writhed on a slew of silk chemises and underthings, squawking and carrying on like a seagull in distress.

Her footman, Ivan, stepped to the man, shooing him away with strongly worded reproofs.

"Oh, do stand down, Ivan, and help the poor man up." Francesca huffed over the cobbles, reaching the man's right shoulder as Ivan reluctantly held the left. "What happened here? Are you all right, sir? Do you need medical attention?" Her propensity to rapid-fire questions wasn't one she'd gathered the discipline to overcome.

It took more strength than she'd expected to lift the surprisingly heavy, incredibly solid fellow from the ground, and he seemed to do nothing whatsoever to assist in his own recovery. The shoulders beneath her hands were padded with too many layers of clothing for summer, making him seem twice his size. It was impossible to gauge his height as he was stooped over so, with a hump on his back beneath his coat that made her own neck ache in sympathy.

"No 'arm done. No 'arm done," he drawled as he tripped and scrambled off his arse to a semi-upright position. He batted at his jacket and backside, releasing more dust into the air than one would collect on the street alone. "It's me damned rheumatism acting up again. Might you get me cane for me, love?" The nail of the finger he pointed with was caked with the same grime as what stained his fingerless gloves. She didn't want to consider its origin.

"Of course." She stooped to retrieve it and extended

it, careful not to touch him. "Are you sure you are not hurt?"

"No more than me pride," he said rather sheepishly as he hobbled about, treading on a few of the garments that had escaped their wrapping.

Francesca did her best not to wince.

"My Mildred, she's always after me for not watching where I'm going. Thick as a mooring post I am, that's what she says." He looked down and gawked at a pair of discarded drawers, which were now soiled from the road and the soles of his patched boots. "What's all this?" He stooped to scoop up the delicate silk, and bent again to yank at the skirt of her ball gown, which was still mostly in the box until he got his hands on it.

Inspecting it with one wide eye, he turned his attention to her with the narrowed gaze of a detective. "Are you going to some posh to-do later? You're a fine lady, i'nt ya? I can tell."

It took no great investigative mind to decipher that. "A ball, in fact, if I can clean my gown by then." Impatience threatened to seep into her tone as she reached for her dress. It had cost a fortune, and now the cleaning would, as well. She might have to wear another for tonight.

A crowd had begun to gather after a fashion, couples and businessmen passing by more slowly to gawk at their goings-on.

Francesca would be humiliated, if she were prone to such ridiculous emotions.

A dingy smile split the man's face, revealing three blackened teeth Francesca couldn't bring herself to look at. "Whar now! I fink you'll be the prettiest thing at the . . . wait a tic. Do I know you?"

"I don't believe we've been introduced." She began to inch toward her carriage as Alexandra, Cecelia, and the footmen did their best to reclaim and reorganize the boxes.

He wagged that large, dingy finger dramatically. "You're famous or somefing, ain't ya? I've seen you in the papers?"

"That isn't likely . . ."

"Why!" His face lit with recognition. "You're that prodigal countess. Mont Claire it were, weren't it?" He slapped his thigh. "Well diddle me giddy aunt, I'll have to tell the missus I was run over by royalty."

"Hardly royalty—"

"And if it'll make you feel better, she'll wallop me another good one for ya. A brigadier general is my Mildred, keeps me on my toes so she don't smash them with those giant clodhoppers, God love 'er."

Cecelia was unable to hide a snort of hilarity from behind Francesca as they helped the footmen stuff everything into the carriage to sort out in a less public location.

"Well, sir." Francesca reached into her purse, extracting a coin. "Please accept this as a gift for Mildred, along with my apologies for the fall." She didn't know whose fault it had been, but she was ready to be done with the entire business.

"That's too kind, my lady, too kind." He snatched the coin from her and studied it with almost insulting exactitude.

"Not at all," she murmured. "Good day, Mr. . . ."

"Thatch, Mr. Edward Thatch." His hand snaked out with astonishing speed and plucked her gloved fingers for a kiss.

"Mr. Thatch." She suffered the kiss, which lingered a bit too long, before pulling her hand back.

"You enjoy your ball, my lady," he said, tipping his cap.

"Thank you." Francesca batted away her footman's hand, sending him up to the driver before mounting the first carriage step.

"Dead men tell no tales," came Thatch's raspy voice from behind her, lowered to an intimate whisper. "But watch the shadows for ghosts, they'll spill your secrets quick enough."

A chill pinned her, paralyzing her spine for a breathless moment before she whirled around. "Why would you say—?"

Life teemed on the street, but the rheumatic Mr. Thatch was nowhere to be found.

Chapter Five

No matter how the Devil of Dorset scrubbed at himself, he couldn't wash away the imprint of Francesca Cavendish. Not from his nostrils. His hands. His lips.

And not for lack of trying. He'd stripped off the wig and prosthetic nose first upon bursting into his Knightsbridge row house. He'd cleaned the black polish from his teeth before shucking everything else and diving into the shallow bath he'd ordered.

She'd only touched his shoulder through ridiculous layers, and he'd only kissed her glove.

But she lingered all over him. *God*, did she stay with him. In every conceivable way. Her fragrance remained long after she'd gone. Not a perfume, but something softer, more honest: laundered linen and citrus. It stripped away the stronger scents of the city in favor of her pleasant one.

The sound of her. A voice so wry, it rasped with

deviant mischief, woven from moonlight's melody juxtaposed with a confident derision not often found in a female.

And then there was the feel of her. Not that he'd sampled enough of that to know. She'd helped lift him from the ground, which was no mean feat as he quite possibly doubled her weight.

Such strength for a woman with no more physical substance than a weeping willow strap.

What did she taste like?

The question struck him with such longing, such unabashed hunger, he swallowed twice.

The Devil of Dorset ran slick, soapy fingers over his chest, cresting the ridges of his ribs and angling south, to where his cock pulsed beneath the water, swelling for the umpteenth time at the very thought of her.

Francesca Cavendish.

They'd shared a space before. He'd been introduced to her earlier that year at the Duke of Redmayne's spring soiree. He'd kissed her glove then, and that contact had electrified him. So much so that he'd almost let his guard, and his act, slip.

Almost.

This time, he'd prepared himself. Or so he'd thought. He tried all he could to mentally talk himself out of his attraction. The woman possessed none of the sexual characteristics attributed to a temptress. No curves to speak of, only long, supple limbs. She was neither demure nor submissive, but often indecorous to the point of rebelliousness. Her smile was wide, her jaw sharp, and her gaze assessing. She spoke with conviction and unrestrained, forthright confidence.

No man listed such things when discussing the perfect mistress.

And yet . . . she was a woman passed around from man to man like a delicacy to be sampled only by the most fortunate.

The thought released some heat and pressure from his cock like a valve, dispersed it through his veins in a parody of . . . of what? Anger? Possession?

The hand low on his belly curled into a fist before it ever reached its wicked destination.

Francesca Cavendish was dangerous. Who'd have ever guessed?

The last time they'd interacted, he'd been Vincenzo de Flor, the Count Armediano of Italy. Black-haired and swarthy from months in the sun. He'd carried himself as a descendant of Roman gladiators and gods naturally would. Cocksure and foolhardy. Overly so. He'd been investigating Cecelia Teague's intended, Lord Ramsay, in regard to the Crimson Council.

Subsequently he'd found that Ramsay's superior, the Lord Chancellor, had been the villain all along.

He had been a true devil that night. Flirting with and scandalizing Cecelia Teague, enraging Ramsay in the process.

Normally, he would have enjoyed himself, but not with *her* in the room. Only steps away. Sharing air and space. It was all he could do not to become distracted as the sound of Francesca's bawdy laugh, unrepentant and decidedly unfeminine, shot waves of pleasure chills down his body.

He'd caught her eye a few times. That is, he'd caught her looking. At him. Like that.

Like she was the sun, and she already knew he was a mass of ice and ash and shadow, just waiting to be pulled into her orbit. Yearning for a touch of her warmth.

Which was strange, because the Countess of Mont Claire, while known for the heat of her bed, was equally as notorious for the ice in her heart.

He reached for his own brand of cool composure, and found it dispelled by the inferno she'd ignited within him.

He couldn't forget . . . that he didn't believe she was who she claimed to be.

And the one way he would find out was to get her naked and inspect every inch of her lithe and creamy body.

Galvanized by the thought, the Devil of Dorset stood, stepped out of the bath, and whipped from the rack a towel with which to dry himself.

Who would he be to her now? Who would she desire? Who would she let get close?

The devil, as they were wont to say, was in the details.

He flipped through the mental files of who'd already claimed to have had her. Most recently, Lord Colfax.

The thought of the disgusting old sod heaving himself between her thighs forced him to fight an acid retch threatening to escape his stomach.

What could the man possibly have done to seduce her? It had made sense when she'd left the Savoy luncheon with Terence Folsom for an afternoon tryst some weeks ago; he was a randy young buck with an elegant manner and a winsome smile.

George Randle had lifted a few eyebrows, as he was a portly fellow, but his wit and wealth seemed to make him a favorite with dames and debutantes alike.

No one had believed the inbred libertine earl, Henry Blankenship, when he'd claimed to have spent the night with her, but then he and Percy Morton had exchanged notes on her lovemaking. That had shocked the ton double, because everyone had whispered that Morton was an invert, only interested in bedding other men.

The list of her lovers became only more varied and bizarre from there.

It was enough to put a man off his dinner. Not only that, it made his job all that much more difficult . . .

How did one seduce a woman with unpredictable tastes? She certainly didn't have a physical type. Nor did she prefer the young or the old. Swarthy or pale.

They'd not all been titled, either, her irritatingly various lovers. One was an officer of the court. Another a banker who, in turn, knew a speculator who'd claimed to have shared her with his twin brother.

Most of the others had been lords.

All of them had one thing in common. They'd wielded a great deal of influence in their spheres. More than they ought, in general.

Was it possible Lady Francesca Cavendish was impassioned by power?

Because power he could do.

He stood in front of his mirror, studying a body hardened with it. Of course, even as he dried the dips and swells of his muscled form, he understood that power was so much more than brute strength.

It was control. Discipline. Wealth. Influence. Charisma. It was the command of oneself and others. Power was fear and love, envy and adoration.

And he could manipulate all of these.

The question was, How could he flex his power for her, specifically? In what way would she react to him? Which power would put him above the pack?

He stared at the features he detested, hair he always covered, the eyes that haunted him in suffocating nightmares.

He hated the man in the mirror, as much as he hated the one in his memory . . .

All of this was his fault.

Blinking the thought away, he went to work.

Becoming someone else wasn't so hard. Certainly, the props and prosthetics helped, but that would truly fool no one for long. The true art was in the small things. The thrust of his jaw, the shape and movement of his brows, tension in his lips and cheeks. The muscles too minuscule to define working to create an entirely different person with unrecognizable mannerisms. When one was familiar with another, it was more than their face that sparked recognition; it was also the way in which they stood, the movements of their limbs, their tone and inflection. The undefinable energy or lack thereof.

What would the countess prefer?

Should his mouth be hard, tight, and uncompromising? Or lackadaisical and debonair? Was he born to power? A lord, perhaps, with an entitled swagger and a bombastic wit. Or did he capture it? Consume it? A politician? A sober, cunning, nay, *conniving* magistrate with his eye on the queen's bench?

Hmmm . . . a solicitor could ask more questions without being suspected of anything, which aided his cause. On the other hand, a lord would get to drink more . . .

That decided it. He reached for the ginger wig and the pale powder, having not lost all of his tan he'd gleaned from his months of preparing to become the Italian count.

His hand paused before it wrapped around the powder as he noted he'd missed a few fingernails in his scrubbing. His hands were still those of Edward Thatch, the rabble-rousing East Ender with a loose tongue and an excellent ear to the ground.

As he meticulously groomed his nails, he caught himself glancing at the mirror. At eyes he wished he could change with the rest of him. Brown, with flecks of gold and green. His only real liability, the one recognizable thing about him. Through them, the Devil of Dorset always peered into the world.

He truly could look like anyone. Everyone. And no one.

But his eyes remained the same.

A question whispered through him, beleaguering his breath.

Who are you?

He always answered the same. *I am an imposter. Because I cannot be who I was.*

Francesca Cavendish had been a sweet, amenable, softhearted girl.

She wasn't sweet anymore. But she'd been kind to Edward Thatch . . .

A kind imposter with a kind mouth.

The kind of mouth he wanted wrapped around his cock.

Fucking hell. He turned away from the mirror before he broke it.

He'd always had a cold streak. Where was it now? He needed it back, so he could reveal her, so he could break her. Because it was more than bloody likely another woman claimed her name. She was missing something Francesca Cavendish had. A dark freckle, almost a birthmark, on her top left lip. She was nothing like he remembered, like he'd imagined, and he'd imagined plenty over the years.

He needed to get to the ball, to get to the bottom of the mystery that was Francesca Cavendish.

As luck would have it, both of the men he'd built identities for had received an invitation to Cecelia's ball, and, as per usual, only one of them would attend.

These men never ran in the same circles, for obvious reasons.

The Countess of Mont Claire wasn't the only motive for attending the function.

Sir Hubert, the former Lord Chancellor, had been interrogated for weeks now. He'd given up the name of his cohort who'd trafficked the underaged girls from Cecelia Teague's enterprise without her knowledge.

Lord Brendan Murphy. A general in a hidden army who'd also been invited to Miss Teague's little soiree. So many questions would be answered today, at a philanthropic event for helpless women and children, no less.

How apropos.

Since Lord Brendan was Irish, the Devil of Dorset decided he would go as a Scot. A marquess. Higher up in the hierarchy, but with a penchant for vice and villainy.

Vice was where the devil found his darlings, after all, and Lady Francesca knew that more than most.

The Devil of Dorset had answered to many names in his lifetime. He'd chosen to be nobody, and could thereby be anybody. A specter in the dark and a man no one would miss when his sins finally caught him up.

But to Francesca Cavendish, he'd once been Declan Chandler, and the few short years at Mont Claire had been the only happiness he'd known.

She might not be the girl who'd stolen his little-boy heart all those years ago, but at the very least he could seduce a fantasy before he ruined a fake.

Chapter Six

Francesca elbowed the Lord Chief Justice of the queen's High Court in the ribs as she scanned the ballroom. "Take your eyes off your intended for two consecutive moments and tell me which one is Lord Brendan." she demanded.

Cassius Gerard Ramsay, *Ramsay* to those knew him, rubbed at the spot on his Viking-wide trunk where her bony elbow had jabbed.

"He's over there, with the wispy beard and the waistcoat that only fits in his most confounding fantasies." Ramsay might as well have pointed outright for all the subtlety in his gesture, and it took everything Francesca had not to shush and grapple her best friend's fiancé.

"Look away, you dolt," she hissed. "I see him plain as day."

Ramsay wrinkled his nose with apparent disgust,

an oddly boyish gesture for a man as imperious and imposing as he. In that moment, Francesca objectively understood Cecelia's attachment to him. The man was tall and wide as an American redwood with a sense of humor to match, but his ice-blue eyes and tawny hair rounded out his stern—almost savage—features in a way that wasn't . . . completely oafish. She supposed he might be attractive, if one found a Scottish barbarian giant alluring. Which she didn't.

"You're still staring," Francesca admonished though clenched teeth as she widened her smile for anyone who might be watching. "You're going to ruin our introduction if you're so bloody obvious."

Ramsay's features maintained their grimace of disgust. "Are ye certain ye want to leave with him?" A visible shudder rippled through him. "He's just so . . . ugly."

"I see that Cambridge education granted you descriptive eloquence, my lord." Francesca rolled her eyes and smirked, but sobered when she met his earnest look of concern.

Uncomfortable with the sentiment, she slid her gaze away. "I'll be fine. I always am."

"If ye say so." He cleared his throat uncomfortably. "Cecelia worries about ye, is all."

"Cecelia worries about everyone. It's alternately her most irritating and wonderful trait."

At that, Ramsay let out a commiserative chuckle. "Ye'll forgive me for asking, Countess, but how are ye going to seduce a man whose taste runs to young girls? Ye're not exactly . . . that is to say . . ."

"I'm a dried-up old spinster?"

His perpetually grim features twisted with chagrin. "I didna mean to imply."

"Don't overcontemplate this, but I have my ways." Setting her glass of wine on the tray of a passing footman, she swiped another of the glorious vintage and drifted away from Ramsay and toward her mark.

Lord Brendan Murphy. He was high up in the council, and she and Ramsay both knew it. They suspected he'd had something to do with the recent debacle with Cecelia's business, and all Francesca had to do was wrest the proof from him. One way or another.

He was on her dance card in three waltzes, but half of the game of seduction was proximity. Eye contact. Complimentary glances. Coy smiles. All that boring tripe.

She skirted the edges of the dance floor, nodding at chaperones and wallflowers to her right and leaving plenty of room for the swirling couples on her left.

Cecelia waltzed with a somewhat clumsy man Francesca didn't recognize, who was a good three inches shorter than her. The disparity in height didn't seem to bother her good-natured friend or the partner, though a quick glance at Ramsay told her the surly Scot didn't appreciate where the shorter man's eyes kept landing.

Cecelia's generous breasts.

Smothering a smile, Francesca sipped her wine and turned toward Murphy.

Before she could close in on her prey, a familiar feeling lifted the fine hairs on her body. A strange dichotomy of warmth and chill. Something like the gaze of a god, or the presence of a ghost. It struck a chord of awe in her, and a bit of fear, if she were honest.

Turning, she used a sip from her champagne glass as an excuse to scan the teeming, glittering, whirling mass of revelers.

There. Across the ballroom. A man stood out by standing still.

He stared at her from the shadows of deep-set eyes.

And just like that, in an overheated room over-filled with people, they were utterly alone. She and the ghost.

Francesca blinked a few times to be certain he wasn't, indeed, some figment of her imagination or truly a specter of the dead.

No, he was still there. Staring.

Strangely discomfited, Francesca affected an air of nonchalance. When others would have retreated, she lifted her glass in a slight toast.

I see you. I see you watching.

Her next thought was to wonder how on earth she'd missed him before.

He had harsh-hewn features that contrasted with his immaculate, elegant attire, and a commanding brow. His nose was bold rather than broad, and his mouth defied description. It shouldn't have tempted her. Not as hard as it was.

Hard like his gaze.

He was a hard man all over, it appeared, and extraordinarily fit. Not as monstrously big as Ramsay, or as tall and rangy as Redmayne, but a man of medium height, bred to stand in a crowd not above it.

The pallor of his skin, the perfection of his slick auburn hair, and the sartorial grace of his stance seemed incongruous with the rest of him, somehow. Like he'd once been a wild thing only recently tamed. A sportsman, maybe?

The man was, in a word, striking.

In response to her gesture, his lip quirked, and his angular chin dipped in a nod. He drifted forward with faultless poise, exuding an overabundance of authority and such inadvertent menace that people melted aside before he took a step. Both repelled and entranced, the crowd moved away from the force of his dynamic presence, and only then did they look to see what had prompted them to instinctually do so.

Some of them seemed to know him, and he murmured a returned greeting to a few as he passed.

But he didn't stop for anyone until he'd reached Francesca.

No, he didn't tower like Ramsay, but he hadn't the need. Everything about him bespoke domination. Power. Unequivocal strength.

Something deep, deep within Francesca trembled. Not with fear, per se. It was more feminine than that. Abruptly, *ridiculously*, she wanted to purr at him. To do all the things she'd done before to attract a man.

To see if she could cast a spell as powerful as his.

Francesca abandoned her glass of wine so he wouldn't see it quiver.

Here was a man who would smell her weakness, and at the moment that weakness began in her knees and worked its way into all sorts of alarming places.

"Dance with me," he ordered.

Francesca rarely responded to commands, and this one was no different. The issuer didn't have to know, however, that her lack of response was an involuntary mutism caused by his astoundingly seductive Scottish brogue. His voice was smooth and dangerous and beautiful, like molten ore hardening into weaponized steel.

"Dance with me," he said with an air of someone unused to repeating himself.

Francesca adopted a demeanor of disinterest to cover his effect on her. "You're not on my card, sir." She turned away from him, stepping toward Murphy, but the ghost stayed with her as if he'd anticipated her move.

"Do ye care about any of those men on yer card?" He reached out and flicked his thumb over the ribbon tied at the wrist of her glove on which the filigreed card dangled.

"Not particularly." Dear Lord, had her voice ever sounded that breathy before?

"Then forget them, and dance with me."

He stood close, too close. Awareness of his proximity threatened to overwhelm her. Instead of retreating, as her instinct bade her to, she stepped in.

"And just who are you, that you're so impertinent?" she demanded. "Surely you're aware it is against protocol to dance with a man to whom I've never been formally introduced. You do us both a dishonor."

The dark and wicked shadows in his eyes jangled her nerves, but an impish charm almost concealed those shadows enough to convince her they hadn't really existed at all. "Since when have ye cared about protocol, Lady Francesca?"

He had her there. Since never, that was when. She did what she liked when she liked, and the devil may take the consequences.

She was at a disadvantage, here. He knew such things about her when she didn't even know his name. In fact, she couldn't decide what unsettled her most: That she had been waylaid from her private mission. That he was asking her to dance in this impolite way . . .

Or that she was tempted to say yes.

More than anything she'd been tempted to do in years.

She looked up at him and found the lure of an adventure she hadn't yet enjoyed. A flirtation she'd never allowed herself to have. When one chased a singular goal, all other idle pursuits seemed to just disappear. Her every interaction had been calculated, save for those with Alexander and Cecil. Her every desire stashed on a shelf deep within herself, deep enough to have gathered dust and been forgotten.

"My lady?" The man held out his hand, and Francesca was suddenly aware of everyone looking.

Cripes. These Scots. They certainly did breed a specific sort of man. Sensual and arrogant. Bold to the point of impertinent.

And this one wielded a smile that would disarm the most protected of hearts.

Francesca doubled the guard on hers, throwing in a few ramparts and spikes . . . maybe a moat for good measure.

She took his hand and led him to the dance floor, where the musicians had struck up "Blue Danube."

Often while dancing, Francesca found herself leading. This time, she had no choice but to follow along as the strong arms clamped around her might have lifted her feet off the floor had she allowed it. The circle of his embrace was unlike any space Francesca had occupied. Here she had no need of her control, which was just as well because he quartered her none. The muscles beneath his jacket bunched and flexed as he led her through a flawless waltz. Her body responded to his slightest lead, deftly gliding through the motions with a grace she'd never possessed before. One his sinuous guidance lent to her.

Just who did this man he think he was?

"I'm Lord Preston Bellamy. Marquess Drake."

Francesca blinked up at him, reassuring herself she hadn't spoken aloud.

"I'm—"

"Oh, I ken who ye are."

"Not enough to know I detest being interrupted." She'd intended to sound coy, but a sharp edge bladed her voice, conjured by her discomfiture.

"My apologies," he murmured.

She caught it then, a flash of uncertainty—no, something else—something stronger. Anger perhaps? Men didn't like to be corrected by a woman. A spinster, no less. Most especially a marquess, her social superior.

The instantaneous flare of emotion smoothed back into a more pleasant expression of interest and charming curiosity.

A facade, to be sure. Francesca had donned enough of her own to recognize one. So, what did the intrepid Drake want with her? Being the unattached Countess of Mont Claire came with the occasional nuisance of a penniless, titled, fortune-hunting suitor. However, she prided herself on detecting their desperation from across a crowded room like this.

No, her awareness of Preston Bellamy, Lord Drake had nothing to do with desperation. He'd the power to arrest her attention from across the room, without her even looking at him. His smile was open but his eyes as mercurial as the cosmos, and possibly just as fathomless. He'd the title of a lord and the trapezius of an ironworker.

So she had his name and knew nothing more than before. "Are you a friend of Lord Ramsay's?"

"Ramsay is a man famously without friends," he replied.

Francesca's brow twitched. "That isn't an answer."

If he was surprised that she didn't allow him to be coy, he didn't show it. Turning his head, he found Ramsay in the crowd. "I would say Lord Ramsay knows me better than anyone else in this room."

If a man could sound duplicitous and truthful at the same time, he did.

"What part of Scotland do you hie from?" she pressed.

His hand slid down her back in a barely perceptible caress, sending a thrill through her spine. "The part that worships strong, crimson-haired women as goddesses in scandalous pagan rites."

Another non-answer. Though one that evoked all manner of delicious and dangerous images.

Trouble. This man with his whiskey and moss eyes and winsome wickedness would cause her no end of trouble. She should walk away from the dance floor this instant. She opened her mouth to claim a twisted ankle, or an overheated headache, and make her escape.

"How would you describe these rites, my lord Drake?" The question slid out of her before she could call it back.

His head dipped toward her. "My vocabulary almost fails me."

"Do try."

The words dripped from his tongue like honey. "Dark, rhythmic, writhing, slick, and hot."

Francesca looked up at him sharply. He'd claimed to know her, but had he any true idea, he'd realize she was not so easily seduced by warm, scandalous whispers in her ear.

And he left no doubt that seduction was his aim.

The clenching of low and luscious muscles belied her thoughts, and she decisively ignored them.

Drake interpreted her glare correctly and straightened. "Drum music pervades these traditions," he explained seriously. "Ye'd find an entire town, the lords and ladies, the peasants and the priest dancing around a bonfire or two. I imagine a woman like ye has never seen the like."

She loved to dispel the preconceived notions of a man with little imagination. "I have, in fact."

"Oh?" That spark returned to his eyes. The honest one. "Do tell."

"In the Carpathian Mountains lives a tribe of nomads who are only half Romani. The other half are picked-up vagabonds and vagrants from every corner of the Continent and beyond. Their drums are vast and varied. Their dances unlike any you've seen in this world." One night, the rhythms of the Romani had taken her away from herself, had woken the woman inside of her.

She felt those beats rise within her now. Thrumming a thread of temptation she'd ignored for so long.

Serana had told her to beware a man who could weave such masculine magic. For he was a tiger, and she was a dragon.

The two were opposing forces. They'd destroy each other in the end.

"Is that where you went? The Carpathian Mountains?"

She blinked up at him. "I'm sorry?"

"After ye left England, as a girl," he prodded. "The ton has been talking of little else but yer return to London. But when they discovered ye alive . . . alive and far away all those years ago, speculation abounded."

Something told her to tread carefully here. "I spent some time in boarding school in Lake Geneva, where I met the Duchess of Redmayne and Miss Teague. After that, we studied at the Sorbonne for a time, but I found a scholarly life and I didn't suit. I wanted to see the world. I lived in Morocco for a while, Algiers, St. Petersburg, and the Far East to name a few."

"How very strange."

"Strange?"

"Most women travel to Paris or Rome or Milan. New York, perhaps. Egypt, if they're feeling adventurous."

Her chin lifted a notch. "I am not most women."

"Nay, nay ye're categorically not." A shift in his voice made it impossible for her to look up just then. Some strange meaning as rich and thick as Devonshire cream. "What brought you back home, if I may ask?" The question lightened his tone, and she was grateful to follow suit.

"Weddings."

"Yer own, I heard whispered."

"Obviously not." That painted a smirk on her lips. "Never my own."

"Never?" He raised a brow at that.

"I'm more stallion than broodmare, I'm afraid. I'll never be saddled with a husband."

A dimple appeared next to his mouth, softening the hard lines slightly with brackets of levity. "One need not be saddled to ride."

She bit down on her cheek, fighting the response he so expertly evoked in her. An answering mischief, a womanly wickedness.

"I ride with a firm hand." She met his eyes with challenge. "I fear you'd have a difficult time keeping up."

"Some men enjoy a firm hand." He leaned down, his every muscle tense as he pulled her hips scandalously close to his. She'd branded him a hard man, and now he branded her with his intimate hardness through their unimaginable layers of clothing. "I've been told a night with you is incomparable," he murmured boldly.

She covered the effect he had on her with her razor tongue. "Strange, I've never been told anything about you."

To punish her, or maybe to demonstrate his strength, the Marquess Drake twirled her and led her through a complicated bout of steps that brought them physically even closer together at the finish.

A group of sparkling revelers burst into applause.

"It was ye, my lady, who turned to find me in the crowd," he reminded her.

"I sensed you." Oh Lord, she'd said too much. "I sensed you watching me. Staring."

"What sensation did I evoke?" he queried. "A chill?"

Quite the opposite, though she'd die before admitting it. "Why did you approach me?"

"I only answered the invitation in yer eyes."

"Don't be obtuse." She rolled said eyes and maneuvered much-needed distance between their bodies. She couldn't think with him so close. She never had a difficult time keeping her wits about her, but at the moment, if she began a battle of wits with Lord Drake she would be outgunned, outmaneuvered, and outmatched.

And that just wouldn't do, not until she'd regained her composure.

"I wanted to know who ye were looking for, that's why I was staring."

The honesty in his voice gave her pause, likely because it was the first time she'd truly felt it from him.

"What makes you think I was looking for someone?"

"Were ye not?"

"What business is it of yours?"

His voice dropped. "Were ye looking for me, Francesca?"

"Hardly." She tossed her head and snorted with a laugh that was meant to be insulting. *Had* she been searching for him? Had she been looking for one man who would tip the world off its axis with little more than a dance?

No. No, she didn't need a distraction. Didn't want a flirtation. Not a real one. She had work to do. "You are too familiar, Lord Drake, as I've not given you leave to use my name."

"I apologize once again, my lady," he said *unapologetically.* "Perhaps ye can tell me who it was ye were searching for. I could help."

"You don't seem like a man who helps anyone but himself."

"Allow me to surprise ye, then."

Francesca famously kept her cards close to her chest. No one peeked at her hand until she played it. But what if . . . this once . . . she could glean information by giving it? "I imagine you've heard about the fire in which my family perished some years past."

Though his face remained carefully blank, she noted the spark of interest in his hazel eyes. "Aye. Everyone from here to Peru has heard about it."

"Well, I am still investigating it."

"Ye believe it was set on purpose?" His brow wrinkled as if she'd been the one to surprise him. "I always thought it might have been."

Her awareness of him sharpened, focused. "Did you?"

"I wondered, how did an entire household perish in a fire in the middle of the day, with no survivors? Not one person had the time to run out, to break windows? Doesna seem likely."

"There was one survivor," she murmured, keenly feeling the weight of guilt she'd carried around for decades now.

"How?" The word was the first raw sound made by his throat, which had seemed coated in silk until this very moment. "How did ye survive?"

"That's not a story for a waltz," she said. "But I will say you're the first person I don't believe is an absolute idiot in a long time."

"That was almost a compliment, my lady."

She looked up at him then, stared at him with the same intensity. Studied him. Absorbed him. Admired him with unrepentant candor. "So it was."

He leaned in, the fragrance of clean cedar and a hint of musk eliciting a deep breath. "I'd kill for another," he said in a dangerous voice.

Would he? Something about him seemed lethal, which bemused her utterly. He was the very picture of an elegant lord. And yet . . . to imagine him slicing through his enemies wasn't at all a stretch.

She conjured a compliment. A safe one. "You are . . . deft on the dance floor."

His victorious smile caused her stomach to flip. "I'm deft at just about everything."

"Except modesty," she said wryly, trying not to be charmed by his confidence.

"Modesty is tripe," he declared.

"Is that what you really think?"

"Aye, a man is his achievements. So why must he hide them? Why must he pretend they belong to someone else, or that he hasn't earned his accolades? I find that weak."

"One must wonder if you hold the same standards for a woman?"

His smile dimmed. "What do ye mean?"

"We are categorically expected to be modest, in every sense of the word. Some of our attributes we are born with, and others we must work very hard to attain. But a woman must reject her compliments. Must act and dress with modesty above all else . . . or she is ruined."

"There's no reason for ye to be modest," he said earnestly. "Especially not with me." He twirled her again, angling for a corner of the dance floor. "In fact, I'd be grateful if ye were the opposite of modest, as I'd like to discover every one of yer attributes."

"I think you are proposing something, my lord Drake," she said rather breathlessly.

His eyes darkened, deepening as the onyx of his pupils dilated with powerful emotion. "I can offer ye no proposal, but a proposition."

She let out a noise of surprise. "You are bold."

"Are ye?"

"Infamously so."

"Good."

Francesca found herself swept from the dance floor with a well-timed whirl. She couldn't say how he threaded them through the throng of people, but suddenly they were bursting forth from French doors onto a garden patio dripping with gardenias, lilacs, and hydrangeas, their sultry nectar perfuming the chilly night air.

Francesca had no time to enjoy the respite of the out of doors before she found herself crowded between a rock and a hard place. The rock being the stone of the manse, and the hard place the entirety of Lord Drake's body.

She barely had a moment to take a breath before that hard mouth clamped over hers.

Francesca stilled. She'd been kissed before, of course she had. She'd kissed a number of men recently, because the situation called for it. Because she needed what they could give her. Information. Confession. A weapon to use against them in condemnation.

But this was different. Her first kiss, truth be told. The first kiss she'd given to a man for no other reason than she wanted to. And oh, how she wanted to.

Especially now.

His mouth, that hard, stern mouth, was both ardent and coaxing upon hers as he immediately nudged her lips open with passionate impatience.

Once his tongue swept inside, however, a tenderness emerged in his kiss that both thrilled and addled her. He secured her firmly between his body and the wall, though his arm burrowed beneath her, supporting her head and protecting her from the abrasive stone.

What did she do with a gesture like that? She'd always assumed consideration and passion were mutually exclusive. Men tended to shore up that opinion with every interaction.

But this. This was . . . extraordinary.

His tongue caressed her everywhere in warm sweeps of silken exploration. He kissed as though they'd shared this intimacy before, and an intimacy far beyond this. He kissed like a lover, like a man who'd claimed her already and promised to do it again.

Francesca found she had no idea what to do. *She* generally controlled a kiss, maneuvering her utmost to keep an unwanted tongue from finding its way down her throat or unwanted hands from her breasts.

But his movements were neither too busy nor too wet. His breath was sweet and intoxicating, his scent blood-heated and masculine among the blossoms.

The bristle of his chin scratched at her cheeks as he dragged his mouth across her lips, eliciting a quivering little moan from her chest. It escaped as a soft breath, and he drew it into his own lungs, releasing a dark sound in reply.

She felt that sound echo in the deep places of her body that ached to contain him.

Francesca couldn't regain control of this kiss because he dominated it. He drove his need into her mouth, her body, against her hips.

Suddenly overstimulated, Francesca might have turned away, but his hand slid up to her jaw, cradling it as he devoured her mouth, her will, her wits, and every coherent thought in her head.

He was a marauder, this man. He consumed everything about her and replaced it with a wanton desire for more. More of him. Of this. Of them.

Had she gone mad? Had he?

His hands were suddenly everywhere, his kiss becoming a wild thing, losing that sense of seduction and control and bleeding into the barbaric. His fingers trailed pathways of shimmering sensation down her neck, her clavicles and shoulders. Hot and restless thrusts of his tongue almost distracted her from their journey to her breasts.

At that, awareness slammed back into her. Awareness that she was outside in a garden instead of where she needed to be. That this was not the man whom she should be kissing and coercing. That she couldn't seem to stop riding his thigh as his lips dragged from hers to paint a moist trail to her throat.

"Tell me yer name," he said in a soft groan before he bent his head to taste the leaping pulse at her neck.

"F-Francesca Cavendish." Lord, but she almost forgot her name when his mouth skimmed her collarbone, trailing the essence of heat across her skin.

"No, my lady," he murmured. "Tell me who ye really are."

Chapter Seven

Francesca's heart, heated by his kisses and caresses, dropped into her stomach, now a ball of ice and stone.

"Is this why you brought me out here?" she demanded. Any moment she would push him away. Just as soon as she wasn't still boneless and breathless from his artful seduction.

"There are speculative whispers that ye're an imposter," he breathed in her ear. "I hear them in dark corners."

"I have no doubt you spend a great deal of your time in dark corners, sir, but what on earth could make you believe the claptrap you hear whispered there?"

"Because I knew her," he murmured, swiping a thumb over her jaw, as if his words were ones of affection rather than accusation. "That is, I'd had the occasion to meet Lady Francesca as a child. She was charming, amenable, and you . . ." He astonished her by nibbling at the very same jaw he'd caressed, kissing away his words.

"Are neither?" she finished as wryly as she could while his mouth made its artful way back toward hers. This wasn't a conversation with which she was unfamiliar. She didn't find it difficult to prove she was a countess; she had the appropriate airs and graces, along with a swaggering confidence generally only belonging to nobility.

Or lunatics.

However, if someone had known "sweet, amenable Francesca" . . . they irrevocably asked some form of this question.

How did such a soft, delicate, good-natured little girl grow up to be . . . well . . . *her*? Outspoken to the point of insolent. Brash, independent, opinionated, educated, and, worst of all, unmarried.

Well, perhaps that was no longer the worst of all her sins in the eyes of society. They could now add promiscuous to the list.

Promiscuous and wanton, apparently, as she shouldn't at present be enjoying an interrogation by a man who held her captive against a wall.

"She had a beauty mark above her lip," Drake murmured. "Right here." His mouth brushed softly against the corner of hers, lifting shivers from her soul.

"It faded," she whispered, turning her head to seek his kiss.

He drew away, but only slightly. Enough that his features remained unfocused, unless she concentrated on just one. She looked into his eyes, of course. Those supposed windows to one's soul. Except in this case, they were infuriatingly opaque. For shame, they couldn't even seem to decide upon which color to be.

"It's my experience such marks and moles have a way of becoming more dramatic with age, rather than fading," he persisted.

"I don't remember being introduced to you as a youth." She lifted her hands to his chest but didn't push. Not just yet. "Furthermore, I don't have to prove to you who I am."

But she did. She should, if she wanted her ruse to work.

"But ye can," he said.

"How?"

His hands slid down her shoulders, skimming her ribs. Spanning her waist. Francesca remained utterly still.

"She was injured when we met," he recalled aloud. "She'd fallen on something sharp." He'd begun to gather her skirts, the hem sliding past her ankle, then her calf. "A knife in the kitchens had sliced into young Francesca's thigh deep enough to require stitching, and I remember hearing her crying through the whole of the east wing."

His words conjured the memory from deep in her childhood. Francesca had been eight, Pippa only six, and the young girls had used the distraction of their parents' important guests to raid the kitchens for sweets. Had those guests been from Scotland? She couldn't remember.

The slide of her hem over her knee dumped her into the present moment. This was something she'd forgotten, a scar of Francesca's she didn't yet possess.

He continued, "The cook was a bit of a scatterbrain, I was told—"

Francesca lifted her knee with as much speed and power as she could muster, aiming for the impressive flesh between his legs.

She'd never met a man who could dodge her agile movements, until now. The blow landed on his inner thigh, and he did little more than wince.

Lord Drake, it appeared, was a man used to pain.

Francesca didn't give him time to answer her attack with one of his own; she followed up with a blow to the solar plexus that should have doubled him over.

Should have.

He released her with a grunt and staggered back a few steps, but other than that the marquess seemed unfazed.

"Mrs. Hargrave was an angel, you pompous twat!" Francesca balled up her fists, dropping into a fighting stance, ready to deflect or absorb any retaliation he could muster.

If this man hit her, she would be in trouble. His fists would land like hammers, and she wasn't certain her bones cold take it.

"That 'scatterbrained' woman is the reason I'm alive," she spat, palming the knife in her pocket. "So you will keep a civil tongue in your head about her or I'll relieve you of it."

"Forgive me." The Scot held up a hand as if to ward her off, the other rubbing at where her knee had connected with his thigh as though trying to erase the pain. "Forgive me. I forgot myself."

"Yes, well . . ." Well, she hadn't expected him to

apologize, not after what she'd just done. "I made certain you will remember in the future."

She turned to leave, but he caught her elbow. "Countess . . . Have I ruined this beyond repair?

"Ruined what, I ask you?"

"Us?"

She gaped at the sheer impudent absurdity of the question. "What makes you think there *is* an us? You don't even believe I am who I am. And I've only just met you!"

"You just kissed me—"

"I categorically did not! *You*, sir, kissed *me*." She jabbed his chest with an accusatory finger.

"And I doona think ye wanted me to stop." His voice deepened once more, and he stepped closer. "I think, Countess, ye wanted more than just a kiss."

He thought right, but she'd die before she'd admit it. "If you *think* I'm letting you inspect my leg for your own perverse curiosity, you can *think* again." She wrenched herself away, turning back toward the door.

He was behind her in an instant, moving with that improbable agility of his. His hands shackled her arms, his chest pressed against her shoulder blades, reminding her what a powerful beast he was.

His voice was velvet, though his grip iron. "I find my perverse curiosity has less and less to do with what is on your leg, and more to do with what is between them." His warm breath carried the hot words to her ear, and they landed in her blood like molten fire. The wickedness of them, the abject, unrepentant desire. "I vow not to take one single look at yer legs, my lady, if ye open them for me." His fingers curled around her arms, his desire evident in the latent wildness, the barely leashed restraint.

"Why should I?" she asked huskily, unable, in this tenuous moment, to think of the many, *many* reasons she shouldn't.

"Ye're fond of lovers, I'm told. I hear that the closest a man can come to touching heaven is to be inside ye."

"Don't believe everything you hear."

His chuckle belonged to the devil. "My sins are so many, they'd crush yer average demon, Countess, and a night with ye might be my only chance to glimpse what I'll be missing whilst I inevitably burn in hell." He brushed the soft place behind her ear with his lips, nuzzling into her hair. "I promise to take ye to paradise, to keep ye there with me, if only for a night."

Francesca's insides knotted at the same time her most feminine parts turned warm and liquid, pulsing with an answering ache. The answer was no, wasn't it? This man, he'd never been whispered about, not by the council, not by any of her "lovers."

She didn't understand what was happening. Didn't have time for it. If she took him up on his offer, she'd be exposed, and not merely because she didn't have a certain scar on her thigh. One she'd give herself the moment she reached home.

"We'll do it in the dark. Yer secrets and truths can remain yers, until ye're ready." Drake seemed to take her silence as acquiescence. "Meet me tonight. I'll be at the bottom of the back stairs at half one."

He released her so abruptly, a less dexterous woman might have stumbled. As it was, Francesca reached out to let the stone of the manse hold her up as she watched the wicked Scot saunter back inside.

Francesca grappled with her heart, her lungs. With indecision and lust and fear and yearning. For the first time in her life, she understood. *God!* She'd thought men so simple. So ridiculous, to be led about by her. To be handled so deftly with the promise of a little pleasure. Now it made sense how the body was more powerful than the mind. How need could overcome logic. How desire could excuse danger.

Half one, bottom of the back stairs.

Francesca bit down on her lip hard enough to hurt, gathered herself, and went in search of another drink.

Chandler escaped the dance floor to slide into the quietude of the east wing. Once he found a washroom there, he locked the door, yanked his cravat loose, and greedily gulped air into his lungs.

God damn, but he'd never been so turned on. He was hard enough to punch through marble. His blood simmered with the want of her, with an anticipation he'd not felt since he'd been a lusty lad seeing a naked woman for the first time.

The Countess of Mont Claire. Francesca?

If he thought her beautiful before, she was even more so when she was angry. Her eyes sparked like diamonds cutting into emeralds. Her pale skin flushed, and he would have given his eyeteeth to follow that color below the line her bodice.

A flush of desire? Or of guilt?

When he'd baited her, the melted puddle of warm,

willing woman had frozen to ice and iron in his grasp. He'd instantly wanted her back the way she was, drooping with desire against him.

Desire, and probable deception.

He still didn't believe a word she said. He'd have not been able to seduce her if he truly thought she was Francesca.

Not only was she was missing a freckle on the top left of her lip, but everything about her was as wrong for Francesca Cavendish as it was right for his libido. She was more lithe and nimble than demure and delicate. Strong, sure, and bold. Three things Francesca had never been.

He'd loved the girl for her fragility. He'd spent his youth swathed in guilt and self-loathing for reasons innumerable, and she'd made him feel like he was St. George, the knight in shining armor who could slay her dragons.

But to this imposter, he could be no saint. She stirred ardor and lust with such violence, he could barely contain it.

And with her, he wouldn't have to.

Chandler gripped the sides of the sink, staring at a stranger in the mirror, going over their interactions carefully, word by word.

She'd ignited within him a spark of recognition, hadn't she? Something had stirred memories of their shared childhood.

The years have changed us both, a desperate inner voice contended. *What if she is who she claims?*

Impossible. Wasn't it? Pippa had said Francesca didn't make it.

For the millionth time, he wished Pippa had survived so he could talk to her. Ask her. Delve into her memories.

So the world could have known her endearing exuberance.

He'd tried so hard to save her. He'd done his best. He'd paid for every second of his sacrifice for her in blood, in nightmares, and with his very soul.

Memories, as he well knew, were forever unreliable. His entire life seemed like a struggle against them, and not just memories of the Mont Claire Massacre.

He'd been broken before then.

And the memories of his childhood often threatened to pull him beneath a tide of pain too strong to fight.

Indeed, Mont Claire had been his salvation. Coming from the dregs of despair as he did, even the little cupboard behind the kitchen stove in which he slept had seemed like a lord's lodgings.

Every kind word of paternal encouragement from the butler had glowed in his chest. Every extra treat from the cook or diverting story from the Romani woman who often kept their company had kissed his dark young heart with hope. Those little moments of respite were like the pinpricks of stars on a moonless night. Glittering points of light and warmth . . . unfathomably far away.

Then there had been Ferdinand and Pippa, the surrogate siblings he'd yearned for. They'd taught him what joy looked like. What fun was. They accepted him into their fold like he'd been born into their litter of pups, scooping him into a wriggling pile of giggles, imagined adventures, and ridiculous romps.

And Francesca . . .

Coming from a world so hard and unmerciful, she had been this brilliant splash of color and kindness. He'd sometimes not been able to bring himself to touch her because he was afraid his common fingers would stain her pure, unadulterated loveliness.

How a girl like that could meet her end with such savage violence. How she'd become nothing now but ash and rubble.

His heart became a lead weight in his chest, returning him to the present.

The current Countess of Mont Claire *couldn't* be Francesca Cavendish.

He knew it.

She knew it.

And he'd do what he'd have to do to find out just who the fuck she really was.

He'd get her naked. He'd check every inch of her. He'd find the other marks, the other proof. There was plenty to be had. If she was a liar, he'd expose her lies.

After he plundered what pleasure he could.

After he'd given the pleasure he'd promised.

Yes, they'd both glimpse paradise together before he dragged her down to hell. He'd make certain this was a lie she'd always regret. The temptress couldn't lick the bottom of Francesca's boots, let alone occupy the void her death had left in this world.

Fixing his cravat, he went to the balcony to smoke his pipe and take in the night, biding his time until the appointed hour.

He'd almost made his way through the first smoke before a vision drove him to his feet. He gripped the railing tight enough to take chunks out in his claws.

Brendan Murphy helped the Countess of Mont Claire into his carriage, and they clopped away into the London night.

Fucking hell. She'd never intended to meet him.

Her secret was safe, for now.

Chapter Eight

Two Weeks Later

Telephones were the worst inventions known to man, Francesca decided as she paced the length of her study in her Belgravia terrace. One could have a frustrating conversation with someone else, and it was impossible to throttle them through the wires.

Not that she could get her fingers around Lord Ramsay's thick throat.

"Don't be obtuse, Ramsay," she snipped. "Just get me in the door of the Secret Services holding house, and I'll do the rest."

"I'm sorry, my lady, but it's too risky for us both." Francesca didn't have to imagine Ramsay's fingers pinching the bridge of his nose in irritation. "I'm not even supposed to know about the holding cells and safe houses. Also, ye're asking me to find ye the former Lord Chancellor, for Christ's sake. Do ye not think he's untouchable whilst in custody? If ye wanted to interrogate him, ye should have figured out how before he was arrested."

"We none of us knew of his ties to the Crimson Council then!" She slapped the edge of her desk. "Come on, man. Just leave a door open for me. Better yet, tell me where he is, and I'll do it all myself. You owe me that, at least."

"I. Owe. Ye?" His dangerous tone would have sent any number of men scampering away, but Francesca had never scampered in her entire life, and she wasn't about to start.

"Remember two weeks ago when I gave you Lord Colfax? That was a career-making indictment, and do not pretend otherwise."

"I only indicted Colfax for fraud on the provided evidence," Ramsay argued. "Ye gave me nothing to do with the Crimson Council."

"What does it matter if he's in chains? Soon they will *all* be in chains," she vowed. "But Murphy proved the Lord Chancellor was part of the Triad, and so I have to interrogate Lord Hubert or I'll never get the answers I—er—*we* need."

Ramsay's sigh was a windy sound against his receiver. "Why doona ye tell me what to ask him about, and I'll get ye the information ye need through proper channels. I have a contact inside the Secret Services. A spy who helped me take him down."

"No. It has to be me." She had some questions of her own to ask the bastard. Questions twenty years overdue.

"Lady Francesca." Ramsay's voice had quieted, tightened, to one he might use with a hysterical child. "I respect and admire your dedication to your cause—"

"Oh horsewallop, don't you dare condescend to me, you arrogant—"

"And I truly sympathize with what ye've lost."

"You have no fucking *idea* what I've lost!" What she'd lost was her temper, the one she'd never quite had to begin with. "You have status and wealth and respect. You have Cecelia. You have a darling child, Phoebe. You have what you were born with between your legs to give you a generous head start out of the womb, goddammit. I only have *this*!"

"My woman and my daughter were almost taken from me by the council, if ye remember," Ramsay said quietly, as if her words made an impact, but not the one she'd intended. "And ye ken that ye have more than this mission of yers. More than yer revenge. Ye have Cecelia, and Alexandra. And . . . us."

Us. He meant himself? His brother, Piers?

"You almost lost them, Ramsay," she said, adjusting her tone to match his. "*Almost* being the operative word. But you didn't, you rescued them and claimed revenge on those who would have taken them from you."

Francesca normally fought her emotions, but as they welled into her voice, she painfully allowed Ramsay to experience them. "I can never bring my family back, but I can bring down those who took them from me. Dammit, Ramsay. I'm not asking you to break the law, just to look the other way while *I* do it."

Another sigh, this one more defeated. "Lady Francesca. The Lord Chancellor is many things, but not a fool. If he is not handled by the book, he might be able to use what little influence he has left to lever leniency for himself in the courts."

"Oh, dog bollocks!"

"Ye ken that means he wouldn't pay for his crimes. Not as he should. I willna allow it. And that is my final word upon it."

Francesca curled her fingers into talons. A man had spoken and his word was final. If she heard that one more bloody time in her life, she might shove those final words one final time up their patriarchal arses. No, she'd get nowhere like this. With beseeching, logic, or argument. She needed to change tactics. She needed to trip him up.

"I understand your concerns, Ramsay, but he's not in a prison, I've checked. So surely he's not being kept in a place where I'd be found out. I could dose him with my tonic and he'd be certain my entire action was all a dream. No one else need know about it."

"Francesca." Ramsay dropped all pretense of civility. "Ye canna sneak into a place like Trenton Park. It's utterly guarded, and the balconies are three stories high. I'm sorry. It's just not possible. Ye'll have to find another way."

"Fine. I hope you can sleep tonight, you bloody Scottish blowhole."

This time, his sigh was one of relief. "I'll give Cecelia yer regards."

"Hang your regards, you stubborn bastard."

"See ye at supper, then?"

"I'll be there at half seven," she muttered. "But only so I can poison you."

"Earlier maybe?" Ramsay's tone warmed to that of a friendly acquaintance. "Phoebe is begging for yer help with her archery."

"Fine. Five o'clock."

"Excellent. Looking forward to it."

So was she. Surprisingly eager to see Ramsay's daughter and Cecelia's ward. She'd never been what she would call a motherly sort, but she enjoyed the precocious girl a great deal.

Francesca replaced the receiver and did an awkward little dance of victory. Ramsay, as canny as he was, didn't realize he'd just revealed to her the exact way to get to the Lord Chancellor. And she'd do it, the very next evening. Tonight, she had to dress for dinner at Cecelia's. Alexandra would be there, with her duke, and they mentioned they'd an exciting announcement to share.

A pregnancy, no doubt, judging by the way they'd been carrying on. Redmayne could barely be in a room with his wife without his hands upon her; she could only imagine what they were like alone.

A child was happy news, most especially where Alexandra was concerned.

So why did she feel so despondent? Because the world felt as though it was moving on without her? As much as her friends had said it was impossible, that they were forever a female family, she realized she'd been so naive to think it could be so indefinitely. Cecil and Alexander would be each other's lawful relations, as Redmayne and Ramsay were half brothers.

They didn't have another brother for her, not that Francesca wanted one. She categorically didn't.

She was happy for them. Really. Because they were happy, her Red Rogues. Happy and hopeful for the future, having children, and making plans for adventures with them, with one another.

And of course, they always made room for her at their tables.

But . . . what would she be after all this business with the Crimson Council was over?

She knew she was being maudlin, but she allowed herself to wallow in this moment of self-pity.

For a young woman—well . . . young-adjacent—she suddenly felt very old. She'd been so many places, enjoyed so many experiences and suffered through others. She'd trained with masters of almost every kind of art, from the physical to the mental, visceral, and aesthetic. She'd climbed to the top of things. Ridden to the edge of other things. Crossed nearly every border and pushed the boundaries allowed to a woman in almost all but one arena.

Sex.

Huffing, Francesca bucked her hips away from her perch on the desk and flicked at a tassel on her bronze window drapes. Perhaps it was time she actually slept with one of the men she marked as her unwitting informers rather than drugging them. Biting her lip, she paused. In order to succumb to a man's advances, she'd have to mark a man worth seeing in the nude. She'd have to find hands worth touching her. A mouth worth kissing.

A body worth allowing inside her own.

Now, that did pose something of a problem.

Oh, of course she was kidding herself.

Every time her mind followed this path, its destination was invariably Lord Drake. His kiss had kindled a fire inside of her that'd taken days to quench, one that had addled her into a puddle of quivering female desire.

As far as she knew, he was no one to the Crimson Council. And no one of consequence to her.

Except that he'd promised to take her to heaven.

Francesca bit her lip at the memory of his voice sliding down her body like velvet and vice.

No, no, best to pick someone else. Someone less lethal. Less suspicious. For something told her that the man who lived behind Drake's gaze was too dangerous even for her to handle. And that wasn't something she readily admitted.

Besides, he claimed to have known Francesca. And she had no real way of repudiating that claim.

Which made him dangerous on an entirely different level.

She touched the healing wound on her thigh, the one she'd inflicted weeks ago that would be a scar in a matter of days. She was still furious with herself for forgetting it had existed. When she'd been so careful to take on every slice of Francesca's persona since childhood.

No, the judicious thing to do would be to stay away from Preston Bellamy, Lord Drake.

Drake was another name for dragon, and this city had room enough for only one of those.

Francesca swept out of her study and into the damask-papered hall, calling for a footman. She nearly collided with an older woman as she shuffled around a corner.

"Serana!" She steadied the woman, who was still more elegant than aged, though rheumatic bones kept her from moving like she used to. "I'm sorry, I didn't see you there."

"Distracted by your schemes, child." Serana patted

her on the cheek as she'd done when she was a girl. "I've been bowled over by worse."

Interlocking her arms with her friend, Francesca helped her to navigate the staircase to the ground level. Even though Serana had taken to living in the luxurious accommodations of a countess, she still favored the animal-skin slippers her tribe of vagabonds crafted in the eastern mountains. Warm, light, and utterly silent.

"Are you engaged to go to a party tonight, love? Do you need me to mix you a dram for one of your villains?"

"What I need is a footman to set up the pole vault in the back garden." She bellowed for her butler across the marble-and-parquet entry. Just where was her staff today?

"A pole vault, you say?" Serana wasn't a woman who gave in to surprise, but her eyebrows crawled up her forehead. "Whatever could you need with that?"

"To practice, dear Serana. I'll meet my end as a stain on the cobbles if I don't make my jump."

"Just how far is this fall you might take?" Serana's brows made a significant inversion, drawing together in worry.

"Only three stories," Francesca said, brightening as she spotted one of her footmen. "But I know that part of town, the space between roofs shouldn't be too far. Also, I'll need to borrow a pair of your shoes."

Chandler couldn't breathe. His lungs were full of water and lead and his limbs secured by shackles of bone. He thrashed. He screamed, but only a flurry of moths escaped his mouth. Flying up. Up. Their sounds as loud in his ears as the beat of bat wings. An explosive, percussive sound.

A final sound.

His eyes stung, with tears. With salt. With . . . something strong and chemical.

He'd done nothing, he wanted to scream. He'd done nothing wrong. Not yet. So why did his skin burn? Why did his sins have to be scrubbed away with bristles that felt as though they were made of iron and ice? Why must he die when he'd not yet lived?

Water and Fire. They both burned, didn't they? They burned and tore flesh away from bone. Tore life away from love. And everything he cared about away from him.

And this time, it was his fault. He'd started the fire and now it sped through the Mont Claire estate devouring everything in its path. If only he had water now. If only he could put it out. And save her.

Save them.

Francesca. Pippa. Everyone.

He'd tried so hard. But he couldn't outrun the fire he'd lit. It would catch him. Burn him. Burn this entire city to the ground if he didn't stop it.

The flames licked at the soles of his feet, searing them, peeling the skin and—

Thud!

Jerking awake, Chandler leapt from the chair where he'd fallen asleep with his feet up close to the hearth. He'd a knife in one hand at the ready and another fist balled, prepared to strike.

His chest pulled in lungsful of air in great gulps. His hands trembled slightly, before steadying themselves.

He looked this way and that, scanning the Spartan bedroom for intruders. If he found one, the bastard would bleed.

It took less than a second to realize he was alone.

Always alone.

He emptied his lungs and dropped his arms. It was just a nightmare. *The* nightmare.

Chandler always had a difficult time sleeping when he'd a monster beneath his roof.

A lesser monster than himself. But a monster, still.

Though he occupied the floor beneath the Lord Chancellor, it was as though the man's evil seeped through the rafters above him, emanating into the very energy of the Lambeth safe house in which he was stationed.

Of course, he'd been called upon to supervise the custodianship of the blackguard as the Secret Services did their utmost to unravel the Lord Chancellor's treasonous acts.

He was the Devil of Dorset, the very best.

Even they didn't know the truth about him.

They didn't know what role Chandler had to play in all of this from the very beginning. What past and prejudices he'd had against the Lord Chancellor on every personal level imaginable.

Chandler went to the fireplace and leaned against the mantel with one hand, staring into the coals and letting them dry the cold sweat in which his nightmare had doused him.

An old and familiar rage rose in him like a tide, choking off his breath even when awake, drowning him in fury and washing him in a cold, bleak fervor he'd spent his entire life trying to forget.

To avenge.

He needed to think of something else—anything else. Until he could truly breathe again. Until the rage receded and the tempest stilled. Until he became himself once more.

Whoever that was.

He needed a distraction from the bleak void that threatened to swallow him on nights like this.

A silken fall of vibrant red hair glistened over a pair of eyes the color of the Cliffs of Moher. Pretty pink lips quirked beneath a nose just a little too crooked to be comely.

The counterfeit countess. She was anything but bleak. The opposite of bleak. God, she was . . . luminous. Vivid. Dazzling. Radiant.

So very alive.

Or at least, he'd begun to wish it so.

He just needed to be sure. He needed to see her hand. He wanted to prove her lie, to kill the hope beginning to bloom in his chest.

He needed to touch her again, regardless of her identity.

For something irrevocably told him she was no more a countess than he was the actual devil, but that didn't stop him from yearning to fuck her.

Lord, he really was a devil.

What a word they'd assigned to him in the as-yet-unofficial Secret Services. He'd never quite learned why it stuck. Because he looked like depictions of said devil? Handsome, satirical, and swarthy. Because he was without a conscience, compassion, or empathy for the men he was assigned to punish?

Because he enjoyed condemning those who deserved it. Bringing evil men to their final reward . . .

Someone had to. Someone needed to be a ballast to the weight of rot and malevolence rising in the empire, in the souls of men. Someone must atone.

Who better than he? When he had so much to atone for.

Thud.

Chandler's hackles rose and his knife appeared back in his palm in the space of a blink. He'd thought that sound a figment of his dream, but no. It came from directly above him.

The Lord Chancellor was kept at the other end of the house.

Someone *else* was upstairs.

Fetching his pistol from the table beside the bed, Chandler flung open his door and pointed it down both ends of the hallway. Finding it dark and empty, he turned to a click at the end of the hall from the rooms of Mrs. Kochman, the cook and housekeeper.

"M-Mr. Alquist?" she said in a trembling voice.

"Stay in your rooms, Mrs. Kochman, I'll investigate." He mounted the stairs two at a time, tearing through the third-floor chamber above his. Nothing but an empty cell, awaiting another prisoner of state, or sometimes a refugee for hiding until they could be deported. This was a modern version of the Tower of London, a building in which people often disappeared, one way or another.

Cautiously, he made his way to the Lord Chancellor's cell, a room that might have been the master suite once upon a time, when this part of town was more fields and fewer factories.

A light glowed from beneath the Lord Chancellor's door. Chandler retrieved the key from his pocket and unlocked it one-handed, training his pistol on the hall the entire time. Kicking the door open, he barreled in, thrusting his weight against it lest someone be on the other side.

He found the room empty but for the Lord Chancellor sprawled on the floor.

Chandler ran over and checked the portly man for wounds. A gash on the head, nothing more. He was breathing, in fact, and fighting for consciousness.

"Who did this, you piece of filth?" Chandler demanded. "How did they get in here?"

"The-the—shhh."

The criminal pointed at the shutters of the window before his eyes rolled back in his head.

The roof? Impossible. One of the reasons a man of the Lord Chancellor's station had been stashed here in the first place was that he had an outdoor area from which to see the sun yet remain hidden.

Chandler threw open the shutters and leapt onto the balcony, searching the dark night with the point of his gun. Instead of speaking, he listened to the night. Waiting for a breath, a step, or a presence to manifest.

On his next step, the ground moved beneath his foot. Or, rather, a cylindrical part of it did. Bending, Chandler picked up an astonishingly long stick. No, not a stick. A vaulting pole.

"Fucking hell."

He tore back through the Lord Chancellor's room, barely taking the time to lock the unconscious man inside before he leapt down the entire flight of stairs.

Someone had vaulted—*vaulted*—from the empty warehouse across the lane onto the roof and had planned to use that exact method as their escape.

Which meant . . . whoever had done it was still in the house.

A muffled cry drew him to Mrs. Kochman's room. If they'd hurt the poor, elderly woman, he'd tear them apart. Kochman had likely been around since Waterloo, and hadn't the eyesight God gave a mole rat by this age.

"Mr. Alquist?" The lady's tiny voice rang from the bed when he opened the door. "Someone was in here, Mr. Alquist. They gave me a dram of something and I can't seem to . . . to stay . . ."

"Mrs. Kochman." Chandler ran to her bedside. "Are you all right? Were you poisoned you say?"

"I-I can see sounds in the darkness. They're like colors. Your voice is blue, Mr. Alquist. Like water, but heavier. You're so lovely to look at, I bet the ladies tell you that sometimes. When they take you to bed . . ."

Holy bleeding Christ, she was addled as an Irishman on St. Patrick's Day. He checked her pulse, her breaths, her pupils. She didn't seem to be in any imminent danger. She hadn't been poisoned, but drugged.

A slight creak in the floorboards told Chandler exactly where their intruder had gone.

His bedroom.

Swearing a foul streak as wide as the Thames, Chandler left Mrs. Kochman's side. He'd taken the vaulting pole away from the intruder, and now they were searching for another way out.

An anticipatory smile tightened his mouth.

There was no way out . . . except through him.

The moment he crept back into the hall, a soft and familiar scent teased his body into awareness of a different sort. Citrus and honey.

Chandler shook his head. Now was not the fucking time, and certainly not the place to be conjuring her.

He stalked the darkness, moving slow and soundless, counting the steps he'd memorized to his room. A pistol in the dark was rarely a boon, unless his nemesis had one.

He pressed his ear to the door and listened. A latch was undone and wood scraped against wood.

He knew exactly where the interloper was. He'd somehow found out about the hidden ladder to the observation room on the third floor.

Probably from poor addled Mrs. Kochman. The woman was a legend; she'd withstood torture back in her spy days, or so they whispered at the Secret Services.

But this villain had gotten her to spill secrets.

And for that he would pay.

Chandler palmed his weapon and kicked his own door in. The moonlight provided ample light for him to catch two slim legs dangling from the pull-down ladder.

He lunged forward, caught an ankle, and tugged.

Instead of landing flat on his back, the nimble invader grabbed the ledge of the ceiling just in time, swung his legs out, and kicked the pistol from Chandler's hand.

The weapon went flying, but Chandler had the criminal subdued before it hit the ground. A quick jab to the stomach stole the air from his enemy's lungs and the strength from his limbs. He lost his grip and Chandler caught the body, elbowing them both to the ground and using his superior weight to secure wiry arms behind the man's back in his inescapable hold.

"Who the fuck are you?" he demanded.

The slight figure merely struggled for breath on his stomach, remaining still otherwise.

Chandler extracted his knife, tucking it beneath the man's chin next to the jugular. "Make a move and I'll open your vein."

No move was made. No words were said. What he wouldn't give for his shackles. A rope. Anything. In order to further secure his opponent, he'd have to take the knife from his neck or his hand from where it clamped around two very slim wrists.

No wonder he'd been able to vault. The intruder weighed a bit of nothing.

"Do you have a weapon?" Chandler demanded.

"If. I did. Do. You think. I'd tell you?" The reply was rasped out between pained breaths, in a distinctly *female* voice.

Holy God. Chandler reared back, pulling the knife away. A woman had vaulted into the safe house, drugged both the Lord Chancellor and the housekeeper, and nearly disarmed him.

No one would believe this.

And if he was honest, he wasn't readily keen to have the story told.

While he kept her hands in his grasp, he palmed his knife and lifted up on his haunches to yank the cord from the bed curtains to tie around her wrists.

She had some explaining to—

Her leg whipped around at an impossibly acrobatic angle and kicked him off balance from where he'd crouched.

Chandler could have maintained his hold on her wrists and the rope, but only if he sacrificed his footing.

He chose his footing, as she was a woman, and would be easy enough to grapple again.

No one else alive had ever made him pay so dearly for a mistake in the moment. She swept his feet from beneath him before he'd even regained his balance. He landed on his arse in an indecorous heap. She was with him the entire way, controlling his fall, leaping atop him so her weight, insignificant as it might be, was concentrated on his chest, her legs trapping his arms and her knees threatening to squeeze the life from his throat.

The throat to which she now held his own knife.

"I don't want to hurt you, not for doing your job." Though still out of breath, her words were measured and even. "No one need know I was here. No one need know I got one over on you."

The smug triumph in her voice wasn't required to identify her. Nor was his body's sudden and thorough reaction to her.

Francesca Cavendish.

Or, rather, the woman who masqueraded as same.

Christ, he could have killed her in the dark. His breath trapped for another reason, one for which he wanted her to kill him. He'd done her violence. Punched her in the stomach . . . hard.

She was still regaining her breath.

"I'm sorry I hurt you," he said, reflexively.

She snorted and ground down with her knees, her slim frame a darker shade of black than the night shadows. Her hair was hidden beneath a sailor's cap, knitted to pull down over her ears.

"*You* hurt *me*?" She huffed out a laugh. "Please, I'm not the one trapped."

"I wouldn't say I'm trapped beneath your thighs, my lady, I'm merely enjoying my current situation." His own English accent protected him from recognition as Lord Drake. At least while the lights remained doused.

In reply, the muscles in her legs tightened, forcing a gasp of air out of him in a cough. Instinctively, his hands lifted to the tops of her thighs, fingers digging in, but it would have taken a crowbar to pry them apart, and he didn't want to hurt her.

Lord, she was strong.

"Are you going to be a good boy, and let me go?" she asked huskily, unfazed by his wickedness. "Or will I have to spill blood on your floorboards?"

His blood sped away from every one of his limbs, racing to his cock with dazzling and infuriating speed. Surely that's why he was light-headed.

Not because her knee dug into his carotid.

He took too long to answer, apparently, while contemplating just why her threat of murder gave him such a painful hard-on.

"Did you hear me?" The knife nicked the tender flesh of his throat, and he sobered instantly. "Because it's been a while since I've buried a body, but I'm certain I've not forgotten how."

Chandler did his best not to investigate the intriguing fabric covering her thighs. She didn't wear a skirt, but they were like no trousers he'd ever seen. Er—felt. They clung to her legs like a second skin, but stretched and moved as she did. Cotton perhaps? Lord he'd give his left eye to find out. Or maybe his left arm, as he'd need both eyes to see her.

She was magnificent, this woman. Who the devil was she to have been entrenched in Francesca's life since finishing school? A spy? Did she work for the council?

Gads he hoped not. He'd hate to see a woman he so thoroughly admired hanged for high treason.

"You failed, you know," he said evenly.

"This ought to be rich. Please tell me which one of us is a success and which a failure under our current circumstances?"

"Whether you intended to kill the Lord Chancellor or rescue him, you have botched both endeavors."

Her scoff was a short breath that he could feel through her entire body. Tightening it. "Men have such vague imaginations sometimes."

Chandler could feel every flex of her buttocks

against his chest, every quiver and clench of her thighs as she maintained her balance, her power, her control.

"Oh, I can imagine plenty." Right now, his thoughts were conjuring all sorts of scenarios that had had absolutely nothing to do with the Lord Chancellor. And everything to do with figuring out how to get his head deeper between her thighs.

"Now is not the time to be disgusting or disrespectful," she snapped. "Or must I remind you I'm the one with a knife against your throat?"

Chandler knew he could likely disarm her before she did any lethal damage.

Probably.

However, she'd astonished him more than once tonight with her physical prowess, so it might do him well to be careful.

Just in case.

Besides, he was too aroused to be very agile, and enjoying his position beneath her a little too much.

"I assure you, lady, I have nothing but respect for you. It's been some time since anyone has been able to disarm me, let alone a scrap of a woman."

"A scrap," she huffed. "I've had enough of you. I'll have you know I'm quite heavy enough to manage all sorts of nefarious—excuse me, sir, are you *laughing*?"

The abject outrage in her voice did little to help the situation as spasms of mirth overtook him. "I'm sorry," he gasped. "It's only that I've never heard a woman anxious to claim how heavy she is."

"Well," she growled. "Now I might just kill you for fun."

No she wouldn't. He'd been trained to spot a killer, as murder was rather his expertise.

This woman was many things, but a cold-blooded killer she was not.

"Tell me what you wanted, and I'll let you go," he offered simply.

"I'll tell you this, I got what I wanted, and you'll let me go, regardless," she said. "You haven't a leg to stand on."

No, but he had a cockstand hard enough to support his entire weight.

"I'll let you go if you kiss me," he breathed.

He didn't see her fist coming at his jaw until it connected with astonishing force.

And then she was gone, as was the front-door key she'd picked from his pocket without him even knowing.

Chandler lay there in a daze. Not because of her blow, which smarted, but because he was an amalgamation of pain and pleasure. A confusion of awe and enmity.

God, she was magnificent. He wished he could think of another word. But there it was. She was a magnificent liar, creature, criminal, and—he was certain—lover. She had physical capabilities so many did not.

And he could only imagine how that interpreted in the bedroom.

Or wherever else he could have her.

He let her go because if he went after her, the urge to pull her back on top of him might prove overpowering.

She was after information from the Lord Chancellor; all he had to do was ask the man what it was she'd demanded of him.

And then Chandler would not only have a leg to stand on, but a leg up on her.

Chapter Nine

Less than a week later, Francesca found herself in the arms of a devil.

Lord Luther Kenway, Earl of Devlin, waltzed her expertly around the Marchioness of Davenport's ballroom, gazing down at her as though she were the only woman in the world.

Francesca, however, could barely bring herself to look him in the eyes for several reasons. The chief one being that she kept inadvertently searching the ballroom for a certain intriguing, infuriating Scot.

But, alas, she didn't see Lord Drake anywhere. Chances were, he didn't run in circles quite so illustrious.

"Are you looking for someone, Countess?" her dance partner astutely inquired.

Francesca mentally admonished herself to pay attention to the task at hand, and batted what she hoped were flirty lashes. "Forgive me, my lord, but I'm a bit awestruck by your attentions, and I'm doing what I can to compose myself."

"I don't believe that for a moment." Kenway patted her rib cage in a rather fatherly gesture, and then pulled her closer in a way that was anything but.

The Earl of Devlin was handsome in that disarmingly attractive yet subtly menacing modality that left a woman breathless. Even the debutantes in their first seasons cast their eyes in his direction, even though he'd probably lived a half century at least.

To distract herself from her racing thoughts, Francesca listed what she knew about him. He'd married young to a beautiful country baron's daughter and had sired three children, a son and then twins, a girl and a boy. Some years ago, his wife had apparently gone mad and drowned their three children. The tragedy still kissed his every interaction in society, even after all this time.

Such a pity, they'd say behind their fans. *Wed a lunatic and lost everything. Quite probably why he never deigned to marry again.*

Despite all that, he was obscenely wealthy, powerful, and possibly the vilest man alive.

At least according to what she'd gleaned from the Lord Chancellor. While she'd interrogated him at the safe house, he'd revealed to her that Kenway was the top point of the Triad.

It all made so much sense now.

The name Kenway had been spilling all around her Red Rogues for ages, but always in the periphery.

As something like fourth in line to the Mont Claire title, he had been far down on her list of suspects, but because of his tragic past, his philanthropic reputation, and more compelling evidence leading her in other directions, she'd allowed her suspicions to wander away from him.

All this time. She'd been so close.

Months ago, a dead girl had been found in his garden, but he'd submitted to every form of investigation, and they'd found the immediate culprit in Cecelia Teague's own household.

The body had been placed out of spite for the man pulling the strings of many a marionette.

Why hadn't she pieced that together before?

The Lord Chancellor had been another angle of the Triad, and because of a recent death by natural causes, the conclave was in search of a third. They'd several candidates, many of them astonishing, and a few of them surprised her not at all.

When she'd asked the Lord Chancellor if Francesca's father, the previous Earl of Mont Claire, had been a powerful part of the Crimson Council, he'd shocked her by laughing.

The Cavendishes were not killed for who they were in the council, he'd slurred up at her, *they were killed for the secrets they couldn't keep. Every person in that household had become a liability, and so they were dealt with.*

Further interrogation had been interrupted by that skilled and . . . perverse agent of the Crown.

Blast that man, whoever he was.

What she didn't know didn't matter. Not tonight. She had a name. Luther Kenway. She was in his arms. The waltz would soon be at an end and she'd done nothing to further their acquaintance.

Speak, Francesca, speak! she bade herself. *Say something witty, or snide, or flirty, at least.*

But she could only peek at him from beneath the shadows of her lashes, because being in his arms made her soul cold enough to lock her muscles with shudders.

This was who she'd been waiting to meet for nearly twenty years. The man most likely responsible for the death of her family. Who'd gone unpunished for so long.

Or had he?

She gathered the courage to scrutinize him. He'd lost all three of his children in such a horrific manner. Perhaps the tragedy had driven him to become a monster. Or perhaps as a monster, he'd driven his wife to do such a shocking and terrible thing. Who could say?

It didn't matter now. He was her enemy.

But what sort of enemy was he? An idealist? A pervert? A tyrant? Did he lead an organization that had become corrupted, or had he corrupted his followers?

"I know what you're thinking," he murmured with a tender sort of condescension.

"You couldn't possibly."

"That we should marry."

Francesca would have stumbled had he not rescued her with a dashing twirl that might have been the reason any normal woman would have appeared breathless.

He was nothing if not effortlessly deft.

Had he just proposed marriage in the same tone one might propose a game of whist?

"I-I beg your pardon?"

Lines appeared at his mouth and eyes that made him somehow look younger as his features were touched with amusement. "Logically, it makes a great deal of sense for us both."

For a woman used to being two steps ahead of her opponent, Francesca found it that much more disconcerting to not be caught up. "But I-I've only just met you."

"Certainly. But we're getting along, aren't we?"

"That's hardly grounds for nuptials."

His lip curled in an oddly familiar gesture. "I'm next in line to the Mont Claire title after you, and seeing as how we're both without an heir, it might behoove us to make one."

Francesca gulped. To the say the prospect repulsed her would be akin to saying the ocean was large or that hell was hot.

"I thought you were fourth in line. Or was it third?" she corrected.

"After two very unfortunate deaths, my dear, it would seem I am your heir."

The blood left her face as she realized he didn't even bother to appear as though the deaths weren't anything but fortunate where he was concerned.

These deaths—they had to have been decidedly recent, or she'd have heard about them. If she didn't accept his proposal, would the next untimely demise be her own?

"You don't want me for a wife, my lord." She injected a coy bit of modesty in her voice, remembering what Drake had said about the word. "I'm a tired old spinster."

He hid his lips next to her ear so no one could read them. "I find you a wickedly desirable woman with an appetite that I'm told rivals mine," he breathed before pulling back and affixing a delighted and fantastically artificial smile on his lips. "And I like to think I'm not without my charms."

"Indeed." He possessed every charm in the world, and he revolted her in every conceivable way.

"I see I've startled you," he noted almost fondly.

Startled? A larger understatement had never been made.

Suddenly Francesca could not breathe. Her corset tightened and tightened until she felt as though her ribs would pop and stab her lungs. Or maybe one already had. The dazzling chandeliers above her blurred and drew strange halos on the ceiling with tails dragging behind.

She was suddenly worried that she'd lost her hearing, but it was when he released her and bowed that she realized the music had stopped.

"Think about it," he murmured as he led her from the dance floor on limbs gone completely numb. "I'll be in touch."

Air. She needed air.

Suddenly Alexandra was there, linking their arms and strolling back to their circle with the appearance of ease. "You look pale, Frank, are you all right?"

Still unable to speak, Francesca shook her head.

"Here." Alexandra took a glass from her husband as they drew near. "Have some water."

"She doesn't need water, she needs this." A snifter of scotch was shoved into her hand by Cecelia, and Francesca tossed back the entire thing in one gulp.

"What happened?" Cecelia touched her elbow, and Francesca could see that she wanted to show more concern and affection, as was her way, but understood the possible implications if she did so. She'd stoke Kenway's suspicion and the speculation of the ton.

"What happened?" Francesca kept her back firmly to the room as she fought for composure. "I choked, is what happened. I choked like a coward, extracted exactly no information from him, and then he asked for my hand in marriage."

"He *what*?" Alexandra put a nervous hand to her mahogany ringlets, as if Francesca's pronouncement threatened to relieve her of her very mind.

"He's now first in line to the Mont Claire title, and he intimated that our child would be the perfect heir." Lord, but she needed another drink.

"You've only just met!" Cecelia had reached out for Ramsay's steadying arm, and he stepped in protectively.

"That's exactly what I said to him."

"That rat devil of a bastard." The Duke of Redmayne's swarthy complexion was lent an even more exotic appeal by the onyx of his beard. It contrasted with Alexandra's milk-white skin, which was paler these days, due to her condition.

Francesca had been right about a child, though Alexandra and Piers were waiting for a few more weeks to make an official announcement. She wanted to be happy for them, but she now knew what world their baby would be born into.

And who the villain was.

Redmayne, never a master of subtlety, scowled and made to advance toward the floor. "I'll have a word with Devlin, and if he balks, I'll have his tongue."

"Not now, dear." Alexandra's gentle, staying hand was all it took to pull her husband back. "Do you think he knows what you're about?" she asked Francesca.

"I think he got rid of everyone else in his way and would have already made attempts on my life if he saw me as an impediment." Francesca felt an awareness on her skin, an invisible tug on her neck to turn back and find what danger lurked behind her.

But she knew. She'd left him on the dance floor only seconds ago.

Ramsay, often the cooler head of the two brothers, touched his chin, adopting a pensive posture. "The question ye must ask yerself is, what does he want with the Mont Claire title? He's worth more than ye are as the Earl of Devlin. He's more powerful and politically connected. And he's done little to move upon the Mont Claire estate ruins, yer fortune, or *ye* until tonight."

"Yes," Cecelia agreed. "Why now?"

Francesca let out a deep breath and closed her eyes

against the concerned and pensive gazes of her nearest and dearest. They were all so brilliant. So wonderful and helpful and priceless to her.

She never should have gotten them involved.

This was becoming too deep and too dangerous.

"Oh, Mr. Chandler!" Cecelia greeted warmly, glancing over Francesca's shoulder. "I hardly recognized you in that—"

"My apologies, Miss Teague, I think ye have me confused with someone else."

Francesca froze when Cecelia uttered the name Chandler, and then melted at the familiar Scottish brogue.

"I am Preston Bellamy, Lord Drake. Ramsay and I sparred in Scotland once, and it was a draw. I believe he owes me a rematch."

"So we did. So we did." Ramsay's features shuttered as their assembly did what they could to dispel the tension of their previous conversation for the sake of the interloper. "Nice to see ye again, Drake. May I introduce Their Graces, the Duke and Duchess of Redmayne, and ye remember my fiancée, Miss Cecelia Teague."

Francesca narrowed her eyes. As far as she knew, Ramsay was undefeated in the boxing ring. "I don't remember you and Ramsay in Scotland recently," she remarked to Cecelia.

"Oh, it must have been ages ago." Cecelia was good at a great many things, but lying was never one of them. She turned to their guest before Francesca could follow up with another question. "Have you met my dear friend the Countess of Mont Claire? Francesca, this is . . . Lord Drake, apparently."

Francesca's lips warmed at the memory of his kiss, and she pressed them together before turning to face him. "We've met." She held out a limp gloved hand.

"Only the once." His firm hand gripped hers with a strength he barely seemed capable of restraining. Francesca looked up into dark-hazel eyes brimming with meaning even as he kept his tone lighthearted. "I was hoping to meet again before now, in fact we'd made plans to do so."

"I'm sorry to have dashed your hopes, my lord Drake, but I had a previous engagement, and I'd already let you divert me from it for too long." Francesca wrinkled her nose in a half smile, half grimace. Just as relieved for his distraction from her predicament as she was irritated at his presence.

His answering smile was full of masculine arrogance. "It's good to know I'm diverting."

Upon rolling her eyes, Francesca caught both of the Red Rogues' questioning glances.

"I'd like to take ye, Lady Francesca." His gaze traveled down the length of her scarlet gown, leaving trails of fire in their wake.

"I beg your pardon?" Or, rather, she'd give him a chance to beg for his.

"For a turn 'round the garden, of course," he added, addressing her circle. "If ye can spare her for a quarter hour."

Ramsay shifted uncomfortably. "It wouldna be proper . . ."

"But I suppose it's up to her, isn't it?" Redmayne cut his brother off and tilted one scarred brow at Francesca. She was often very glad she'd relinquished her betrothal with the duke to Alexandra, but there were moments like this when she realized they'd have found a kinship if the situation had been forced.

"My lady." The way Drake murmured the words whispered through her, heating the chill Kenway had left in her blood. "Walk with me? I would . . . discuss something with ye."

She hesitated. Lord, she couldn't handle another proposition tonight. Or, God forbid, another proposal.

Her eyes flicked toward Kenway, and she found him watching them with acute interest.

She stared at him defiantly, transmitting a lie. *I'm not afraid of you.* To illustrate her point, she tucked her hand in Drake's and *she* marched *him* toward the garden.

Francesca assumed that the tension in his grip conveyed surprise until he disavowed her of the very notion by crowding her into the first dark nook he found and crushing his lips to hers.

Any thought of resistance evaporated as she succumbed to the mouth that had haunted her thoughts since the last time he'd stolen a kiss.

Chandler's heart pounded with such force, he wondered if it would seize. He was distantly aware of her sound of surprise as he roughly pulled her shock-stiffened body against his. He pried her pliant lips apart with his mouth and plunged inside to feel the velvet silk of her. To taste what he'd craved for weeks now. He kissed her with exacting thoroughness, licking into her mouth in sure glides, enjoying the spar of her tongue and the instant reaction of her entire body.

She came alive in his arms, returning his kiss with unabashed pleasure and hungry inquisitiveness.

Dare he suppose she'd craved him, too?

Her hands worked their way beneath his coat, exploring the ridges of his ribs before working over the winged muscle of his back.

He hadn't brought her out here to kiss her. It'd just—happened. When he'd seen her earlier, in the arms of the devil . . . a primal need had taken hold. A need to stake his claim.

He reached for her wrists and gently drew them from inside his jacket, bringing them together between their bodies before he tore his mouth from hers as if fighting a powerful adhesive.

Before he took this any further, he needed to know one thing . . .

"Tell me ye've never taken Lord Kenway into your bed." He'd meant it as an order, but it escaped closer to a plea.

Her eyes turned from liquid to gem-hard in a second, narrowing with suspicion. "I do not see how that is any of your business."

Could she not be stubborn for the sum total of one breath? He drew himself up, meaning to intimidate the answer out of her if need be. "Tell. Me."

"I owe you no such answer."

"*Francesca*," he growled.

She wrenched her hands out of his grasp and ducked under him, out of the nook and back onto the veranda. "Why does it matter to you so much who I've taken as a lover? I'm sure you've heard I've had many, as have you."

It mattered. It mattered so bloody much.

"Not. *Him*."

"I never assumed *you* slept with Lord Kenway," she said flippantly.

"Dammit, woman, this is no time for japes." He was so utterly affected, his accent almost slipped. "Is he or is he not yer lover? Tell me or . . ."

"Or you'll what?" She stood highlighted by the night sky, moonlight shimmering off the scarlet silk of her gown that did nothing to dim the vibrancy of her hair. She might have been an ancient goddess, demanding her blood sacrifice.

One he might have been eager to give, if she were who she claimed to be.

She licked her lips, her eyes affixed to his mouth as she repeated the question. "Or you'll what, Lord Drake?"

"I'll leave." It would have been a ridiculous threat, if he didn't see the answering lust in her eyes.

"The door is right there." She called his bluff.

Damn her.

Instead of making good on his threat, he strode forward, gripping her arm. "Promise me ye willna be with him." Not the man who was responsible for the Mont Claire Massacre.

"I'll make no such promise, and furthermore, I'm still stymied by the fact that you would presume to care. We are almost strangers, you and I, regardless of the intimacies we've shared."

Chandler stared down at her, transfixed. With her slim nose flaring and glare snapping with emotion, her energy crackled around them as if she could pluck it from the ether and use it against him. She wouldn't be seduced. She wouldn't be intimidated. And she packed one hell of a powerful punch for a woman so slight.

For anyone, really.

So how did he get through to her?

Chandler changed tactics, trying something he almost never did.

The truth.

"Francesca . . . Ye don't know me, but I'm a monster. I am a man with dubious contacts, limitless legal protections, and power in almost every corner of this city from the lowliest rookery to the very throne room, do ye ken?"

Her eyes flared, and she nodded, but she remained silent as if she knew he wasn't finished yet.

Power, he remembered, was something she was attracted to. Seduced by.

"I'm dangerous, woman, can ye not see that? I'm a wealthy man whose currency is not just money but secrets and blood. Do ye understand what I'm saying to ye?"

"Stop asking me that, I'm not an idiot." She tried to pull her arm out of his grasp, but this time he didn't allow it. "Are you trying to frighten me?"

"Yes, dammit!" He shook her a little. "Because ye should be frightened."

"Of you?"

"If that's what it takes." He released her and made to run his hand through his hair before he remembered the wig and let his fist fall to his side. "If a man like me tells ye to stay away from Luther Kenway, ye should obey."

"Oh. Bey?" Her jaw jutted forward, and a stubborn line appeared between her brows. Her own small gloved hands knotted into fists. "Obey?" she repeated with no small amount of incredulity.

"He's a criminal, Francesca. If I'm any kind of monster, then he's a nightmare. One of which you could never conceive. He'll rip ye apart just to see what ye have inside."

Instead of afraid, she looked . . . intrigued. "How do you know this?"

"He'll go through ye like a tempest, leaving nothing but devastation in his wake," he pressed on, ignoring her question. "Women are not people to him, they're not even whores. They're just . . . insects. Butterflies maybe, to be skewered and displayed in a shadow box." Unable to keep himself from touching her, he seized both of her shoulders, this time with the tender restraint she deserved.

"Please. *Please*, if ye never follow another man's edict in yer life. Just heed this one. Never be alone with Lord Kenway. Not for a minute. I will not allow—"

"Not *allow*?" The muscles of her arms tightened as if she was preparing to resist. "Who are you to presume to tell me what to do?"

He dropped his forehead to hers, a gesture incredibly intimate for a stranger. If they were, indeed, strangers.

And yet, despite her claim and the truth of it, he didn't want this woman to fall victim to Kenway as so many others had.

"Francesca . . ."

"No." She wrenched away again. "You answer *my* questions, Lord Drake. What aren't you telling me? Why do you care?"

"Because I want . . ." He dropped his hands, unsure of how much more truth he could give her.

"You want to fuck me, yes, you've made that abundantly clear."

"I want to protect ye," he thundered after taking the space of a blink to recover from the crass and intriguing word tumbling from her mouth. "I think ye're flirting with a danger ye don't understand."

"Then tell me, in no uncertain terms, so that I understand." She made a gesture for him to go on before crossing her arms over her chest. "Tell me what you know."

"All I can tell ye is that I know enough to warn you away from what you're trying to do." He'd never been so frustrated by his charge, so uncomfortable with the lies his vocation required from him.

"I'm *trying* to celebrate my friend's forthcoming baby announcement. I'm *trying* to make the most of being a wealthy, unattached countess in a world that would confine me in every fathomable sort of prison." She stepped toward him, her gaze turning soft and liquid. "And if you'd stop telling me what to do for two goddamned seconds, I'd try to seduce a rather suspicious Scot."

He froze. "Ye'd . . . What?"

"You are dangerous, so you claim. So powerful?" She raked him with a sneering glare. "Prove it, Lord Drake. Show me just exactly what you can do."

Chapter Ten

Francesca read nothing but secrets in Drake's stormy eyes. Secrets her instincts screamed at her to uncover.

Luckily for her, uncovering secrets from men who claimed to be powerful was a formula she'd perfected over the past few years.

This man, however, was different. His power was more than a claim, but self-evident in every aspect of his being.

He restrained that strength as his fingers bit into her shoulders. "Ye need to be very certain of what ye're offering, my lady. If ye take me to yer bed, it willna change anything."

She stalled. It'd been the first time one of her seductions had been met with a warning. A cryptic one at that. Why were men so often wrong? Of course it would change *everything*, at least for her.

"Well," she answered with a coy and practiced quirk

of her lips. "I was rather hoping you'd take me to *your* bed."

"Bloody Christ," he cursed, before all but dragging her toward the back stairs that would lead to where the carriages waited to take their masters and mistresses home at the end of the evening.

Francesca floated on her slippers, feeling like she imagined Icarus might have. Daring to fly too close to the sun, hoping not to fall out of the sky before her purpose had been attained.

And her *immediate* purpose had become finding out just who this Lord Drake was. This man with "dubious contacts" and "limitless legal protections whose currency was not just money but secrets and blood." This man who knew Luther Kenway intimately enough to warn her away from him, despite the earl's more sterling reputation.

He'd warned her as if he cared, which was very probably a lie.

And yet . . . a sincerity had emanated from him, not just during their conversation but during their kiss, as well.

A man's mouth often lied, but his body rarely did.

He kissed her like he couldn't help himself, and Francesca intended to use that against him.

Even as her own body threatened to betray her.

A flurry of butterflies erupted in her stomach as they crunched over the drive with ever-quickening steps. Francesca was able to pause long enough to bid her driver to send her excuses to Alexander and Cecil, and to tell them with whom she was leaving.

She made certain Lord Drake marked the precaution she took.

If something were to happen to her, the remaining Red Rogues would do anything to avenge her.

Not that she couldn't take care of herself.

She'd a dram in her pocket and weapons on her person, prepared for just such an occasion.

Drake less lifted and more crowded her into his well-appointed carriage. With a motion equally graceful and fluid, he settled himself into the plush champagne velvet seat and pulled her atop him, affixing his mouth to hers before she could object.

Not that she would have.

Francesca was used to eager men; it was why she generally took her own carriage to such a seduction. This time, however, she'd been afraid to let Drake out of her sight, in case he slipped through her fingers.

In case she lost her nerve.

And if she was honest, a part of her had hoped for this exact moment. This man. This kiss. This hunger. The headiness of it threatened to overwhelm her. The danger somehow intensified her desire.

Though she was atop him, Drake claimed and maintained control of their passion. He kept her busy with his lips as he split her thighs over his lap. Her skirts created a lake of crimson that threatened to drown them both.

He breathed in the slight gasp she emitted as their bodies molded. His big hands cupped her hips, pulling her bottom against his thighs. His sex unrepentantly found hers through the layers of their clothing, and he pressed his hips forward even as he guided a roll of her pelvis, grinding against her in a shockingly intimate parody of what he thought they were about to do.

She should be afraid. Of his need, of hers. Of his size and her recklessness. Of the unrelenting strength rippling in his shoulders as she clutched them for purchase.

Of the way his eyes were always shifting and suspicious, as though he knew the world should trust neither of them.

He gave her no time for fear, distracting her as he nibbled and sampled, then devoured her with a surge of his tongue before retreating to drag his passion-slicked lips across hers.

His body was impossibly hard and tense and his mouth demanding. His hands, though, were languid and patient as they smoothed up her back, managing to both hold her aloft and caress her at once.

Overwhelmed, she broke the seal of their lips to take in a full breath. At just that moment, they passed a streetlamp, and it slashed a golden light over his features.

Francesca's heart stalled. She'd caught him in an unguarded, ephemeral instant. And beneath the look of sweltering, savage lust, she read something she'd not expected.

Hope.

Longing, perhaps. Not the bright, lovely wish one sees on the faces of children. But the stark, careful yearning of someone who is starving and desperate. Who looks for kindness without really expecting to receive it.

He hadn't meant for her to see the expression, of that she was certain, but she couldn't pretend it hadn't been there.

Because it nearly melted her heart.

Or broke it.

"Christ, woman," he groaned, his voice guttural and his accent less tangible in the dark. "You'll ruin me."

Only if she had to.

Only if he was a man worthy of ruining.

She brushed the shadow of his cheek with searching fingertips for a strange and tender moment, wondering why that look seemed so familiar. Why it tugged at places inside of her turned to ash ages ago.

He surged beneath her touch, capturing her mouth in a wild, wet kiss and pouring unrestrained lust over her bones like molten fire.

He didn't want her softness. Didn't need to be tender or vulnerable. This man's desires were hard and hot and punishing.

His body rolled beneath her, hips grinding up and *up* as his wide shoulders fell against the back of the carriage, sprawling her more absolutely atop him.

Gasping at the instant pleasure against her core, Francesca's hips made jerking little motions against the hands that locked them in place. Never had she felt this. Never had she been so exposed with all her clothing on. So intimate with a man.

Awareness of every part of herself distracted her so fully from any logical thought. The muscles of her abdomen clenched and worked as she rocked intimately against the barrel of his erection. Her hands kneaded his shoulders like he was a kitten being stroked. Her thighs held her weight, trembling but strong as they bracketed his strong legs.

Who was she?

In his arms, she had no idea. She'd never met this woman before, so unleashed and uncalculated.

Who was he that he could wreak this kind of havoc upon her?

What was he?

A friend? An enemy?

That's what she needed to find out. Why she was here in this carriage. She mustn't forget that. She wasn't here for the sake of her seduction.

But information.

Even as she did her best to collect the ice around her heart, her body heated to such a degree she'd no sooner summoned it than it melted into a puddle.

She was so wet. Drenched, in fact. She could feel it against her intimate underthings, absorbed by clean cotton.

Gods, but she was in trouble.

His breath panted out of him in puffs of warmth, fragrant with wine. As they moved together, devoured each other, Francesca heard it begin to catch in his chest. And then his throat. Moans of desire at first, and then demands.

His fingers found her garters before she'd even been aware they'd slipped beneath her skirts.

"No!" She clenched her thighs, lifting herself away from him. "That is. I mean. Not yet. I don't want this to be finished too soon. Not in the carriage."

She needed to get into his house.

"Oh, Countess." A soft chuff growled out of him,

perhaps a laugh but not quite. He brushed his rough cheek against her smooth one before dipping to breathe in the scent of her neck. "I plan for ye to finish *many* times before this night is over. Why not start here?" His fingers crept no higher, but their calluses abraded at the flash of thigh between her drawers and her stockings.

"I can feel yer heat through these," he breathed, toying with her undergarment. "Ye'd come so fast. So hard. I'd have to carry ye upstairs and give ye time to recover before ye did it again."

Francesca had to gather every bit of her will not to give in to the cajoling in his voice. She reached down and took his wrists, unable to meet her fingers around them. He allowed her to lift them from her thighs and imprison them out wide against the seat back, like a penitent nailed to a Roman cross.

"I want to wait," she leaned in to say against his ear. "To come with you. I want to watch your pleasure."

He made a short noise of amusement. Not quite a laugh, not quite a groan. "Is that what ye like, my lady? To watch?"

"I like a great many things," she hedged, boldly stopping his lips with her own. Taking his kiss from him while keeping him a willing prisoner.

He could have overpowered her at any time, but it seemed to please him to indulge her.

She counted upon that indulgence to save her later.

The carriage stopped rather abruptly, nearly sending Francesca tumbling off his lap. Drake caught her, and she righted herself, leaping away from him before the footman turned the latch of the door.

The same footman accompanied them up the steps

and acted the butler, letting them into the redbrick row house.

"Thank you, Howard." Drake nodded to him.

The marquess resided close to her own terrace, though Francesca didn't remark upon it as he swept her through the dark, quiet grand entry toward the marble stairs.

White sheets covered everything, as if his home had been furnished with ghosts. Francesca paused at the door to a long dining room with a forlorn table. "How long have you been in residence here?"

"I'm only visiting for a short time. I'll be bound for Edinburgh soon, unless I've a reason to abide." The look he gave her brimmed with meaning, and something else.

Something so opaque she couldn't identify it.

Despite her suspicions, the warmth of a blush spread through her extremities.

Don't fall for this, she recriminated. *This isn't real.*

Her body didn't mark her as he swept her into his arms and conquered the stairs two at a time. His steps echoed like gunshots in the eerie quiet of the house. No, not quiet. Emptiness. She knew, somehow, that they were utterly alone. No maids, footmen, or under-butlers slept beneath this roof.

No one to hear her scream.

The thought was at once erotic and alarming, as was the manner in which he kicked open a bedroom door, deposited her on a cavernous bed, and maneuvered himself between her legs before she could think to stop him.

He covered her body as he captured her mouth,

claiming it so utterly, her head emptied of thought and her body brimming with need.

Would succumbing to this all-consuming lust be such a sin?

While he supported his weight with one hand, his other caressed her cheek, her jaw, and fluttered against the corner of her lip before gently drawing her mouth open to resume the damp exploration he'd begun in the coach.

His mouth. His hard, wicked mouth. She'd never experienced its like. It yielded against her lips with surprising smoothness, the pressure perfect and passionate.

Oh, the things he might do with that mouth.

Should she? Should they . . . ?

No.

If Francesca had been alone, she might have slapped herself, just to break whatever spell he weaved with the promise of pleasure.

No. Not until she knew who he was.

Until she could be sure of what he wasn't.

"Wait," she whispered. The slight pressure of her hands levered him away from her, which made her feel a great deal safer.

At least he listened. He didn't insist. So many men wouldn't hear those words from her. *Wait. No. Stop. Don't. Not yet.* She had to learn—to train herself—to be physically agile, strong, and devious in order to avoid so many awful situations.

But with one word, one press of her hand . . . he stopped.

He waited.

It ingratiated him to her a great deal.

"It . . . it's too dark."

"I do my best work in the dark."

Of that, Francesca had no doubt.

Lowering his head, he ran questing lips along her jaw and sifted down the column of her neck.

He made it to the bodice of her dress with little caressing kisses before she could muddle together any reason. "But it's cold. Are you not cold? Mightn't we have a fire laid in the hearth?"

She felt rather than saw his frown against her clavicle, and she had to ignore the insistent press of her beaded nipple quivering just below her plunging neckline.

"Ye're cold?" he murmured, certainly thinking about how late in the summer it was. Or how warm and flushed her skin felt by his. "Doona worry," he rumbled. "I'll keep ye warm with my body. Besides, with the amount of physical activity and friction we're about to—"

"Just a lamp then," she insisted. "Or two. I want to see you. Like I said. To see . . . us."

"Well, in that case." His breath quickened in the dark, as if the thought tempted him a great deal. He heaved himself away from her, and she marked his shadow as he went to the mantel for matches.

"Might I ring for a drink?" she asked, palming the tonic in her pocket. The glass felt as smooth as a well-told lie.

"No need. There's several on the sideboard," he answered.

What a relief. Summoning her last reserves of will, Francesca sat up and waited for the strike and flare of the match in order to assess her surroundings.

He'd lit the first lamp as she found the sideboard with four separate decanters upon it. She went to it, pouring them both a glass of whiskey, and anointing his with a healthy dose of the sleeping draught.

When she turned around, he'd lit two lamps on the mantel and one on the nightstand.

The bedroom was so perfunctory. So utilitarian. Large, masculine furniture in various shades of boring. The bed was nice, though, likely carved back when the Scots and the English were considered enemies.

He whipped the match in the air a few times to extinguish it and set it aside before stalking toward her with the grace of a rawboned jungle cat.

The lamplight gleamed from the striations in his eyes, turning them a wicked sort of amber. Almost the very color of the liquid in the glass she extended to him.

"Fortify yourself, Marquess," she said playfully. "I don't intend to be gentle."

His eyes flared as he took it and tapped the rim of hers with his own. "I wish I could say ye'd surprised me, my lady."

Francesca paused and watched him toss back his entire drink in one swift motion.

A bleak note had underscored the heat in his words.

Francesca—the real Francesca—had been a gentle girl . . . Were they both thinking it?

He didn't give her time to ponder, as he nudged her glass. "Drink up, Countess. Ye'll need it to melt yer own fortifications."

She studied him over a sip before setting the glass down on the nightstand. Advancing on him, she pressed her hand against the mound of muscle on his chest and pushed until the bed caught the backs of his knees, forcing him to sit.

Lifting her skirt, she climbed atop him, careful to keep the pocket with her pistol out of his reach. Settling back on his lap, she wished like hell she didn't feel as though this was the exact place she should be. With him. Over, beneath, or around him.

Belying her words, she pressed her mouth gently to his, bracketing his jaw with the palms of her hands. It'd been so smooth at the beginning of the night, and was now stubbled with a dark shadow.

One with very little auburn.

She kissed him with protracted intimacy, wondering if she'd ever again get the chance. If this was goodbye to a pleasant fantasy before she found out what kind of monster he really was.

It was bliss, this. The not knowing. Bliss and torture.

Slowly, his muscles uncorded one by one, his mouth becoming less coordinated, his hands falling to his sides onto the bed.

"What . . ." He pulled away, looking at her with an amused sort of surprise. "What did you . . . ?"

Francesca slid her hands to his neck, cradling it as he gently leaned back, his heavy body rolling vertebra by vertebra onto the mattress until he was completely prone, his knees still hanging off the side.

Unconscious.

Francesca looked down at him from where she straddled his lean hips and felt a pang of remorse. Or perhaps something as strong as regret. Lord, she hoped her instincts were right about him, because if he was any kind of innocent, she was the villain here.

Best she find out sooner than later.

Francesca dismounted him as one would a horse, fully aware that her entire body protested. The room *was* rather chilly without the heat of his skin, summer or no.

It took her no time to tear through his house, and she learned more from what she didn't find than what she did.

Which was next to nothing.

The library was full of untouched books, and she wandered through kitchens that weren't just tidy, but empty. Unused. The larder bereft of food. She searched beneath furniture covers for bodies and in closets for skeletons.

Nothing. Nothing but mothballs and the faint scent of desolation.

By the time Francesca reached the study, she was certain of one thing: Drake might own this place, but he certainly didn't live here. She supposed some bachelor gentlemen, and even nobles, preferred to sleep at their clubs when in town, making use of club staff instead of bringing their own.

But not marquesses. A man of his station required a full retinue, and a house of this size required constant upkeep. Accounts. Ledgers. Banknotes and bills. Each household often had a steward or at least a solicitor. Someone to keep the paperwork in order, even if a marquess was impoverished.

She found the study as empty as the rest of the house.

Frustrated and intrigued, Francesca slowly made her way back to his bedroom.

He still lay upon the bed, looking angelic, really, in a sinister, star-of-the-morning sort of way.

She drifted to the bedside and leaned her shoulder against the pillar at the foot, studying the enigma before her.

Francesca had never really noticed how perpetually clenched his jaw was until she saw it now slack with slumber. Lord, but he was beautiful in that way men were. Stark angles. Broad planes. Lean muscle.

She shouldn't be staring. Furthermore, she shouldn't stay. She feared him so terribly only because she wanted him so much. He was older than she'd first assumed. He had creases branching from his eyes she hadn't previously noticed. Perhaps because of the flattering lighting, or because . . . wait. Was that—?

She drifted closer and snatched the lamp from the side table to hold it closer to Drake's face.

His eyelids danced with dreams, and from the furrow of his brow, Francesca guessed those dreams were troubled. But that wasn't what kept her gaze locked to his face, his eyes in particular.

Reaching out, she brushed at a gather of substance in the grooves of skin at the edge of his eyelids before examining her thumb.

Powder. The kind ladies used to cover blemishes and imperfections.

Was he so vain? Or . . .

A groan escaped him, and then something of a protest in his chest. A bark of anger, subdued by his compelled sleep.

"Nothing will make it right. Nothing will bring them back," he mumbled. "I'll kill you for what you did . . . For taking them from me. I'll avenge . . ."

Francesca reached into her dress. Extracting her pistol, she aimed it right at his temple. Her finger caressed the trigger, but her hand trembled too much to shoot true.

It didn't matter. He deserved to be shot.

And she deserved a goddamned medal, as she'd been correct about him from the start.

In his sleep, his Scottish brogue had melted into a proper English accent.

Which meant he wasn't who he claimed to be, either.

Chapter Eleven

Something had crawled into Chandler's mouth and died. He forced a swallow over a dry tongue and put his hand to his pounding head, trying to summon what reserves of strength he had to open his eyes.

When had he fallen asleep? What time was—

Francesca.

Consciousness slammed into him with all the weight of a sledgehammer, forcing his lids open.

He looked down the length of his prone body, noting the barrel of the pistol first, and only then the lovely woman attached to the trigger finger. His eyeballs ached as he bounced them from thing to thing, gathering what information he could.

More lamps had been lit. His wardrobe had been gone through, as had the drawers. His wig hung on the arm of the chair she'd pulled up to occupy as she trained the little gun right between his legs.

Bollocks, he'd been caught out.

"Tell me who you are, or I'll shoot off the very thing that makes you a man." She extended her arm to punctuate just where her pistol was aimed.

Chandler fought the reflex to jerk his legs closed.

"Did ye drug me?" he rasped from a throat made of wool.

"Impressive that you can still pretend," she said with unwavering control. "You must feel like death has taken residence in your skull."

She wasn't wrong. "What did ye use on me?"

"You wouldn't know it," she snapped. "And you can drop your accent, I've uncovered your deceit."

He stalled, sifting through his muddled thoughts to find a reason for his wig. "I doona ken what ye think ye know—"

"I know you talk in your sleep."

Chandler froze. Did he? He'd never allowed himself to fall asleep next to a woman before. What had he said? What had he revealed in his sleep?

"Who are you?" she repeated.

Chandler could only stare at her a moment. Not out of fear, but of awe. Christ, she was even more magnificent when angry. Her porcelain skin stretched across a perfect bone structure with tension and determination. Her eyes glittered diamond-hard without a trace of fear. Her hand was steady, her aim true.

She could be Athena if she had a bow. Lithe and strong and deceptively dangerous.

He pushed himself to his elbows with great care and instant regret, if only to get a better look at her.

"I'm what you are," he answered in his own

British accent. "I am a lie. A ghost. I am anyone I need to be."

She snorted her derision, which was the last thing he'd expected, tossing her head like a displeased filly. "If you insist on feeding me these non-answers, I might as well shoot you in the head and see who comes for you. Then I'll interrogate them."

"You'll get answers from none of them. We're trained to be interrogated," he replied with a flippancy he didn't feel. "What did I say in my sleep?"

Oddly her gaze softened a bit, as did the white of her knuckles on the pistol. "You spoke of vengeance," she answered gently. "Of loss. Who was taken from you? Are they why you are pretending to be a marquess?"

"It was nonsense," he hedged, thinking that she'd never answered his accusation of her being as much of a liar as he.

"It didn't sound like nonsense."

"Don't you ever have nightmares?"

Her jaw jutted forward, and a flash of emotion washed her face in anguish for a moment before it disappeared. "My entire family is dead. Why look further for a nightmare than that?"

Why, indeed?

"Tell me who. You. Are." Her pistol cocked in the silence between them, a cold and final sound. "I will not ask again."

She would do it. He read murder in her eyes. Such a foreign and troubling sight on such a slight and beautiful woman. Could it be that the truth lived in that pain? Could she possibly be a girl who once watched men in masks massacre her entire family?

The ice encasing Chandler's heart cracked just a bit, as it struggled to reawaken something he'd lived so long without. Hope.

"I didn't lie when I told you that I am a ghost." To combat the indecorous threat of actual emotion, he pushed more insouciance into his manner. "I have it on official record that I'm dead. Twice, actually. A third time will barely make a dent." He waved his hand. "Pull the trigger, if you must."

Her frown deepened, settling heavily on such finely crafted features. "You're saying you'll not be missed?"

"Men in my line of work rarely are."

"And what line of work is that, exactly?" She looked more triumphant than sympathetic. "Are you, what, Crimson Council? Is that why you've warned me away from Luther Kenway? Do you work for him?" She leaned forward, obviously excited when he'd expected some sort of anger, or at least fear. "Am I getting too close to the truth?"

She was. She was getting too close . . . to everything. To him.

His body stirred, despite his malaise.

"If I were such a man, wouldn't I lie about it?" he asked testily.

Her fingers snagged his notice as they traced the line of her bodice, the beading rough, and the skin as soft as hand-whipped cream.

Chandler's dry mouth flooded with moisture. Had he been able to sample any parts of her flesh before the tonic had pulled him under? His unrequited passion told him no.

She extracted a wicked-looking blade from a sheath

in her décolletage. "You'll tell me the truth, of course." She stood, her pistol in one hand and her blade in the other, rising like a goddess of the dark, of war and desire and needful things. Approaching, she pressed each one of her weapons rather painfully against his kneecaps. "You'll tell me now as you are, or under duress, I care not."

Christ. His cock stirred, thickened. In moments she'd be able to see what was becoming a vicious erection. "Some men appreciate duress," he answered. "As I'm certain your bawd friend—Cecelia, is it?—could tell you. Duress is a sexual commodity. She sells it with some frequency, I imagine . . . illegally."

"You keep Cecelia out of this." To his utter astonishment, she reached out and struck him across the cheek with the butt of her pistol.

His head swung to the side, and he tasted blood from a split on the inside of his cheek.

"I swear to you, if you threaten her, I'll fucking send you to hell with only half your bits attached to your body, do we quite understand each other?"

Chandler wiped at the blood on his lip, staring at her mutely. Magnificent. Impressive. Brilliant. He couldn't find enough words to describe the sheer stunning gloriousness of her.

He decided to be done with deception, to a point. "I'm not Crimson Council. But, like you, I'm after them."

"Why? Why, then, pretend to be a Scottish marquess?" she demanded.

"The same reason you pretend to be a countess, I expect. It opens doors."

She wound her arm back, preparing to strike him

again when she paused. "But people at Cecelia's ball knew you. They recognized you as Lord Drake. How did you—?"

"I *am* Lord Drake—"

"But—"

"I am also Lord Andrew Barton of the Cambridge Bartons."

Her brow quirked, and she lowered the gun to merely point at his chest. "The reclusive baronet who only shows up for his seat in Parliament?"

"I'm Nathaniel Butler, merchant of Drury Lane, James Lancaster in the East End. And you'll recognize this one." He scrunched up his left eye and talked out of the right side of his mouth. "Me wife, Mildred, thanks yew, kind lady, for your generosi'y."

Her features instantly brightened, suddenly shining with astonishment, though her weapons never moved. "Edward Thatch! I cannot believe it."

"Thank you." He summoned a smile. "Can I trouble you to fetch me some water there, I'm halfway to dead with thirst."

She sheathed her knife in its enviable scabbard and backed to the sideboard. Selecting the entire pitcher with her free hand, she returned, plunked it on the nightstand, and backed away. The pistol's barrel never left his vitals.

Chandler sat up to reach for the water, ignoring the swimming in his head as he cooled his throat with a few healthy gulps.

"Do you fancy yourself a pirate?" she asked when he finished, wiping away a drop from the corner of his mouth with a sleeve.

"I'm a spy," he confessed.

She shook her head. "You've distinctly picked your monikers from famous—or infamous—pirates."

"Privateers," he corrected. "And I cannot very well name myself after spies, now can I? If they're famous, then they're obviously terrible at their jobs."

At that, Francesca laughed.

And the world paused to hear it.

Chandler stared at her, gun in hand, head tilted back and a little to the left, exposing the white column of her elegant neck. Her face crinkled from somber to adorable in the space of a smile.

Something about that laugh twisted inside of him a feeling of fondness he'd not had since he was a boy, enjoying the only carefree years he'd experienced before the fates turned on him.

Could it be . . . ?

"Are you anyone else?" she asked almost gleefully.

"A few people," he answered honestly. "Most of them foreign. A German officer, for example, Klein Heinzlein, or an Italian count . . . one who is acquainted with a certain scarred duke of ancient Redmayne heritage."

She gasped, and for once was completely speechless for longer than the space of time it took to fill her lungs. "Count Armediano?" she whispered.

"Al tuo servizio, signora."

"Holy mother of Minerva, I can't believe I've met you so many times and never suspected a thing . . ." She lowered her gun, but only a few inches, her features shining with an admiration that stole years from her countenance. "You're incredible."

His lip twitched with the genuine threat of a smile.

Her unabashed compliment meant more to him, somehow, than a slew of official commendations he'd received over the years. "Those are just the personas I maintain with paperwork, residences, and societal contacts." He was in danger of bragging, but he couldn't seem to help himself.

Why did he want to impress her? Did this mean he was beginning to believe?

"I'd be mad to believe you," she said with an incredulous shake of her head. "And don't think it's escaped my notice that you still haven't told me who you really are."

"You knew me once," he murmured. His heart ceased to beat as he contemplated his next move. What if she failed his test?

What if she succeeded?

She frowned, her eyes shifting away suspiciously. "You told me we'd met in my childhood, but I'm sorry, I still can't recall you."

Chandler wished his fingers were steadier as he held them out to her, palm up.

"What about now?"

Chapter Twelve

Francesca stared down at his hand for what felt like the space of a blink but could have been an eternity. Her vision narrowed, tunneled. Dimly, she heard her name being called. Felt her arm drop to her side and the hammer release from her pistol.

Her limbs went numb, then disappeared. Little tingles of sensation crawled over her face, her scalp, and rose gooseflesh over her entire body.

You knew me once.

Long ago, Declan Chandler and Ferdinand had snuck out of the house to romp in the woods in the dark. Young Francesca had been afraid to go.

But Pippa, she'd yearned to be invited with all her little-girl being. They'd promised to take her, but ultimately left without her. They'd played at being werewolves and bayed at the moon. They'd sliced the flesh of their palms and comingled their blood, solidifying a blood-brotherhood.

Pippa had been incensed upon waking the next morning—nay, she'd been livid. She'd cut her palm to match them, but had accidentally done the left hand instead of the right. She'd demanded that the entire clan do it again, but they refused her. She'd demanded to know why she'd been left out. They'd told her she was too young and loud and would have revealed them to the entire household. That she was a girl and not welcome into their brotherhood. Ferdinand had said she needed to learn to be a better lady. That she needed to change if she wanted anyone to like her.

Declan hadn't agreed, but he hadn't said anything against the young heir to Mont Claire, either.

That day had been the first time she realized that who she was as a person might cost her something as intrinsic as love. That she'd have to choose between her nature and what others desired her to be. Because girls, ladies, didn't act like her. Didn't have her ambitions, her proclivities, nor her curiosity.

At least, they weren't supposed to.

It had been the worst day of her young life.

Up until the massacre.

To fill her astonished silence, he said, "Do you remember when Ferdinand and I did this, you were so dismayed. Disgusted. You dressed us down as you dressed the wounds."

Not her. Francesca. *Francesca* had been disgusted.

Pippa had been enchanted and jealous.

"Declan?" Holy God, how many times had she said

that name to the dark, aching, praying, *yearning* for an answer. "It's . . . not. How could it be? You were shot in the back."

It took her a humiliatingly long time to realize that her eyes kept blurring because of tears. She blinked them away angrily, wishing they would stop stealing away the precious sight of the tiny scar on his palm. A scar no less than biblical to her.

She closed her fist around the matching one on her hand.

"My shoulder, mostly, and with a shotgun at long range," he explained. "I was able to run into the dark, though I had to get pellets picked out of my flesh. Even my side."

Stowing the pistol back in her pocket, she rushed forward and seized the palm. She dropped to her knees and kissed the little fissure again and again. Tasting the salt of her tears. Of his skin. Of her pain.

She covered her eyes, then her mouth, tears gathering like little gems in her lashes.

She didn't care that she'd surrendered her dignity, her vanity, and her secrets. She didn't care if he was good or bad, he was . . .

Declan. *Alive.*

Even in her thoughts the name washed her with such a swath of emotion she feared she might drown in it.

She looked up at the man who stared down at her with a guarded, almost uncertain expression, and swayed a little. Making sure her desire didn't deceive her, she drank in the sight of him. Examined him with all the scrutiny of a detective.

His hair was darker than it had been as a boy, cut in

shorter layers to hide its tendency to curl. He stood so much taller and wider than she'd ever expected the lean lad to become. And the pallor of his skin had given way to swarthiness. He'd come to Mont Claire with shadows in his eyes, and those shadows had darkened then been joined by others. The hazel of his youth had become more brown than green, especially in the dim light.

The cruel slash of his mouth, set as though a sarcastic sneer would appear any moment, was new. He'd been a kind boy, if a little melancholy and broken-hearted, but his smile had been earnest.

The proud brow and stubborn jaw, however, were unmistakable.

How had she not seen it before?

He'd been the ghost she could sense in the room.

She scrambled to her feet, surging against him. Enfolding her arms around him in an embrace she'd never thought possible until she crawled into the grave after him someday.

"Declan Chandler, I cannot believe . . ."

His arms came around her in the manner of a man who was unused to this honest sort of affection, but after a moment he gathered her up into his lap, this time cradling her as one would a sweetheart, not necessarily a lover.

"Francesca." His voice was deeper than before, rasping with unspent emotion.

A pang of pain and regret needled beneath the word. The name was not her own, and it would kill him to find that out.

She should tell him.

But she needed a moment longer to bask in his nearness, in his regard. She'd yearned to be Francesca in his eyes almost all of her little-girl life.

What was a few more minutes?

"Bloody hell," he groaned, kissing the top of her hair. "I didn't believe it was you until now. Do you forgive me?"

Swallowing around a lump of sadness and dread, she turned her nose into his chest, inhaling the warm, masculine scent of him. Memorizing what it was like to be held by the ghost of the only person she'd ever truly loved. His flesh was like iron stretched over the mounds of his muscle, and she could have pressed her cheek against it forever. Listening to the sound of his heart. That percussion that had once kept her alive. Kept her going in the worst possible moment.

"Declan . . ." she began. "I'm not the child you knew. In fact—"

"No, you're all woman now." He slid a rough finger under her chin and lifted her face toward his.

He searched her eyes, looking past the tears gathering her lashes together to the soul mirrored within.

Whatever he read there beckoned him, and he lowered his head to kiss her.

Lifting her, twisting them, he rolled her beneath him, settling his weight gently atop her without breaking the seal of their lips. This time, his kiss was different. Better, if that were possible. A tenderness that hadn't been there before melted her into a puddle of emotion and threatened to evoke even more uncharacteristic tears.

When had been the last time she'd cried? She

couldn't remember. Of course, with him kissing her like that, she could barely remember her name.

Her name! *Pippa*. Not Francesca. Pippa Hargrave.

She had to stop this before it went further. Didn't she?

Gasping in some strength with a breath, she pushed him away and wriggled a bit to be free of him. "Declan. I—It's been so long. I have to—"

"I know." He panted, pulling away. Running a hand through his hair and rolling his fingers into a fist to tug at his nape. "Forgive me, I just . . . I forgot myself." He reached out to help her into a sitting position before he left the bed and staggered a few paces away. "Francesca, I want you to know I've spent my entire life trying to find proof of who was responsible for the Mont Claire Massacre."

The news cheered her a little. "As have I, in fact—"

"It was the fucking Hargraves. They're the reason we lost everything."

Chapter Thirteen

Francesca couldn't have been more shocked or cold if a bucket of ice water had doused her.

"C-come again?"

"Charles and Hattie, of whom you are so fond. Well, Charles, at least, though he rarely did anything without his wife's permission. *They* drew the ire of deadly men." He turned around with disgust etched upon his features. "Of the council in particular, and because of their stupidity—"

"H-how do you know this?" she asked in a voice so small, it might have been that of a child.

His features darkened, the shadows pulling around him as if his anger could chase away the glow of the lamplight. This man, *this* Declan, was not recognizable. He was furious. Malevolent.

Violent even.

"There was a man that day of the massacre, an

American. Alfred 'Alfie' Tuttle. I found him. I interrogated him, and I made sure his blood spilled when his information didn't." A slight bit of his composure returned. "He confessed, eventually. And then he hanged."

"Good," she replied before she could hold it back. Alfred Tuttle had killed Francesca and Pippa's own mother. They'd been avenged, at least.

"What did he say against them? The Hargraves?" She did her utmost to ask this as though she wasn't one of them.

"He said Charles and Hattie wrote a missive to the authorities and signed it with the Cavendish seal, though it's unclear if they were ignorant of the fact that the Crimson Council has its fingers everywhere, in every civil and private sector, including Scotland Yard."

"Including the Secret Services?"

He crossed his arms and gave her a mulish look, but eventually had to concede. "If the Crimson Council infiltrated the office of the Lord Chancellor, it would be remiss of me to think we were immune. We're not even technically a branch of government yet."

"So you're angry with the Hargraves for going to the authorities?" she reasoned. "Even though you are one? Do you know why they went?"

"Anger is a wasted emotion," he said. "But did you not hear me, Francesca, the Hargraves took the Cavendish family seal—*your* family seal—and wrote a fraudulent missive that got everyone killed."

"Have you seen the missive?" Her own arms crossed over her chest, as she was suddenly cold from the inside out.

"I've requested the paperwork through the proper channels. It was taking longer than expected, so I went to the records office at New Scotland Yard and they'd told me the case was misfiled at a storage facility in town, and there's no way to find it without looking through every single paper."

"Then let's do it." Francesca stood. "Where is the storage facility?" She had to know if what he was saying about her parents was the truth. She remembered them so fondly, but through the eyes of a girl still aged in the single digits. She'd not been old enough to uncover their sins. Surely, they had no idea what their actions might have wrought, and if they were fraudulent, they must have had a good reason.

Unless . . . they didn't.

Unless they weren't good people.

"Who is to say that the bastard Tuttle was telling the truth?" she said desperately. "Perhaps he sent you on a fool's errand, or he protected the council even under threat of death. You don't know if they had something on his family or—"

"Francesca." Though his voice was gentle, there was a thread of steel in the way he said her name.

She bit her lip.

"Paperwork regarding the death of an earl and his family wouldn't be sent to a dusty storage facility; it'd be sent to an official office—hell, the bloody palace—to be kept in books for British aristocratic progeny. They'd have released it to you, even, before they dared to lose it. Do you understand what I'm saying?"

She did. But she didn't want to.

He pinched the bridge of his nose. "The verification of the truth is in the fact that it's being covered up. Surely you can see that."

"That's not an absolute," she said obstinately. "I'll not believe it until I see my father's . . . seal for myself." She was going to say *handwriting*, Charles Hargrave's handwriting.

He stepped forward, looking as if he wanted to reach for her, but didn't allow himself to do so. She was glad. She couldn't take his kindness right now. Nor could she refuse it.

"Why are you being so stubborn about this?" His tone was gentle, though his words were not. "It's an answer, Francesca, a direction. We're one step closer to putting it to rest."

Why was she being so stubborn? Because she'd just received the most incredible news followed by the most devastating in the space of five minutes. Because she couldn't face telling this man—who used to be the boy she loved—her real identity if he thought her parents were culpable for their shared tragedy. Because she needed to know the truth. All of it. Because she wanted to understand who Declan had become before she trusted him with her most closely guarded secret.

And her own brand of fraud.

He deserved to know, didn't he?

Her conscience pricked her as she looked into those eyes that had seemed ancient even when he'd been a boy. That once held a lifetime of pain in their young depths, but now only reflected the flames.

Anything beyond that was opaque.

Did he, though? Was her reason for telling him any better than her reason for keeping her deception? She'd come so far and was so close to justice; what if her revelation was enough to ruin that? What if he was angry enough at her, at her entire family, that he exposed her legally? Publicly? Not only would she lose her title, which wasn't of much consequence, but it would go to Luther Kenway.

The Earl of Devlin had said as much.

And since when did she take anyone but Cecil and Alexander at their word? Certainly, she'd been enamored with Declan Chandler as a girl, but what sort of man had he become?

A ghost. Like her. A spy.

A professional liar.

"Tonight at the ball . . . Cecelia called you Chandler." Her eyes narrowed and her jaw tightened as she braced for her own uncomfortable truths. "Do they know who you are? Have they known all this time?" Because if they did, she'd kill Ramsay first.

"No one knows who I am, not really." Another of his non-answers.

Francesca considered throwing something at him.

He must have correctly calculated her expression because he elaborated for once. "I wasn't having you on when I told you I was a spy. It's my official job. I work for the Secret Services and everything. I met Ramsay when your friend Cecelia ran afoul of the Crimson Council. I helped him save his beloved and imprison the Lord Chancellor before he could finish his plan to kill your friend and use her business to traffic young girls. I'm a hero really," he flashed her a jaunty, arrogant smile. "Unsung, of course."

"Is that why I could never find record of your name?"

she asked. "I looked everywhere, just in case you'd survived. Or in case you had family somewhere. Or even a family plot in which to bury an empty casket, but it was as if Declan Chandler never existed."

"I'm Chandler Alquist now," he replied. "For the sake of my job."

"Alquis." She left off the *t* on purpose. "Anyone."

"Of course you know Latin," he grumbled.

"I know Alexandra Atherton." The brilliant duchess was the only reason she could passably speak the queen's own English. Let alone the other languages she'd drudged through during her tenure at finishing school.

Francesca realized she and Chandler were facing each other, standing not five paces away, each with their arms crossed against the other, protecting themselves.

But from what?

"There's so much to say . . . I don't know where to start." Chandler was the first to let his arms down, dropping them to his sides. It was the first time she'd seen him hesitant. Uncertain. She should say something kind. Put him at ease.

"I didn't know you were alive, but you must have known I was," she realized aloud. "Why didn't you come to me?" Oh bollocks. That had sounded more plaintive and demanding than she'd meant it to.

But she burned for the answer.

His face smoothed to blank before he turned away and went to a hat rack standing sentinel next to the door. He shucked his evening jacket and waistcoat and flung them onto one of the many solicitous arms. "The other night, I scuffled with a woman who'd broken into the safe house where the Lord Chancellor is being kept . . . you wouldn't know anything about that, would you?"

That was him?

Oh, they'd get to that, but she wasn't going to let him get away that easily. "You didn't answer my question."

He whirled around. His countenance wasn't just dark, but demonic. His brow was cruel and his eyes no longer burned. They were cold. Hard. Abysmal. "Are you ready to give me all your answers, Francesca?" He advanced on her, that predatory swagger returning. "Do you want to explain how you survived? What you saw that day? What knowledge you've gleaned since then and what you've done to get it?" He stopped only when he towered over her. A smarter woman would have stepped back. Retreated. But Francesca wasn't in the habit of yielding ground. "Are we ready to rip our truths open and bleed them all over each other? Is that what this moment is for?"

They held gazes. Everything both spoken and unspoken filled the spaces between them, threatening to drive them apart.

She looked away first, deciding to yield something else. "It was me the other night. At the safe house . . ."

He chuffed out a breath. "I won't ask you where you learned to fight, or to vault, not tonight," he said wryly. "But I will ask what the hell you were doing there?"

"Same as you. Searching for answers."

"And?"

"And, what?"

"And did the Lord Chancellor provide you with any?" he asked impatiently.

Francesca chose her words very carefully. "He told me a little about the power structure in the Crimson Council. He said there is a Triad and at the time of the massacre, there was a vacancy in the third spot. As there is right now." She could feel her own dark desires gathering on her face. "It seems there will be a second opening as well, if fate is kind and the Lord Chancellor hangs."

"A vacancy . . ." Chandler tapped his chin thoughtfully, and Francesca wondered how she'd ever thought the large hand with its calluses, rough skin, and a network of veins only dissected by scars could belong to an aristocrat.

"A vacancy they thought to fill with several people we know. Some of whom are dead."

That sparked his attention. "Such as?"

"Cecelia's aunt, the obscenely wealthy Henrietta Thistledown, known to all as the Scarlet Lady, for one. Lord Ramsay, for another, as he was the Lord Chancellor's protégé."

"Did Ramsay know of this?" he asked alertly.

Francesca shook her head. "He knew nothing of the council until he ran afoul of it."

"Strange, then, that they'd consider an outsider for their leader."

"They want power, and he has it in spades."

His lips twisted into a wry grimace. "Now that Cecelia is the Scarlet Lady, and she's attached herself to Ramsay, they'll be an unstoppable force, God save us all."

Francesca agreed with a fond noise before she lit up with an idea. "Was it possible Cavendish—my father—was a part of the council? That he wanted to be on the Triad?"

Chandler scrutinized her from beneath a lowered brow. "Your father?"

"The Lord Chancellor said that at time of the massacre, the place in the Triad was open to two individuals. He intimated one of them *might* have been the Earl of Mont Claire."

"And the other?"

"The other was Kenway, which is why I singled him out tonight."

"*Fucking* Kenway." Lashing as quickly as a viper, Chandler reached for the glass on the nightstand, turned, and hurled it into the fireplace.

It shattered with a disproportionately loud vibration, echoing his fury through the room before the shards fell to the ground in sharp aftermath.

The fit of pique seemed uncharacteristic, and Francesca desperately wanted to go to him. She sensed that he needed to find his composure, that he wasn't ready to face her without it, so she waited for several beats before voicing her thoughts.

"Is it possible that the Cavendish household was massacred because they got in the way of what the Earl of Kenway wanted? Not because of the Hargraves?"

He took two deep breaths and then exhaled mightily before touching his chin to his shoulder to look back to her. "It's a theory."

"One you're ready to embrace?" She did her best to keep the hope out of her voice.

"One I'm ready to entertain."

She frowned. "It's like you want it to be their fault. Hattie and Charles Hargrave were the loveliest people. So good-natured and kind. If they had something to do with the deaths, it couldn't have been by design—they died, too." Sighing, she added. "It's strange that the Lord Chancellor didn't mention them to me."

"I know you were fond of them, and Pip. I was, too. But if they'd never said anything, the household would still be alive. If they knew anything about the council, they knew that to mention it was to toy with death."

"Sounds like a lot of supposition to me."

"Just trust me," he said. "It isn't."

Trust me. He'd said that before. He'd shoved her in a tree and then told her to trust him.

And they'd lost twenty years.

"I gave you the information you asked for," she said. "It's your turn."

"My turn?"

"To trust me. To tell me what you know."

He turned away from the destroyed glass and reached out, grazing her cheek with the backs of his fingers. "I trust no one," he said as if it were a regrettable, unchangeable fact. "A symptom of the industry, I'm afraid."

"But . . . you know me. I'm your friend."

"I am not a man who is allowed friends," he said, as though not just telling her, but reminding himself.

She wanted to be angry, but she felt akin to him, sometimes. She had the Rogues, but she also left them out of so much of her life. For their own good.

"Well then, I'm the enemy of your enemy, and that means . . ."

"You are still someone who can betray me."

Taken aback, she huffed, "I would never!"

"I believe even you, yourself, aren't aware of the depths of depravity of which you are capable. It is my design to keep things that way. To not pull you into my world."

She was aware of her capabilities. She'd hidden more bodies than your average countess. Not as many as Elizabeth Báthory, but still.

"I'm already a part of this. You don't get to decide for me what I am capable of or not." It was a churlish comeback, and they both knew it.

His eyes upon her were assessing, and then appreciative. "You've managed to surprise me thus far, I'll give you that."

"And what does that mean?" Dammit, her arms were crossed again.

"Francesca." He brought his caressing finger down her jaw to her chin, lifting it up with a firm but gentle press. "If I don't tell you anything, it's for your own good."

"My own good?" She jerked her head away. "You *must* be joking."

He shook his head. "This is an official investigation. You don't understand what I must do next."

"Then *tell* me, Declan."

"I'm *not* Declan anymore. I never really was."

"Fine." She threw her arms out. "That's all right with me. You can be anyone you choose on any given day and I'll be there for you. We are not like others, we never have been and especially cannot be now. We wear our pain as armor, don't we? We use it to make us strong and decisive and to do what must be done." She went to him, putting her hands against his chest, letting the warmth of his core seep into her cold fingers. "Our shared memories can purify our bond and our shared purpose can perhaps heal us one day. It's all right if you're not Declan. I'm not exactly Francesca, either. I'm—"

"No." He took her hands from his chest and firmly put them to her sides. "That isn't how this works. That isn't how *I* work."

"I'm telling you it doesn't matter."

"It fucking matters to me!" he thundered, raking a hand through his disheveled hair. "I do dark things, and I will keep doing them. Things that would haunt your nightmares for years to come. Things that make me wonder if I'm becoming the monsters I've fought for so long. *That* is my reward for cranking the engine of this empire and for keeping the Crimson Council at bay."

When she would have said something, he held his hand up to silence her, and then out as if he would touch her before curling it into a fist. "In that darkness, I've held a glimmer of light in my memory. *You*, Francesca. You were so soft and so kind . . . the purity I fought for. That I avenged. And it is a hard thing to see that purity dashed."

"Dashed?" she echoed.

He looked away from her then, and something within her shriveled.

"I'll answer one question," he said darkly. "I didn't come to you all those years ago because I didn't believe you truly existed, and I didn't want to see who was parading as you. And now that we—" He let out a breath that sounded as if it carried the pain of dashed dreams. "You have your own darkness. I cannot add to it, and I cannot watch you do the same. You've become . . . this . . . this . . ."

"This what?" she asked from between clenched teeth that held back a slew of curses and a storm of feminine fury.

"Well." He made a curt gesture. "You've been relieved of your innocence, or you gave it away, I don't know which. And because of your vengeance, your reputation is in tatters and your bed acquainted with so many men that—"

Francesca slapped him. Not to shock him, nor to silence him. But to strike him. To shame him for the words both expressed and left unsaid. "How dare you? I've *seen* what a girl looks like when her innocence has been taken. And it is hard and ugly and a right bastard to try to regain. I've seen those who give up their purity for the sake of greed or spite or pure malevolence. I am ashamed of nothing, and those who think I should be can go hang. You included."

She turned to the nightstand and finished her scotch in one gulp before turning back to find him in much the same posture as before. "I'm no longer a child who must be protected," she said, her decisions remade and her courage reconstituted. "I am a woman in search of answers. A professional liar, same as you. I've trained for this my entire life. Allowed myself to want for nothing else but truth and justice for those who are dead, and I'll get that with or without your help." She gathered her skirts and made to sweep past him. "I suppose we'll just have to stay out of each other's way."

"Francesca, wait—" He reached for her arm, but she jerked away, backing toward the door as she added an addendum to her rant.

"I imagine you're not paragon of chastity," she spat. "My purity and my virginity are not one and the same. It doesn't matter how many men I've had, I am fucking pure as the driven snow, and no one will make me feel otherwise."

She turned her back to him, putting both her hands in the pockets of her gown to keep her fists from flying in a rage.

"Francesca." He stormed after her.

"Don't follow me," she snapped.

"I'm not letting you leave until you hear—"

"Hear *this*." She extracted her hand from her pocket, turned, and pulled the trigger of her pistol right next to his ear. To add injury to insult, she stowed the weapon and performed some kind of two-handed punch to his solar plexus, stealing his breath as well as his hearing.

By the time the ringing cleared and he was able to fill his lungs, she was long gone.

Chapter Fourteen

Francesca did her best not to scowl as Alexandra's arrow hit closer to the mark than her own. Either the Duchess of Redmayne had been practicing in her spare time, or Francesca was losing her edge.

Probably both.

The Red Rogues had taken a short holiday away from the city, boarding the train out of London to Dorset, where Castle Redmayne hulked like an ancient sentinel above Maynemouth, a lovely fishing village turned tourist destination on the Devonshire coast. The women stood in the southern sunshine at the ruins of an old fort above Torcliff, one that had been built by Redmayne's ancestors after their victory at the side of William the Conqueror.

They'd set up an archery range in the abandoned courtyard to take full advantage of the last of the decent weather before summer gave way to autumn, as it threatened to do.

The stone walls of the fort protected them from ocean breezes as they practiced their archery. The gallop from the castle to the fort over the lush, verdant grasses of Maynemouth Moor had invigorated Francesca, but still had done little to lift her spirits.

She hadn't seen Declan Chandler for days, and it was starting to get to her.

She pulled the veil of her riding hat down further against the high sun, hoping those clouds in the distance would be blown this way so she could stop bloody squinting. The call and reply of seabirds was more of an assault on her senses than a boon, and she couldn't seem to conjure anything but resentment for the rich scents of briny sea air, loamy grass, and horses.

Some of her favorite things.

It's not that she expected the world to match the grey of her mood, but she certainly wished it would. The uncommonly good weather and the general happiness of her loved ones were things she ardently desired, and couldn't bring herself to even pretend to enjoy.

She occupied a world where Declan Chandler was alive . . . and rather than a joy, it was a maze she couldn't see through. A wall of obstacles built by evil men, forces beyond her control . . .

And her own deceit.

"I worry about your plans to attend this function thrown by Lord Kenway, Frank," Cecelia said from where she grappled an arrow from her quiver in the corner and did her best to nock it with clumsy fingers. A brilliant, graceful woman was she, until competition was involved. Then she lost all sense and didn't have the coordination God gave a lump of clay. Finally, Cecelia gave up and lifted her gaze to Francesca's. Her high color set off the sapphire blue of her eyes, though whether it was from exertion or the sun on her uncommonly fair skin, it was impossible to say.

Francesca had explained to them the invitation she'd received to attend a very exclusive function at Lord Kenway's estate the following Saturday.

"Of course you're worried," Francesca replied, reaching into her own quiver. "I'm quite convinced that you've taken on fretting over us as your second vocation."

"It was my first before I became a card sharp." Cecil smiled that sweet, disarming grin, and laughed off the jibe with her characteristic good humor before she sobered. "But didn't you mention your Chandler told you that Kenway is more dangerous than your workaday villain?"

"He's not my Chandler."

Alexandra, who'd gone to Cecelia to help her, sent a level look from beneath the robin's-egg blue of her riding hat and veil, but kept her own counsel.

"Whoever's Chandler he is—and whether it's his first or last name—I still wonder if it's not a good idea to heed him in this case."

Francesca's lips tightened. "You have no idea how much it would gall me to heed any word out of that man's mouth."

This time, it was Alexandra and Cecelia who shared a look.

Francesca pretended not to notice, testing the tension on her bow.

"He was the most important person in the world to you at one point," Cecelia persisted. "Surely one conversation couldn't have changed that."

"It didn't. Twenty years changed it. Changed us." Francesca leaned her bow against a railing and peeled her riding jacket down her shoulders, shucking it before the sun cooked her in it. "He's not the boy I knew, nor is he the man I thought he'd grow into." She yanked at her necktie and popped open the first buttons of her chin-high blouse.

The same was true for them both, she supposed. So maybe it was better this way. Perhaps he was wise to never have come for her, because he'd been right all along. She wasn't who she claimed to be.

And telling him could ruin them both. "Before I knew about Chandler's survival, Kenway was always my aim. I mustn't be distracted from that," she said, pulling the bowstring back and letting her arrow fly. It landed the third right out, an even worse shot than before. "I still have a job to do. That hasn't changed."

"No, of course not," Cecelia placated her, pulling her veil above her hat rim and blowing at some errant fringe. "But to attend a function, a strictly Crimson Council function, alone. It seems rather . . . reckless, that's all. Perhaps you should at least tell Chandler that you'll be there, for safety's sake."

"I will dance a naked Irish jig on Prince Albert's grave before I ask that man for help." Francesca knew she should chew on the practicality of Cecelia's gentle suggestion, but her pride rejected it as violently as bad oysters. She'd not really hurt Chandler that night in his room when she'd discharged her weapon. He'd let her escape. He could have easily caught her, found her in the subsequent days.

He could have apologized for being an ass.

She might have even offered an apology of her own.

Emphasis on the word *might.*

Alexandra handed the bow with the nocked arrow to Cecelia and patiently helped her with her form as she drew a bead. Cecelia, who was almost never unladylike, whooped in victory as the arrow actually hit the side of the target rather than glancing off the grey stone walls as it had all afternoon. It landed nowhere close to the markers, but Cecelia was the sort to celebrate personal victories rather than ones over other people. She always felt guilty for winning competitions, and generally made certain she never did.

"It does appear that your and Chandler's current paths are aligned," the duchess finally weighed in as she adjusted her glove. "Perhaps, now that cooler heads prevail, you can at least discuss it with him, maybe plot some contingencies should aught go awry."

"Do you not remember what he said to me?" Francesca snatched up her weapon again. "I refuse to align myself with someone who would *malign* my parents, condescend to me, and then proceed to shame me for my reputation before even asking if his assumptions were valid in the first place!" She grabbed an arrow so violently from her quiver, it snapped.

Alexandra's lips twisted into a wry grimace that wrinkled her freckled nose, making her appear ten years younger. "That was rather poorly done of him."

"Though there aren't many men alive who wouldn't have done the same," Cecelia chimed in.

"Do not tell me you're defending him, Cecil," Francesca snapped. "You wouldn't abide that sort of thing from Ramsay, and Redmayne wouldn't dare."

"Touché," Alexandra conceded.

"I wouldn't think of defending him." Cecelia puffed out a defeated breath. "It's only that, well, people say rather awful things sometimes when they're jealous. Things they don't mean."

"He meant it," Francesca grumped.

"I suppose I just felt that you two finding each other after all this time . . . Well, it was all rather romantic. Something like fate." Cecelia sighed the last word with dramatic nostalgia.

"We don't believe in fate," Francesca muttered.

"But we do believe in second chances." Cecelia reached for her waterskin, which was filled with a lovely Viognier, and took delicate sips before handing it to Francesca. "And you two have such a history."

"I've always hated history." Francesca enjoyed the wine that tasted of exotic pears and summers in the south of France before passing it along to Alexandra, who waited to have the alcohol safely in her grasp before she retorted.

"The only people who say that are the people who hate their own history."

Francesca's next arrow missed its mark, but Alexandra's comment had been a bull's-eye.

"Chandler and I . . . our history is built on lies," she lamented. "He believes my actual parents are the reason our childhoods were taken from us. He believes I'm Francesca."

Alexandra drew up on her right and Cecelia on her left, a post they often took when together, the most distraught of them bracketed in the middle of their abiding devotion and undying protection.

"We're all women who are acquainted with carrying our secrets and sins . . ." Alexandra drifted off, no doubt thinking of the man they'd all buried so long ago. The man who'd raped her at seventeen. The man she'd killed that very night when Cecelia and Francesca had helped her bury the body. "They do not make us villains."

"He thinks I am a whore."

To her astonishment, Cecelia shrugged. "Ramsay assumed I was the whore of Babylon. He now respects the women who work for me, so I'm convinced hearts and minds can be changed. It's not an insurmountable obstacle. It just takes a bit of creative navigating, is all."

Francesca vehemently shook her head. "I refuse to prove my virginity to him."

Cecelia further surprised her by laughing. "Not of your virginity, dear, but of his own perception. It shouldn't matter to him whether or not you've had lovers. He certainly has had his share."

"How do you know?" Francesca whirled on her, suppressing the urge to shake her friend or interrogate her. Had she heard anything? Had he been to her establishment? Did she know a woman who'd enjoyed him in bed?

The thought made her sick, which made her cross.

"He has a very cocksure manner, doesn't he?" Cecelia looked into the distance, as if Chandler, himself, was standing there. "He walks as though he is a man who has pleasured many women. Who enjoys doing so. Who is proud that he can."

Francesca screwed up her nose. "You can tell all that by a man's walk?"

"Of course not. But there are certain things about the language of the body." Cecelia made an insouciant gesture. "I've collected certain odd bits of data from my current vocation as the Scarlet Lady, and subsequent analysis has required that I excel at reading men. Their tastes, proclivities. When not to let them in my establishment. Who and what they'd want to be offered." She ticked these off on her fingers.

"Why, then, does *he* get to walk like he's a lover, and I am expected to hang my head in shame?"

"Because you are a woman, obviously."

Francesca ripped off her gloves, quite finished with enjoying herself. "That isn't good enough. Not for me."

"We're getting off track here, Frank," Alexandra said. "You are considering infiltrating the society that thinks nothing of enslaving little girls. Of burning entire households down to protect their interests. Our immediate concern is your survival."

"That's your immediate concern, not mine," Francesca remonstrated. "I'm resolved, ladies. I will see this through or die trying. Best you get on board with that, or get out of my way."

Cecelia retreated slightly as if she'd been slapped. Alexandra did the opposite.

Francesca felt immediate regret, but her lips didn't seem capable of parting for an apology. Instead, angry tears stung at the corners of her eyes, and she had to turn away from them both.

It was Alexandra's hand that landed on her shoulder, gently and unthreateningly.

"You survived the unthinkable," she ventured. "When you go through something like that, it tempers you. It can break you down or forge you. It folds and shapes and sharpens you into something new, a weapon perhaps, and that is no small feat. But—"

"My mind is made up." Francesca said. "I didn't tell you two my plan to have you talk me out of it. I told you for the very reason you want me to tell him. In case . . ."

"In case you're killed?" Cecelia threw her hands up.

"I'm not going to be killed."

"You don't know that. What if they find out? What if they've found out already? You could be walking into a trap for all you know."

"Or they could be inviting their demise right into their lair. I appreciate the vote of confidence, you two."

Alexandra put up a staying hand. "We're not saying that we don't trust your skills."

"But no one should have to stand alone," Cecelia added.

"What if we attended as your guests?" the duchess offered. "Redmayne and Ramsay have both been courted by the council . . ."

"You weren't invited," Francesca said. "They'd suspect something."

"We could send protection?" Cecelia presented.

"I don't need it."

"You've done it for us."

"That was different."

Alexandra made a caustic noise. "How, exactly, was it different?"

"In each case, the threats to your lives were in the shadows. Mine has a face. A name. A tangible reason. I know what I'm walking into."

It was an absolute lie, but . . . in for a penny and all that.

"But you don't know their motivations, not when it comes to you. And you don't know what information they have on you."

"That's what I intend to find out, and if you love me, you two, you will do nothing to stop me." Whirling on her heel, Francesca stormed toward the archway, above which the ceiling had long since crumbled.

The women who had loved her stubborn hide looked after her silently until she'd mounted her horse and spurred it in the direction of the hills.

Alexandra released a calming breath. "Lord, but she could start an argument in an empty room."

Cecelia's face glimmered with concern. "Should we . . . do something? Tell someone?"

"She'd hate us," Alexandra said soberly.

"I'd rather have her irate than dead."

Alexandra thought for a moment, then brightened. "Lord Kenway's estate abuts the ruins of Miss Henrietta's School for Cultured Young Ladies, does it not?"

Cecelia caught her smile as if it were as contagious as the unspoken idea. "It does, indeed."

"She may think that she's walking into the lion's den

and will emerge unscathed. And while she might be alone, she will not be without backup."

That decided, the remaining contingent of the Red Rogues packed up to go back to the castle.

They had secret arrangements to make.

Chapter Fifteen

Francesca noticed Luther Kenway's butler was blindfolded before it registered that he was also stark naked. She stood at his threshold, seized with astonished indecision.

"I'm . . ." She'd quite forgotten why she'd come. In fact, she'd forgotten her name.

"Countess, welcome. Do come in." As stately as any yeoman, the man stepped back and widened the door for her, sweeping a grand gesture toward the interior of the Kenway estate.

Swallowing a surge of nerves, Francesca picked up the hem of her crimson garment and entered as he bade her.

She wasn't certain which disturbed her most: the blindfold; the nudity of an elegant, if portly, man well past his prime; or her own ensemble, a shimmering robe the color of the devil's own blood, and an intricate porcelain mask hand-painted by a masterful artisan in the form of a fox head.

Francesca paused on the landing of the grand entrance and absorbed the cornucopia of curiosities before her. She hadn't exactly known what to expect when she'd made her way through the London night following the exact route her invitation had specified. She'd been unable to identify travelers with a similar possible destination, and she would have, as the hour was late for the beginning of a soiree of any kind.

A midnight masquerade, it seemed.

Devotion. It was the only word on the invitation upon which the map had been depicted.

On her arrival, she'd been ushered through the gate by a man in a black robe, and directed to a dark fabric tent where her costume had been draped from a rather eerie-looking mannequin. She'd donned it, as directed, abandoning her clothing to the makeshift dressing room. It was a long affair with a grand train. A hood covered her hair, and behind it an adornment that would have done Queen Elizabeth proud sprouted from the shoulders and framed her features, creating the perfect canvas for her mask.

She'd felt rather silly drifting up the grand walkway in nothing but this gossamer robe and disguise. Had she still been a girl, she might have been enchanted. But as a woman possessed of almost thirty years, she couldn't quite imagine what she'd get up to in a fox mask. Or perhaps she didn't want to. She was just glad the only light to guide her glowed from the steps of the manor, and she'd followed it like the proverbial light at the end of a dark tunnel.

To a destination unknown. Feared. And perhaps hoped for.

"My lady," the butler murmured unobtrusively. "You are welcome to go inside. Barclay and Smythe will provide you with refreshment, and whatever else you desire."

Francesca swallowed around a dry tongue. Barclay and Smythe were two silent sentinels bracketing the entrance to the grand hall. They, too, wore nothing but blindfolds, though it was immediately apparent they had fewer years than the butler and decidedly more physical vocations.

Her neck was going to ache by the end of the night with the immense effort it took to not look down.

Beyond the guards, bodies clad in robes similar to hers mingled beneath chandeliers with only a few candles to illuminate them. The gas lamps remained unlit.

The revelers might have been ghosts. Specters of scarlet iridescence, their robes dragging behind them across the dark parquet floors like slicks of blood in the moonlight.

Objectively, the tableau was as beautiful as it was bizarre.

"Are you not going to announce me?" She turned to the butler, who shook his head.

"A woman of your eminence needs no introduction." He bowed, a most supplicant motion, and again gestured toward the ballroom. "Do enjoy yourself, my lady, and may I be the first to say we are most pleased to reintroduce the Cavendish line into the council."

Francesca's blood cooled. Chilled. And her entire body bloomed with hair-raising gooseflesh.

Unable to thank him, she inclined her head and had to look away as he turned back toward the door, presenting her with a decidedly hairier back end than she'd been prepared for.

As she neared the arched entrance, it became apparent that Smythe and Barclay were not the only—footmen?—in service thus attired. Or rather, *unattired.*

Others stood at strategically placed intervals around the room. As still as statues, they were offering trays to the guests. Some laden with goblets of drink, others with succulents and hors d'oeuvres.

A few serving women hovered around the frozen footmen. They made certain silver trays were filled and artfully arranged, that the men were coiffed and their blindfolds secure. They silently took empty goblets from guests and offered linens or refills with gentle gestures and pleasant, questioning eyes.

These women were also brazenly naked but with one marked difference.

Rather than blindfolded, they were gagged.

In the flowing sleeves of her robe, Francesca's fingers curled and tightened until her nails dug against her palms.

She'd wondered why such a concealing costume didn't come with gloves. Now she knew. They wanted nothing to impede tactile sensation.

The council didn't sample merely what was on the trays of the footmen, but anything else they wished to put their hands on. Every sort of body imaginable was on display. Pale, dusky, or dark. Slim, stocky, soft, or solid. Elegant or rough.

Francesca did more than stare. She gawked, feeling

guilty as she did so. Were these people here of their own volition? Not only women scored the footmen's backs with their nails or reached between their legs for a feel. For a stroke.

But men did as well.

Likewise, the serving girls were idly caressed and handled, and they bore it patiently. Gladly, it seemed, pausing their work to make themselves available.

The chamber quintet on the corner of a raised dais were likewise nude, in fact. Just about anyone who would have been considered service staff performed their duties without a uniform of any kind.

Many other guests turned when Francesca entered, and she immediately realized why. Beasts of every genus and species were represented in the room, but no two masks were alike. She spotted a bear and a bee, a stag and a snake, and just about everything in between. Each mask was a work of art, a white porcelain base with vibrant details done in monochromatic tones. Not all robes were crimson. A few were a ghostly shade, not white and not quite silver. Only a handful, though, were adorned with the same hood and stiff collar as hers.

A status symbol, it seemed, though one she didn't understand.

Did they know who she was behind this mask? Did they know one another? How many of them would she pass on the street and recognize as an acquaintance without knowing what they got up to at night?

How many of these people were responsible for the Mont Claire Massacre, or knew about it and did nothing?

She suppressed a shudder at the very thought, suddenly very aware of how alone she was.

Serana knew of her whereabouts, of course, and so did the Rogues, but that would do blessed little to help her if things went sideways.

She'd made peace with her fate before she'd stepped a foot on the Kenway grounds, so there was only one thing to do.

Plunge into the crowd as if she belonged there and get what she came for.

Walking with an affected air of superiority, she went to a large Moorish fellow who stood taller than most. He had the loveliest, smoothest complexion she'd ever seen, and his shoulders and head gleamed even in the lowest of light.

She did her best not to peek . . . down below and failed utterly. It wasn't that she'd never seen a naked man before; of course she had. But she'd always averted her eyes. Despite her boldness in so many aspects, the vulnerability of these people made her want to squirm.

Uncertainty tugged at her. Was it disrespectful to be curious? Was it awful to look?

Probably.

But she looked. And she'd be lying if she claimed not to like what she saw. Not just the African with the impressive physique, but also the slim and pale androgynous man with the long waist to match his impressive sex. He contrasted splendidly with a rather square fellow with a wealth of hair, bulky muscle beneath a healthy layer of padding, and what she considered to be a much less intimidating organ.

The women intrigued her, too, all told. The differences and similarities. The placements of their hips and breasts. The abject wickedness of so much flesh on display, and the anonymity her mask provided.

No one knew where her eyes drifted, and there was a certain freedom in that. She'd be lying to claim that freedom didn't titillate her somewhat.

Even as something primal in her responded to the situation, she shriveled from it, as well.

The others gathered, maybe seventy or so in number, greeted her in reverent whispers. No one called her by name, but they seemed to understand she had a "my lady" status.

She nodded and returned their greetings with a low murmur, somehow feeling that she'd stumbled into a church. She didn't want to meet the God to whom these people swore fealty. The one who gagged women and blinded men, who displayed them vulnerably and subjected them to objectification.

A familiar feeling swept over her on the tail of that thought.

The breath of a ghost on her back. Not quite chilling, but neither was it warm. Warning bells clanged in her head, in her body.

At least, by now, the sensation was familiar, and always accompanied by a subsequent encounter with Chandler—or whomever he pretended to be at the moment.

Was he here? Was that the danger she sensed?

She'd been doing her utmost not to think of him these past weeks. Not to want. To yearn. To seek him out and . . .

And what? Apologize? Explain? Confess?

Francesca shook her head and lifted a glass from the

proffered tray. The mask she wore left her lower lip exposed, and the goblet conveniently fit to her mouth so she could drink.

She used the sip as an excuse to survey the gathered crowd in low light.

The figures in white were few, maybe seven, and it appeared that some of them intended to make their way toward her, drifting through the river of red like specters swimming upstream through a lake of blood.

Their masks were all the same. Stags. Great, sharp antlers branched from their crowns, holding the hoods in place.

They seemed all like rather large men. Security, perhaps?

"I wasn't certain you'd come."

Francesca whirled at the disembodied voice, nearly colliding with the footman from whom she took her wine. Next to him, a figure with the mask of a lion tilted his head down to look at her. He had a high collar behind his cape, as well. And his mane was extraordinary, reminding her of the sun.

Not Chandler. Her shoulders fell.

Luther Kenway.

Francesca did what she always did when she was frightened: She lifted her chin, squared her shoulders, and bared her teeth.

Figuratively, for now.

"I would have RSVP'd if you'd have preferred, but alas . . ." She let the insinuation drift away. When he didn't reply, Francesca continued. "You certainly went through a lot of costuming trouble for someone you weren't sure would attend." She took another drink.

For a man with so much money and influence, he had shit taste in wine.

"I said I wasn't certain you'd come, but I'll admit I was confident." The mask lent his voice a certain growl, as if the soul of the lion did, indeed, inhabit his body.

"And what inspired this confidence?" she asked, turning so she stood shoulder-to-shoulder with him, rather than facing the frightening mask.

"I know you are an inquisitive woman." His lips, both foreign and familiar, drew into a tight, almost cruel smile. "I know you couldn't help but indulge your curiosity."

Something about the way he said this rankled at her.

What else did he presume to know about her?

"So *this* is the Crimson Council." She surveyed the room with an unaffected air she didn't feel. Hard to believe she'd finally made it.

Now how could she irrevocably destroy it?

"All this could be yours," he murmured.

She looked up at him sharply.

"My dear Countess, you must know that I do nothing by degrees, and I did not offer my proposal lightly. I think we could be good together, you and I."

"I think you mean I could be good for you."

He tilted his head in an almost doglike gesture of confusion. "Are you saying I have nothing to offer you that you would want?"

She shrugged "I am already a countess, so you could offer me no higher title," she pointed out. "And while you may be wealthier than I am, I have enough money to last me generations. I have no interest in politics, not really. And if I were to marry you, what is mine would become yours. How exactly, is your proposal supposed to tempt me, Lord Devlin?"

Instead of angering him, as she'd suspected she might, he indulged her with a sound of amusement. "A privileged woman, indeed," he said blithely. "I'm curious, then, as to why you would attend my fete."

"Perhaps to see what else you had to offer." She tilted her head coyly and was rewarded with the sense her answer pleased him.

"My lady, I can offer you what you most desire. All you need do is tell me what that is."

The truth. Justice. No, more than that, revenge.

"Freedom," was what escaped her lips. And the truth of it resounded in her soul.

"Look around, my dear."

She did. And what she saw confused, intrigued, and sickened her.

His hand landed on her shoulder, and it took every ounce of will she had not to duck away from it.

"Freedom is exactly what I'm offering. It is what these devotees of the council seek."

She looked up in genuine amazement. "I would have thought power. Or wealth. Political influence or—"

He shook his head both immediately and violently the moment she began to speak.

"Our wealth helps us to gain our influence," he conceded. "And therein we find power . . . but I'll tell you a secret, little vixen." He leaned closer, tilting his head down as if the lion and the fox might kiss. "Power is an illusion, one we certainly maintain as a tool to accomplish our main objective, one that aligns with your own."

"I'm . . . not following."

"Freedom," he said, his voice ardent as he nudged her toward the dais, where a sensual cello refrain drifted around them.

"Nothing about this room speaks of freedom to me." She gestured with her chin to a gagged woman offering her wares to a group of guests.

If Francesca watched for too long, she feared she'd become violently ill.

"Think, my lady, about where we have been told for centuries upon centuries that our loyalties must lie? Think about the order of importance."

When she said nothing, he elucidated. "Your God first, then your nation. Family. Community, and then, finally, the individual." He paused, turning to face her. "What does that sort of philosophy get you?"

Francesca frowned. She wasn't particularly religious; nor was she patriotic. She was British because she was born so. Anglican, perhaps, because of the traditions of her ancestors. But she'd seen too much of the world, of humanity, of spirituality to believe in or completely discard almost any possibility. She had no such creed, and told him so. "I wouldn't know. That isn't how I live."

"I know." He held up a finger as if to say, *Ah-ha*. "You live to please only yourself."

"I wouldn't say—"

"Oh come now, you do not have to pretend here. You are of a like mind to us. To live crimson is to live without shame."

"Crimson," she repeated, running out of patience. "Why the crimson? Does it represent the devil? The church? A pagan god, or demon perhaps? Is it something to do with Britannia, herself?"

She drew herself up short. Drat, she'd begun to rapid-fire questions again.

Instead of seeming frustrated or insulted, he seemed fascinated. Francesca didn't know whether to be relieved or mortified.

"Think about the color red, Francesca. It's the color of extremes. It captures our attention, and it warns us of danger. It represents all things visceral and primal. Blood. Danger. Violence." He stepped in closer. "Passion, seduction, and even love. It colors the flags of nearly every powerful empire, and yet it denotes districts in which we try to contain our vice in every European culture. We give red roses when we are in love, and we see red when we are about to take a life in anger. Why, Countess, do you think that is?"

Stymied, Francesca only shook her head.

"You've purloined it for your own moniker, I'm told. You and your red-headed rogues."

A beat of terror thumped behind her ribs. It wasn't as though she hid her relationship with the Rogues, but neither did she advertise it.

If he knew about the Red Rogues . . . then he'd been watching her. Listening to whispers about her.

But how closely?

"Why hide behind your ridiculous masks if you do nothing to be ashamed of?" she demanded as if she didn't already know.

His fingers tightened around his glass, his only outward show of emotion since she'd arrived. "Because." He thrust his strong chin toward the milling crowd, even as a restlessness pervaded the room. "Our *ridiculous* masks remind us that behind our civility, every human is just an animal. And animals all have certain primitive understandings."

"Such as?" She injected insouciance into her voice to cover her excitement. Finally, some answers.

"Survival is our first instinct, to be sure. Those in power convince the masses that they allow them to survive. They pretend to help, to sacrifice the good of the few for the many and so forth . . . but it is they who hold sway over our lives. They who squeeze the life right out of us. They take from us what we are at our most base. Our most honest and raw form."

"What are we?" she whispered.

"Dear Francesca, we are desire."

She was so deflated, she puffed out most of the air from her lungs before she echoed him drolly. "Desire?

"Yes." He nodded. "We are beings of need and of want. It is that simple."

Francesca clenched her jaw. Her thighs. Her fists. Frustration thrummed through every sinew of her body. "You mean lust?" she huffed. "Tell me you didn't go through all of this hoopla to invite a throng of perverts to just one more Caligulan orgy." She said this as if it was a waste of her time. As if she'd been to several and they now bored her to tears.

It *was* a waste. She could think of no greater rubbish than if the entire Cavendish household had been snuffed out because of the earl and countess's adventurous sex lives.

Nothing could be so laughably tragic.

"It's so much more than that," Kenway insisted. "We

have urges, Francesca. Instincts. Ones we are forced to quell by the strictures of society. What are we behind the frippery that confines us and the machines we create? Unapologetic carnivores. Predators. We crave dominance. Power. Glory. Blood." He looked over at her, and his eyes seemed to glow from behind the see-through linen. "And yes. Fucking. We desire pleasure and progeny. Immortality."

A distinct chill cooled her frustration. "And . . . you have convinced these people that you will give them this . . . freedom?" To do what?

"No, this philosophy, this council, was around long before I joined, long before I rose to power. No, Francesca, my job is not to give people these things, but to train them to take it."

"What?" She stared at him, aghast.

He stepped closer. "If I desired you, what's to stop me from taking you right now? Do you think these people would lift a finger? Any of them?"

She searched the crowd, noting that some of them pretended not to watch them while others were actively eavesdropping.

Sliding her fingers into her robes, she found the leather straps beneath which she'd sheathed a knife against her arm. "I would," she said in a hard voice. "*I* would stop you."

His eyes flared. "I know. That's why you are here."

"Is that so?" she scoffed, again trying to seem unaffected, doing her utmost not to be alarmed to notice that the stags in white robes had lurked closer.

"I wonder." Kenway moved behind her, causing her

breath to catch in her throat. "I wonder if you are worthy of the name you claim."

"I will prove to you, before this is over, that I will take exactly what I deserve." From him, she'd take everything. She swore it.

"You've already taken so much, Countess. You've quite the craven reputation . . ."

She thought of Chandler then. Of the fact that he shamed her for her lovers. A pang of sadness sliced through the fear. What a disappointment they were to each other.

Kenway leaned down to whisper in her ear as he gestured widely to the council. "Desire drives you, Francesca, just as it does all of us."

"You have no *idea* what drives me," she retorted.

"Oh, I have some idea." He beckoned the men in white robes even closer. "I invited temptation here for you tonight. To show you what life might be like. Even as a wife of mine, you would be allowed all kinds of freedoms."

"Allowed?" she echoed archly.

"Encouraged," he amended. "You'll be encouraged to take what you want, to indulge, to share it with me. You'll be part of a movement. Of a shift in society so extraordinary, the world will never be the same."

Christ, he wasn't just evil, he was a lunatic. They all were.

"I am not inclined to . . . indulge . . . publicly."

"And so you shan't," he cajoled. "After this one display of devotion."

She swallowed. Hard. "Display? What sort of display?"

"Consider, Countess, how animals live. You are quite the equestrian, I'm told. You know horses?"

"Some," she hedged.

"Does a stallion care about pedigree when he mounts a mare? Does he ask her permission? Do they care who is watching as they rut?"

A horror utter and complete rose within her as Francesca mutely considered her options.

"Do most creatures care about modesty, physical or social? Do they care about the feelings of their prey? Does an eagle feel guilt for the adorable squirrel who is his meal? Does the lion not drive away his offspring to make certain his kingdom is never questioned?"

She fought to remain calm. To not bolt. "S-some would argue we as higher-minded individuals have evolved beyond such base instincts."

"Some would." The men in white robes broke from the crowd and approached the dais. A herd of stags. "And others would say that we are merely the apex predators. That we are capable of such feats. Such unsurpassable godlike feats if we were not tethered by the mythos of the past and those who would keep us on our knees."

"The monarchy, you mean?"

He inclined his head. "The monarchy. Or republics. The church. Every prophet, warlord, and prostitute who demanded someone bow down before them. To kneel."

He moved back into her line of vision, the stags making a half circle around her. "When is the last time you knelt to anyone?"

Never was when, and she wasn't about to start now.

He traced some flare of art on her mask with his fingertip, a tender lion courting a fox.

"Did you know this place has never had a woman in our Triad of leaders? Perhaps it is time that changes."

"Why select me to lead when I've never followed?" she asked. "I'm no devotee of yours."

"Perhaps that's exactly why I'm considering you." He reached out and adjusted her hood, his fingers sliding through her hair.

It took every bit of her will not to shrink from his touch.

"You are bold and worldly enough to lead, but young enough to abide. This council grows stagnant with old men and, to be honest, I'm in need of a physical heir to my earldom, as mine are no longer viable."

At this, Francesca couldn't contain an audible gasp. How could he speak of his dead children like that?

"You have a decision to make tonight, Francesca. You could take the first step toward becoming the most powerful countess in the world. Or . . . the Mont Claire tragedy could be complete."

Simple enough. Take his offer or die.

Evil men called choices like that freedom, and idiots fell for it.

"What must I do?" she asked.

"You must only watch. And then you must decide."

Watch who? Decide what?

He turned from her then and motioned to the stags, two of whom parted from their compatriots to open a cavernous set of doors to a dark hallway. An expectant hush fell over the crowd, and Francesca felt certain the entire ballroom could hear the pounding of her heart.

She didn't know who or what she expected to emerge from the dark hall, but it certainly wasn't the Lord Chancellor.

Had he escaped from the Secret Service? Or had he been delivered to this dangerous, powerful man by agents from within?

As much as Francesca despised Sir Hubert, she fought a spurt of pity. Not because she'd forgiven him his unforgivable sins, but because he appeared so pitiable. To see the man who held an office arguably as high as the Prime Minister, a man who held power over all the courts of Great Brittan, stripped bare and brought so low was less than palatable.

For an old man, he had the body of a toddler, wobbly and potbellied, wrinkled and dimpled at the joints. He walked without chains, cuffs, or ropes. The stags didn't touch him; in fact, it appeared that the Lord Chancellor led them to the dais. The Crimson Council parted for him and then closed ranks as he passed, like displaced liquid forming around a sinking ship.

Francesca was both mortified and mystified. Again, she clung to the knife she'd strapped to her arm, waiting for someone to make a move.

It was the Lord Chancellor who spoke first. "As a member of the Triad, I prostrate myself at the will of the wild. It is our way to prey upon the weak. To cast out from our presence one who has failed us absolutely. I have endangered the council, have profaned its precepts, and in doing so I am condemned by the laws of the realm to forfeit my life."

"What is it you desire?" Kenway asked, his voice

echoing into fractures around the chamber, seeming to come from many directions at once.

"I offer myself in the stead of the sacred seven. I will be the vessel of devotion. The bond that ties our council together. My actions will renew our vow to *Predonius Primus.*"

Predonius Primus. Francesca searched her knowledge of Latin. The alpha predator.

Kenway turned to the room at large. "The actions of this . . ." He paused and raked Hubert with a withering glare. "*Man* robbed us of our sacrifices. The rite of devotion has always been a sacrifice of innocence. Of blood. On this day, unfortunately, we will only be allowed one of these, as innocence is beyond you. But . . . you offer something else that will redeem you, Hubert."

He did? Francesca watched with trapped breath screaming in her lungs. The Lord Chancellor had not one redeeming quality. He'd been a cog in the machine that had caused the Mont Claire Massacre. He'd captured young girls and kept them chained like dogs in the catacombs beneath Cecelia's estate. He'd perverted justice of the realm during his tenure countless times to serve his causes. His and, it would seem, the Crimson Council's.

She'd have not lost any sleep if he hanged in the tower.

So why did the thought of watching him die make her feel weak-kneed?

"In lieu of innocence you offer us influence. May your sacrifice be deemed sufficient."

"May it be so." Hubert lowered his head, and Kenway put his hand upon it as if he were the pope blessing a supplicant.

Francesca readied herself for the worst. Tensed with a frenzy of thought. Would he stab himself? Commit some sort of seppuku, right here in front of a crowd of onlookers?

Or would Kenway murder him in front of everyone?

What would she do in response?

She was supposed to watch. But could she really bring herself to witness a murder? A suicide?

She was in too deep. And she was utterly alone.

Suddenly she wanted Chandler. Because even though he fought with her, he would also fight beside her. This she knew absolutely.

Kenway took a knife out of his robes and held it out to the Lord Chancellor, who took it almost gratefully.

Francesca steeled herself, prepared for the worst. She'd known tonight would be strange, and dangerous. This was the moment she'd hoped for and feared: She was bearing witness to something she could use against them one day. This was what infiltrators had to do.

And she had to remain silent.

The Lord Chancellor held the dagger against his forearm and sliced. Some of the crowd gasped; others remained still as the blood flowed, but not so much as Francesca had feared.

Not enough to be fatal.

He brought the cut to his pale and doughy chest and drew the three-headed snake, or at least, she thought it was. That finished, a bandage was brought to him by a nubile handmaiden and pressed to the shallow wound before the stag-headed men relieved him of the dagger and escorted him out.

They didn't follow him, but closed the door behind him and returned to their half-moon arc around her.

Sacrifice, indeed. Francesca rolled her eyes and let out a trapped breath on a sigh that was equal parts relieved and deflated as the chamber orchestra struck up their seductive melody once again.

If ever there was a good time for an anticlimax, this was it. She didn't have to watch anyone die.

"Do I sense a bit of disappointment in you, Countess?" Kenway drifted forward and inquired sotto voce. "He was your enemy, was he not?"

Francesca knew she must answer carefully so as not to give herself away.

He saved her from having to reply. "What would you have done to him, I wonder? Would you have put him back in the cage from which he has been freed?"

Her temper rose at the thought of his freedom as she remembered those innocent girls locked away for weeks.

"Would you have seen him hanged?" Kenway continued with a malicious glee. "Put him in front of a firing squad? Tell me, Francesca, what your most dangerous desire would be. If it would not stain your soul. Would you watch him die as your family died?"

Kenway knew, she realized with a twist of terror. He knew that she'd found the Lord Chancellor in the safe house and interrogated him for information. Which meant he knew what the Lord Chancellor had revealed to her.

Now more than ever, it was important that she remain unaffected. "What happens to Sir Hubert means nothing to me," she said with as much flippancy as she could muster. "Feed him to the dogs if you will. I've more pressing concerns."

"Such as?"

"Such as the state of these men and women?" She motioned to the naked servants. "You shame and degrade them, and what have they done? Would you do the same to me if I were to accept your proposal? Is this how I would have to show devotion? Because I think not."

A mirthless laugh rolled from beneath his mask, and she wanted to rip it away so she could read the evil in his eyes.

"Darling, there are those who would be always prey. They sometimes devote themselves to the strong, and we allow it. These are our aspirants. They beg to be on their knees for us, so when our time comes to take power, they will be by our side instead of beneath our feet. It *is* how they show their devotion." He leaned closer. "You show your devotion by witnessing what you witness tonight, and keeping it silent."

Bile rose in Francesca's throat. This . . . this was sick. Perverse. Profane. She watched how the crowd now milled with excitement. Little groups began to form, heads together, whispering intimacies in unlikely animalian clusters.

Expectancy still hovered in the air, and it didn't take a genius to guess what sorts of things would happen next.

Her parents had something to do with this? Were they like these servants? The thought made her ill.

"Now, my dear, let us prepare for the next night."

"The next?"

"We meet for three nights every three years for this particular three-part ritual. Of course, the most important work is done beyond these walls. However, three is a very auspicious number, and I daresay the second night is our favorite."

She was almost afraid to ask. "What is the second night?"

"The second night"—he put his hands on her shoulders and gently turned her to face the crescent of patiently waiting stags—"is Desire."

Whatever motion Kenway made from behind her, it was a command.

Because all of the stag-headed men shucked their white robes, uncovering the bodies of seven would-be gods.

Stunned, Francesca gaped.

Exquisite, they were, each in their own way. An overabundance of masculinity, nay an assault of savage beauty. Mounds of muscle shone in the wan glow, creating grooves and shadows as they were flexed and displayed. Each man was larger and lovelier than the last. Some had dark hair, others fair. A few had little at all. Some were older, grizzled and hard. Others young and eager and also—she swallowed as she looked down—hard.

They all wanted her. That much was physically obvious. And for every moment of this night that was wrong, Kenway had been right about one thing.

The power of it was heady.

Francesca still struggled to process it all when

Kenway nudged her forward. "They are here for you, Countess. To tempt you. To pleasure you. They must show devotion by devoting themselves to your whims. You select what you want, *who* you want, and tomorrow, you'll have him, or them. There will be no depravity unavailable to you, and if you do not see what you desire here, it will be fetched for you. This is only the first of the—"

Without forethought, Francesca held up a hand to stop him.

And it worked.

It was so quiet in the room, the whisper of her robes across marble could be heard in the back.

Everything about this night was entirely, deeply wrong. These people did not understand the slightest thing about what it was to be human, their entire philosophy was skewed, but she had to do what she had to do.

And she'd known immediately who she would select.

Who she wanted.

There. Him. Two "stags" over from the left. He was the entity she could feel in a room full of people. He was the skitter of awareness up her spine.

He was not extraordinarily tall, like some, nor did he have an overabundance of bulk. No, he was the perfect specimen. The Vitruvian man. His body was sculpted of different clay than most, perhaps stolen from Mount Olympus rather than the pedestrian earth from which others were forged. When the masters painted gods and heroes of myths and legends, they might have studied his frame.

Testing a theory, Francesca touched a few of the men as she strode by, pretending to test the strength of a shoulder, the firmness of a jaw.

And each time her hand reached out, the stag that had caught her eye tensed even further. His knuckles whitened as his side. A flush stole over his skin, barely perceptible in such dim light.

Finally, she stopped in front of him. Almost certain her suspicions were correct.

As she stood before him, his breath increased perceptibly, and she knew.

She said nothing as she smoothed her hand down the swells and valleys of his powerful arm, stopping to pull his hand to her.

He allowed this, though she could sense hesitance in the rigidity of his every visible sinew.

Silently, as if they didn't have an audience, she opened his palm.

Chandler.

She traced the scar with her nail and looked back up at him. He was good at being a spy. He'd found a way in, just as she had.

She'd known him to be spectacularly fit from when she'd sparred with him, but she hadn't expected such exquisite beauty.

He was glaring down at her now through the slits in his mask covered with iridescent, paper-thin fabric. She wasn't afraid, even when she couldn't see his face.

They'd been wearing masks since they'd rediscovered each other.

She could never read his thoughts, and he never guessed her emotions.

She knew nothing about him really . . . Only that she wanted him. Desired him.

His skin responded to her touch, little bumps of gooseflesh rising to meet her palm. His muscles twitched and warmed wherever her fingertips ventured.

And when she looked down at where their hands were joined, it was impossible to miss another appendage of his. Thick and impressive, jutting toward her from narrow hips lined with lean muscle.

She'd selected him now . . . which meant tomorrow they must—

"Excellent." Kenway stepped behind her, and Chandler wound impossibly tighter, his muscles bunching like a stallion ready to take a leap. Waves of menace rolled from him, emanating with such strength, she was astonished that Kenway wasn't toppled over by the tidal force.

Even she had to stop herself from taking a step in retreat.

"The selection is made," Kenway said with encouragement. "You will receive a summons and a map to the next meeting place."

"We will not be here tomorrow?" Francesca dropped Chandler's hand, and it seemed it would not return to his side for a hesitant moment as she turned to Kenway.

"No, my vixen, needs must that we conduct our rituals in several expedient places."

She merely inclined her head, almost dizzy with relief to find that she'd be leaving this place tonight.

Alive.

Kenway seemed as if he would move on before he paused. "Feel free to take one home with you, if you'd like." He motioned to Chandler with his chin. "Not him of course, but if I know you, you'll want an amuse-bouche before the main course." He leaned in. "Or, perhaps, you would stay here tonight. With me."

Chandler almost stepped out of the circle, a low noise escaping his throat, and Francesca panicked. Her hand collided with his chest, but she softened the touch as she raked her fingers down the many corrugations of his ribs in a show of lust that wasn't exactly a performance. "I believe I will take the night to prepare." She shot Chandler a pleading look from beneath her mask, knowing it was hopeless. "I think we should all recoup and ready ourselves for what we must do next."

If Kenway thought her reply odd, he gave no indication. "Indeed. Until we meet again, my Crimson Countess."

When he left through the same large door through which the Lord Chancellor had gone, the council dispersed in no particular hurry.

Chandler said nothing to her, following the stags in their procession, taking with him any sense of protection she'd felt.

It would be folly to wait around here for him, though Francesca did what she could to linger. Finally she gave in to the parts screaming at her to run. To get out.

Eventually, she followed a couple who kept their arms interlocked as they were ushered down a barely lit corridor. The dim glow hardly reached the walls, but plush carpet muted the sounds of the people being led to who-knew-where.

"The council has become so secretive since those girls were found," the woman in front of her said in muted tones to her companion. "Too careful, if I'm honest. Seems to go against the creed, don't you agree?"

"Perhaps," her fellow replied in a waspish voice. "But think about how many of us have been befallen by some sort of calamity or other. Colfax, Murphy, and scores of others. Not to mention the Lord Chancellor." A shudder went through him. "I'll be honest, whatever befalls Sir Hubert won't keep me up at night. Sometimes the fate of those poor girls has stolen my peaceful slumber in the past. It is a true and ingenious test of our devotion, to watch the sacrifice of innocents, an unnecessary one, I feel. I've always been rather glad it is quick and painless."

The girls he spoke of, girls not yet become women stashed in the basement of the high-end den of vice that had abutted the Kenway estates. The Red Rogues had always assumed the girls were meant to be used as objects for the perversions of powerful men. Francesca was certain Ramsay and Cecelia had saved the young ladies from molestation.

To think there was something worse in store for them. A sacrificial death, perhaps. It was enough to chill the bones.

To wonder if she'd ever be warm again.

"Tosh," the woman reprimanded. "Those girls were always nothing more than immigrants and East End rubbish. The Lord Chancellor was part of the Triad. If he can so be discarded, then we should all fear for our own necks."

Francesca had to stop herself from snorting aloud. The Lord Chancellor, in her opinion, was fortunate to escape with his life. He'd gotten off rather lightly, in her opinion.

For now. She was going to take down the rest of these deviants if it was the last thing she did. The Lord Chancellor would be first on her list.

"We do not protect our necks, my dear," said her husband. "We go for the throats of others."

"Absolutely." She patted the man's arm as they turned a corner and filed through a narrow door to the gardens across which a gate stood ajar.

What they saw through slats in a wrought-iron fence to the north was the only thing that kept Francesca from clawing the insufferable woman's eyes out.

The wet sounds of animals dining slowed the exit of the council as they walked by, each of them pausing to watch the gruesome spectacle.

A pack of hounds fed on fresh meat.

"I suppose we will need more sacrifices in the future," the woman said as she watched for a moment from beneath a mask of a badger. "Other sacrifices . . ." She turned to look at Francesca, her hawk-masked companion following suit. "One wonders, my dear, what sort of dynamic a woman will bring to the Triad, most especially when our Primus has chosen you, and also paid you this tribute."

Francesca couldn't bring herself to summon a reply as she stepped closer to the wrought-iron gate. The bars were cool, even as she wrapped fingers of ice around them.

Tribute?

Blood ran through the grooves of the paving stones as the last of the flesh was torn from a long bone.

Francesca had to swallow several times so as not to retch.

What had she said so flippantly to Kenway when he'd asked her what she wanted to do with the vile Lord Chancellor?

Feed him to the dogs.

Chapter Sixteen

With a traumatized sort of numbness, Francesca dressed in the detached tent and wobbled out into the night. Her carriage awaited her in the drive next door, the ruins of Cecelia's old manor. The rebuild of Miss Henrietta's School for Cultured Young Ladies had already broken ground, but the last of the rubble had yet to be cleared away.

London seemed darker tonight. Quiet and eerie, with the muffled, biting chill of the winter. Or perhaps that was just how she perceived it.

Perhaps she saw in the atmosphere what swirled about inside. She was both a tempest and wasteland after tonight. A storm with nowhere to blow.

But she'd achieved her goals, hadn't she? She'd infiltrated the enemy, and seduced their leader. If she was stalwart, she could break them. So long as she didn't break first.

The gas lamps didn't seem gold tonight, but pallid and wan. They cast more shadows than light, and she kept a firm grip on her knife in case she might need it.

When strong hands grabbed for her and pulled her behind the solid stone security fence of Cecelia's property, she had the blade out and at a male throat in an instant.

"Frank, darling," Alexandra said gently. "I'd consider it a personal favor if you didn't stab the father of my child."

Francesca wrenched herself out of the Duke of Redmayne's grasp and scowled up into his scarred, satirical features. "I'll slice the pretty side of your face if you presume to grab me again," she snapped with no veracity whatsoever to the threat.

"You're welcome." The split in his lip showed as his close-cropped ebony beard parted to reveal one of his rare smiles. He pointed at a post, one she might have walked into if he hadn't have redirected her.

She scowled at it, refusing to thank him while he was being smug.

"I expressly forbade you two from spying on me," she scolded the Rogues, refusing to let them know how knee-wobblingly *glad* she was to see them. "And then you bring these brutes to muddle things up? If I'm discovered because of you, I'll be so bloody cross I'll—"

Cecelia threw her arms around her as if she were a long-lost sister. "We were so worried, Frank." She might as well not have whispered, as the rasp of her voice carried through the night at a regular pitch. "All these people and no lights."

They turned to watch the last few people disperse into the night like Mayfair ghosts. "I've never seen the like. What is going on over there?"

Francesca backed up, right into Ramsay, who wisely stepped back and allowed her to steady herself.

Ramsay, a famous celibate before Cecelia, touched no woman but his own.

Francesca assessed the four faces glowing at her expectantly from what little light shone through the clouds.

Should she tell? Should she confess to Ramsay that the Lord Chancellor was dead, arguably at her command?

As she searched each of their faces, she thought of power. These were powerful men. Redmayne held one of the oldest ducal titles in the realm. And Ramsay, who lorded over one of the most powerful elected offices, was being eyed by the throne as the next Lord Chancellor. Their women were influential in their own rights, Alexandra as one of the few female doctors of archeology in the entire world, and Cecelia a wealthy, brilliant businesswoman—and keeper of enough secrets she might inadvertently be able to tear down the Crimson Council on her own.

Though the sweet woman wasn't capable of wreaking destruction. Not on purpose.

Yes, they were formidable . . . and yet they could never stand against the throng of what she saw in there. They didn't have an army of devotees, nor did they have the kind of killer instincts to burn someone's entire legacy to the ground on a whim.

No, she had to do this herself. She . . . and Chandler.

This had become their destiny long ago, the moment they'd clung together in a fireplace.

"This is the Crimson Council?" Ramsay asked, his features arranged in such a way to show how thoroughly unimpressed he was. "It seems like any soiree dispersing into the early hours of the morn."

Francesca nodded. "Promise me you'll not do anything." She seized his arm. "I've infiltrated them, but not deep enough yet. You must be patient a while longer."

"Like hell!" Ramsay seethed before Cecelia clapped a hand over her would-be husband's mouth.

His eyes burned murderous, and Francesca hurried to mollify him.

"I found something out. We knew they were planning on using the girls they kept in the catacombs beneath your house for nefarious deeds, but I don't believe it had anything to do with sex as we first assumed. I think they were planning on using them for something more occult. Maybe sacrifices."

"What?" Cecelia drew back, holding the back of her hand against her mouth as though she might be sick.

"These bastards don't deserve to live," Redmayne snarled. "Give us names and we'll hunt them down. Tonight, if we have to."''

Francesca shook her head vehemently. "There are too many." She turned back to Ramsay. "I'll tell you everything, but we must wait until tomorrow."

"What is tomorrow?" Alexandra asked.

"A ritual of some kind. Here at the Kenway estate." She gathered her Rogues to her, relying upon them to hold sway over their men. "You have to trust me to handle this. I know what I'm doing."

Ramsay eyed her with a rank glare. "Trust is not a virtue I was born with. Ye'll need to give me more than that."

Cecelia—ever faithful, valiant Cecelia—came through. "You can trust Frank. She's the truest soul in the world." The statuesque woman leaned in and kissed Francesca on the cheek, smelling of chocolate and wine and hope. "We can be here tomorrow night."

"You mean Ramsay and I will be here," Redmayne decreed. "You and Alexandra will be somewhere safe, far away from men who would murder little girls, and from us, when we quite possibly murder them." The father-to-be curled his hands at his sides into fists.

"No, thank you," Cecelia said gently. "We'll be here."

"We'll lock you up if we—"

Alexandra put a hand on her husband's arm, leaning in to press herself against his side. "We've never let a Red Rogue march into danger without us." Her declaration wasn't forceful, but it was final. "We're not about to start now."

"Tomorrow then." Francesca gave them a full salute before she turned on her heel and made for her carriage at full regimental march.

Bless Cecelia and her blind faith. Bless Alexandra and her undying loyalty.

Because she'd just lied to them all to save them from being anywhere near the Crimson Council tomorrow night.

Chapter Seventeen

The very devil rode the wind as it whipped through the streets of London that night. Gusting first this way and then that with the chaos of an angry battle. It carried the scents of the river, of industry and bakeries and chimneys. Fetid things and pleasant things.

The Devil of Dorset identified them all as he lurked in front of Francesca's home.

The structure snuggled with almost defiant cheerfulness against the backdrop of the bleak and lonely night. Little lamps glowed in the front windows, and he wondered if she lit them to give the illusion of a home on alert.

Hers was a modest house for the West End, one with a spectacularly famous garden. It was likely built before the Tudor dynasty and had been lovingly tended to by generations.

He waited to approach until the imminent storm

whipped some sense into him. It wailed and screamed in a voice that matched the bleak howl inside of him. Fury and fear were both such powerful emotions, and they warred within him like a tempest of the gods.

Because of her.

She shouldn't have been at the ritual tonight. She shouldn't have let Kenway touch her. Every breath that man took in her direction was a blasphemy, and Chandler would be damned before he allowed her to be tainted by his evil.

If only he could make her understand . . .

She'd glimpsed the darkness of Kenway's soul tonight, but she couldn't even fathom the depth of his evil. She'd never borne witness to it.

Not like he had.

He closed his eyes, breathing in the chaos while becoming very still. He was a stone. He'd always been a stone. Heavy, hard, and unable to float. If he were to be dropped in the pool of her eyes, he'd sink.

He'd drown.

But the wind could not move him. No matter how it howled and battered.

For Chandler, it was safer out here on the street, safer to endure the tempest than to approach her lair.

And yet.

She had to be stopped, before she ruined everything. Before she distracted him from his ultimate goal, when he was so very close.

Idly, he rubbed at the place where she'd touched his arm, then lifted his fingers to examine his palm in the lamplight. One of his only scars he never regretted.

The mark had meant more to her than he'd originally

thought. Perhaps because her brother Ferdinand's blood had melded with his. Perhaps because it reminded her of her purpose.

A purpose he had to diffuse.

Tonight.

He would breach her gates, so to speak, and scare nine shades of shit out of her. He'd tell her the truth if he had to. If it came to that.

That once he'd been an innocent on the altar of Kenway's sacrifice.

That the Crimson Council had not taken everything away from him once . . . but twice.

That he wouldn't allow them a third chance. Not her. Not this time.

Chandler approached her home, trying the doors and the windows first, gratified to find them locked up tighter than a nun's knickers. At least she wasn't a complete fool. He'd been starting to wonder if she had any sense of caution or self-preservation beneath all that boldness and bravado.

As he made his way around to the back of the house, he ran his fingers along the stone, letting it catch and abrade the calluses on his hands. He'd felt matching calluses on her fingers. Ones that might have been made in a similar fashion as his. With weapons, and weights, and physically punishing combat arts.

He scaled her back wall with climbing picks, planting them into the mortared brick beneath the ivy and levering his body above each one. He held his weight with one hand as he drove the other into the stone, waiting for a gust of wind loud enough to cover the sound.

When he reached her second-floor balcony, he picked the lock and let himself in, careful not to get wrapped up in the white drapes that floated around him like the shifts of spirits warning him away.

The second-floor balcony belonged to a guest room, and he tiptoed through it, avoiding the shadows of furniture, and let himself into the hall.

Her house smelled different from most. Less like flowers and perfume and more like herbs and earth. Had he been blindfolded he might have thought he'd broken into a witch's lair. The pleasant aromatics of magic bubbling in a cauldron over the fire.

He padded up a flight of stairs, following the architect's map he'd memorized of her home that he'd acquired some nights ago from the records office. The master suite looked over the gardens in the back and had its own balcony, though Francesca had erected an iron fence around it complete with medieval-looking spikes just as dangerous as they were decorative.

He'd done his best not to be impressed.

Chandler's heart was not an unsteady organ. It didn't give in to bouts of emotion-fueled pumping. It was a fit muscle, efficient and steady.

Which was why he found it insufferable that its thundering was all he could hear as he put his ear to the door.

Taking a steady breath, he turned the latch slowly and let himself into the darkness.

He was taking a moment to allow his eyes to adjust when a lamp blazed to life with the flick of a switch to reveal his prey.

Or rather, Francesca, her knees bent in a fighting

stance, a pistol in one hand and the glint of something he couldn't make out in the other.

Upon seeing him, she lowered her weapons. "Oh," she breathed in relief. "I had a feeling it was you."

"Did you plan to kill me?" he asked.

She lowered her weapons, setting them on the nightstand. "I just had to be sure. You know. In case it was a murderer or some such unpleasant thing." She bent to straighten the covers of a bed into which she obviously hadn't retired yet and then patted it in invitation. "Here. Sit."

Chandler didn't sit. He stared.

It was widely thought that women were delicate creatures. Like seashells and flower petals. Like things that were easy to break and crush and discard. Useful, pretty. Ephemeral.

If this was so, Francesca Cavendish was a flower made of steel.

A curious ache opened in Chandler's chest, welling from a place that had been drowned in suffering long ago. He'd learned how to hate so early, and how to pluck the weaknesses and flaws from a person with such efficiency, he wasn't certain he was able to do anything but distrust. He was a cynic, a manipulator, and sometimes, when the situation called for it, he was a monster. He never looked at people, but he disassembled them moments after. He poked about their insides to see where the strings were, so he could pull them.

But what he saw before him was an entire woman. A person. Whole and bold and true. The wind whistled at the shutters of her window, but only whispers of a draft got through. He thought he heard her name in the gusts, a portent or a poem, he couldn't be sure.

Was it startling or sensual that not only did she keep up with him, but she was often one step ahead?

Her hair was tamed in a shiny braid that fell over her shoulder like a silk rope. Draped in some sort of green silk harem pants and a kurta she might have picked up in the Far East, she looked both fearsome and feminine. The fabric shifted and shimmered in time with her easy strides, molding to thighs that were long and distractingly lovely.

Chandler suddenly forgot to be angry.

"There was no need to sneak in," she informed him while stowing her weapons in her bedside table. "I would have let you in the front door."

"I wanted to demonstrate how easy it was to get to you," he said. "I needed to frighten some wits into you."

"Your hairstyle frightens me, if that's any solace."

Stymied, Chandler glanced in a gilded mirror across the room. The wind had thrown his hair into startling disarray, as if he'd taken a dunk in pomade and let a chimpanzee groom him.

Grimacing, he smoothed it down and turned to scowl at her. "You can jest, after everything you witnessed tonight?"

Her pleasant mask slipped just enough to announce that she'd been wearing it in the first place. He grasped at the unfettered emotion he read in her expression and advanced. "Are you going to explain to me just what the fuck you were doing at Luther Kenway's home?"

"Same thing as you." She moved to the escritoire by

the balcony window and began to leaf through some papers in an obvious ploy not to look at him. "Infiltrating the Crimson Council."

"You didn't tell me they'd invited you, Francesca." He ate up the whole of her room in a few furious strides.

She stubbornly refused to look up from scanning the paperwork. "You also neglected to mention to me that you'd be there . . ." The words drifted away, as if they hadn't much mattered in the first place.

He stopped in front of her, brows drawing down. "Why would I tell you? You're not—"

"Not what?" She flipped the paper to look at the back. "A man?"

"A *spy*." He snatched the paper from her and tossed it to the floor. "Goddammit, Francesca look at me!"

She did, and the frank assessment she gave him reminded him instantly that she'd seen him naked. "I could be, you know," she protested, jabbing his chest with her index finger. "I'd make an excellent spy."

Of that, he had no doubt. She'd excel at anything she put her mind to. "I'd never allow it."

"Why?" she demanded, her clear eyes clouding with storms.

"Because you'd be bloody miserable, that's why. Everything I am, everything I have, is tied to what I do. A wife, children: I can hope for none of it. Any chance to try was taken from me ages ago."

Her face softened as she reached up to him. "I know. I was there. It was taken from me, too."

No. She wasn't. It had been before then. Before her and Mont Claire and this entire bloody debacle.

God, but he'd been born under a cursed star. He saw

it glimmer in her eyes as she stared up at him. The curse that was waiting to take her from him a second time.

"I suppose there are many things we are both denied," she said. "But we can each claim our vengeance. Together." Instead of backing away from his anger, she leaned in, sliding her hands into his jacket "You can still have me."

"Francesca," he warned, even as his body responded. "Don't."

"We are close, Chandler, I can feel it." Her fingers curled against his chest, becoming fists. "You and I, we can put an end to this. Doesn't that excite you? The thought of victory?" She traced the corrugated ripples of is ribs, eliciting a moan and a shudder of need.

She'd seen his body tonight, and it seemed to have ignited something in her.

He'd wondered what she'd thought of his desire, what she'd felt about his cock straining for her as he stood naked and proud. A stag ready to strike at any other who would seek to claim her as a mate. He would even have locked horns with Kenway. Right then and there. Consequences be damned.

What did she feel, now that she knew what her nearness did to his body?

Every fucking time.

He took her hands and pulled them off him, imprisoning them in his palms so he could think. "You cannot go back there tomorrow."

She gave him a wry glance as she pulled her hands away, hiding them behind her. "Of course I can. Kenway is grooming me for the Triad. This is our in . . ."

She retrieved the letter he'd thrown on the floor, giving him a view of how the silk of her pantaloons stretched over her backside.

He was still swallowing his tongue when she looked over and said, "Not to be unkind, but my infiltration into the Crimson Council is deeper than yours. I mean, you were little more than a party favor." Flashing a roguish smile, she lifted the lid of the desk and put the paper in it.

"It can't be you," Chandler declared.

"Why not me?"

"Because you are . . ."

Her mild amusement turned to mutiny. "Because I'm a woman?"

"Stop saying that, Francesca, you have no idea . . ." Turning, he scored his scalp in frustration, ruining his hair once again. "You have no idea the ruthlessness of this man. The depths of depravity of which he is capable. I mean, he very likely killed everyone you love."

She advanced on him, eyes narrowed into slits of viperous wrath. "Do you think I've forgotten that? You think you're the only one who has sacrificed his entire life for this? I *have* to go back. I have to. I hate them, Chandler. My hate is all I have, and I cannot make way for anything else until it is dealt with. If you cannot handle that, then *you* should be the one to step away."

An impotent frustration welled within him. He couldn't force her to drop this . . . and he couldn't stand the thought of her in danger. Reaching out, he drew a knuckle down the curve of her cheek. "After everything you saw tonight, are you not afraid?"

The jaw beneath his hand hardened. "Aren't you?"

"Of course I am." His answer seemed to startle her, and she blinked at him, mute for a blessed moment.

"Fear is the most primitive emotion," he continued. "But as you know, hate must be learned. You have to experience it. Smell it. Taste it. And I know you have." He stepped closer, framing her face with his hands. "My hate is stronger than my fear, Francesca. I've melded with it and I let it run through me like it is my own blood. But you don't have to. I don't want that for you."

"This isn't about what *you* want." She put her hands on his wrists but didn't pull away. Suddenly her eyes were both bleak and unsure and for a moment, she looked incredibly young. And not at all like the girl she'd been.

"The Lord Chancellor . . ." Her breath hitched. "I thought he'd gotten off easily with that little show he did with the dagger. I thought . . ." She swallowed some strong emotion. "Did you see the hounds? I didn't mean for him to die . . . not like that."

He nodded. He'd seen it, and it had sickened him, despite his acrimony for the Lord Chancellor.

"This is what I'm talking about," he said, heartened that he might be getting through to her. "It's not too late, Francesca. I can get you out of this. I can help you—"

She surged forward, mashing her lips against his, her fingers dropping to his shirt, ripping at the buttons, clumsy with frenzy.

"No." Chandler couldn't believe he stopped her, but he did.

"You want to help me? Then take off your trousers."

He wanted to. *God*, how he wanted to, but something in her frenzy caused him to pause.

Fear. He'd found it. He'd done what he'd come to do. He'd frightened her.

So why did he feel like such an absolute ass? For all the lies he lived, it was time he told some truths. "Do you want to know what I thought when I learned you might have lived?"

"That I was a liar." The earnestness in her eyes was almost his undoing.

"I thought—I'd hoped—that perhaps you'd buried your past. And me along with it. I didn't know if you were real. Maybe I didn't want to know, because if you'd lived, if you were happy, then I could visit you whenever I felt like it. In my dreams. I thought that maybe, this was all worth it if you were happy."

Her chin dipped toward her chest and she stole furtive, melancholy glances at him before her eyes darted away. It reminded him of the Francesca of his youth. A shy, repressible girl with a dainty smile and generous heart.

"I shouldn't have waited to come find you," he said, meaning it. "You've reminded me what I'm doing this for. I think, you're making me believe in the one thing I'd thought I'd never recover. You give me—no—you *force* me to hope. And in order to keep that hope, to do what must be done, I need you alive. I need you safe. You are a rare and incredible creature, you always have been. And Kenway sees this."

He cupped her cheek, hating that behind the strength of her was flesh that could puncture and a skeleton that could be broken. She had the will of iron, but her body was still delicate. "He doesn't just want you, Francesca, I know this. He wants to crush you. He's done it before, and I couldn't live with myself if . . . if anything happened to you."

The smile she attempted was wobbly, as if she knew his words should please her, but they had the opposite effect.

"Francesca." Her name escaped as a tender benediction. "Listen to me—"

"No," she said, cutting at the air with the flat of her hand and jerking out of his reach as she backed toward the bed. Not a retreat, but a regroup.

"You listen," she commanded, jabbing her finger at him before turning away, as if she couldn't think and look at him at the same time. "*You listen.* Kenway is no longer the villain." She paused. "Well, not the *only* villain. They *all* are. If we cut Kenway down, we only succeed in chopping off the head of the hydra, and it'll just grow another." She whirled on him, composure reclaimed into those gem-hard eyes. "I think you know that. We have to do this, to go all the way into the Crimson Council so we may find the roots and rip it out of the earth. You and I.

"If you'd looked for me sooner, you'd have seen me become who I am now. You'd understand that the Francesca you knew doesn't exist. She's dead, Chandler, buried alongside Declan in the ashes of Mont Claire. *This* is what we are." She held her hands out to the side. "This is what we must do: Take down the Crimson Council. Together."

Instead of coming at him, as she'd done before, she held her hands out like a penitent to a priest, beckoning him to close the gap. "Rather than fight me on this, join me. Join *with* me, and I will prove to you that I can do what it takes."

Magnificent.

The word throbbed through him in perfect sync to the rhythm of his heart.

Mag.ni.fi.cent.

She'd been a pretty girl, sweet like spun sugar and fragile as a china cup. His young love for her had been excruciating, because her radiance had illuminated his darkness. He'd never felt as though he could touch her, because everyone would know. He'd leave imprints of shadows upon her perfection and they'd come for him in the night. And who would have blamed them?

And so he hadn't dared to dream.

But now. Now? She was something else. She was no longer a saint; she was a sin. She wasn't perfection, she was pleasure. She wasn't forbidden, she was . . . fire.

She'd become the element that had taken everything from her.

And holy Christ did her flame tempt him like the proverbial moth. Her heat, it radiated from her like that of the very sun. How could she have become this unstoppable force, this marvel of energy and essence that put every other hero, mythic or otherwise, to shame?

Suddenly it didn't matter how many men had had her before, because the answer was none.

She'd had them.

She'd been born a whisper, and now she was a scream. A demand. A fucking goddess in a pair of billowing silk trousers.

Her appetite rivaled that of Kali. Her desire was

worn naked and abashed on her face as she raked him over with rank challenge.

And to think, he'd once been afraid that she couldn't handle him. His weight, his darkness, his need.

But for the first time, Chandler felt a pang of fear . . . *of a girl.* A woman. Of the hunger pulling her skin tight over those perfect bones. Of the honest promise in her eyes, and also of the secrets.

He'd thought it better to be a rock. To be hard and heavy and immobile, and yet . . . he realized he could still be ground to dust. Or even reshaped. If he was stone, then she was water. Nothing was so soft, pliant, and nourishing.

And yet, who could withstand the power of a rogue wave?

Or a rogue redhead.

The most incredible force on this earth, she was. She would claim him, pull him back to the sea from which he wouldn't emerge again. At least, not the same man he'd been before. He would drown in her depths as she devoured him. Body and soul. She'd show him no mercy and offer him no excuses. She would leave him an empty husk and walk away strengthened by their encounter.

Because she was what he feared the most. Both fire and water.

In spite of himself, Chandler took a step forward, and her gaze sharpened. Then he took another, and her eyes flared.

Whatever intent she read on his features caused her to go utterly still. Then, as per usual, she did the exact opposite of what he'd expected her to. Instead of meeting him halfway, or waiting for him to reach for her, she grasped the hem of her kurta and pulled it over her head, uncovering the loveliest breasts he'd ever seen. She stood before him, her back arched and her hip kicked out to the side.

Proud. Challenging. Perfect.

They collided like thunderclouds. All electricity and wild, chaotic abandon. Some would fear to watch it, of that he had no doubt. His fingers tangled in her braid and he couldn't be sure if he trapped her or she'd ensnared him. Her hands scored at the rough stubble of his cheek as she pulled him in to kiss him as if she'd been born hungry for a taste.

As if she'd been waiting for twenty years.

Her hands scraped down his shirt and then tightened into fists, threatening to tear it from his body.

He did it for her.

The sound of buttons clattering to the floor was the perfect percussion to her purr of encouragement, the vibrations of which went all the way to his cock.

He filled his hands with her, his arms, pulling her in and crushing her lithe frame against his thick one. His fingers were bruising on her back, her shoulders, her waist; he knew that.

Neither of them would escape this encounter unmarked.

It was only that her frenzy matched his own. She clutched at him, digging her fingers into the cords and muscles of his back, pawing at him with identical ardor. Her tongue met his, matching him stroke for stroke and plunge for plunge.

Christ, if he was the devil . . . she was a fucking

demon. A succubus. And he was quite suddenly her willing victim.

Chandler finally stopped fighting. He gave over to the hunger, surrendered to his own dark desires, and succumbed to her unspoken challenges.

But that didn't mean he was dormant.

He used his teeth on her lips as he explored her every bare inch of skin with rough hands. He wanted to mark her. To show the world that she might own him now, but he'd claimed a bit of her, as well.

She was all smooth flesh over toned muscle. Not lush, but lovely. Her flares were subtle and her lines sleek. Her breasts small and pert, the nipples pink pebbles begging for his mouth.

All in good time.

Her fingers delved into his disheveled hair, and he growled as her nails scored his scalp. He pinned her to him, imprisoning with one arm as he filled the other hand with her ass covered with that emerald silk. The muscles of her bottom flexed and clenched beneath his touch, and she lifted a leg to wrap around his thigh. Gods, she was strong, and limber as well.

This was going to be as much a fight as it was fucking.

He couldn't wait.

As impatient as he was, Chandler explored the parts of her mouth he'd missed before. Going deeper, thrusting stronger until he felt as though she stole his breath from his lungs and gave it back again.

Finally he tore away, needing to think. To breathe.

"No," she panted. "More."

It wasn't a question, but a command.

And he could do nothing but oblige her. With a

rumble of victory that escaped from somewhere deep, deep inside of him, he reached down to lift her against him, splitting her other leg so they both wrapped around his waist.

In three powerful strides he drove her against the wall, hissing a breath in through his teeth as his sex rolled and flexed against hers, again frustrated by the layers of their clothing.

Yes, they'd been here before . . .

And now he'd get to finish what they'd started.

She wasn't a patient prisoner. She climbed him like a rope, using her thighs as a vise as she hooked her heels around his buttocks and pulled him harder against her, riding him, after a fashion. Her movements were not those of a practiced seductress, but a primal, jolting roll of her body in shuddering successions.

No, he would take nothing from her tonight, but she would take whatever pleasure from him he could give.

And all he could do was be humbled. Grateful. Two emotions with which he was not well acquainted.

Her lips drove against his with such fervor that their teeth briefly met. She kissed like a woman denied too long. As if instead of doing this with regularity, she'd been waiting her entire life for it. Her hands were everywhere at once. His hair, his neck, the columns of muscle bracketing his spine.

She used the wall as a rally point, pushing against it to get closer to him. He pinned her down, grappling her, grinding her, reveling in the little mewls of pleasure she made.

He'd never come like this with a woman. Not without being inside her in some capacity or another.

He wasn't about to start now.

Pushing away from the wall, he rebounded to another surface, the wardrobe maybe, settling back into her with a bruising, straining kiss. When that wasn't enough, he abandoned it to set her ass on the desk and pulled away just long enough to reach between them and tear those fucking silk pants and her underthings down the never-ending length of her legs.

The scent of her filled his mouth with moisture, and he had her spread wide on the desk, his head buried between her legs, before the raw, shocked sound she made even registered.

He dragged the flat of his tongue through the folds of her intimate flesh.

Fire and water, she was. Unbearably hot, and indescribably wet. Here was the spun sugar he'd been searching for.

Here, where she was all woman.

Somewhere in his lust-frenzied brain it registered that she didn't ride his mouth. Instead she became curiously passive beneath his ministrations.

Would wonders never cease?

He laid ruthless claim to her sex with his tongue. Sliding through the ruffles of flesh with strong licks, leaving silken heat and wet promises in his wake. He worshiped the center of her until her hips began to buck and jerk, making him chase her with his seeking lips.

Finally, he pinned her legs wide, needing to dine on her, to drink her desire. This was the only way he could take her inside of him.

Before she returned the favor.

Her fingers fisted in his hair, but she neither pulled

him away nor encouraged him forward. She merely held on. As though she needed something to hold on to or she'd fall.

He'd never allow that. He'd never let her fall.

He wanted to tell her that. He wanted to say so many things. But he couldn't look at her. He couldn't see the storm in her eyes. Instead he admired the pink flesh beneath him. The delectable delicacy of it. He discovered what made her gasp. What caused her to buck and writhe. And he did those things.

Relentlessly.

He sucked at the petals of straining flesh, capturing the tiny bead between his lips and flicking his tongue across it in measured movements so as not to be too much. Her hips rose and she made a jagged sound. Then another.

And then she went silent. But not still. Oh God, never that.

Her every lovely muscle seized and her back arched in such a way he had a momentary worry that it would snap. She pulled his hair so hard, he heard some of it tear, the pain doing strange and wondrous things to his erection.

She didn't merely come, she came apart. He watched her, then, his mouth gentling to elongate the moment for her. Her breasts trembled as they arched to the sky. Her other hand clasped over her eyes, as if she was afraid to look. Or perhaps to look away from whatever she was seeing on the backs of her eyelids.

He kept her locked in that place for as long as he could. Until she found her voice and could make little hitching sounds, until those sounds turned plaintive and she squirmed for escape when the pleasure became too much.

Only then did he pull away to kiss the smooth length of her thigh and wipe his lips with the back of his hand. He stood, replacing his head with his hips between her parted legs. His entire body throbbed in time with his cock, and the look on her face did little to help.

She gazed up at him as though he were a god. And he felt like one, standing over her then. A wild pagan deity, one that didn't bother with mere mortals.

Only her.

The summer storm raged outside, the wind not abating, but gathering strength, as did his need.

As did hers.

She didn't lounge back on liquid bones as some women were wont to do after such a release.

No, she reared up and reached for the placket of his trousers. Her thighs still parted, her limber body able to move in ways he couldn't comprehend. With a few swift movements of her thumbs, she had his trousers open enough to delve inside.

Her fingers closed around his cock, and pulled it free.

He couldn't exactly read her expression now, as the light from the one lamp lit her from behind. It created a brilliant ruby halo around her ruined braid, but left her features mostly in shadow.

She scooted to the very edge of the desk and, once again, wrapped those long, lovely legs around him.

With a lithe roll of her spine she brought her body against him, threading her arms around to pull him close.

Chandler stilled. For all of their frenzy . . . the clutching, seizing, bruising desperation of before, this was something else.

An embrace, perhaps.

She put her head on his shoulder, and then rooted around for a moment, finally landing with her face pressed firmly into the crook of his neck and her hand sliding with an almost anxious repetition along his back.

He wasn't ready for whatever tender thing rose from the void within him, the thing that wanted to hold her back. That wanted to soothe and smooth, to nuzzle and croon.

That wasn't him. It wasn't them. *This* was them. Wet, hard, straining sex.

Christ, he'd barely made peace with her strength, he wasn't sure he could bear her softness.

And so did the only thing could think of.

He drove his hips forward, shoving his full, hard length inside of her heat.

Past a barrier he hadn't expected, eliciting a gasp of pain he'd never forget.

Chapter Eighteen

Francesca bit back the raw cry just as soon as she'd uttered it, cursing herself. She'd known it would hurt, of course she had. She just . . . hadn't realized how much.

She was grateful she knew a bit about combat, and that her training had taught her to fight through the pain, or she'd never have been able to stick to Chandler like a burr as he attempted to jerk back.

His hips levered enough away that he withdrew, and she couldn't deny that her straining body found it a relief.

"Wait," she said. "Wait. Don't stop." They needed to do this. For so many reasons.

"Jesus. Christ. Jesus. *Fuck.*"

She waited patiently as he worked through every curse she'd heard in the queen's own English, and a few new ones, as well.

She breathed in the warm scent of his skin, linen,

soap, and something a little earthy. Like cedar maybe, or pine. Christmas. His scent reminded her of Christmas. Unable to help herself, her tongue escaped her lips for a little taste.

I just licked Christmas, was her absurd thought. Followed by the fact that she wanted to do it again.

He tasted good. He tasted right.

"Jesus fucking Christ, Francesca, did you just *lick* me?"

She drew in a few more lungsful of his scent before she gathered the strength to draw away. "To be fair," she ventured, "you licked me first."

Did he ever.

She'd known of the deviant acts one could perform upon another, being friends with two very adventurous, very well-pleasured women. Also, she was no stranger to a climax, having given herself more than a few.

But she'd never known . . . could never have imagined in any of the many meanderings of her imagination that a man's mouth could be so incredibly wicked. That the euphoria he elicited could be so absolute as to be unbearable at the end.

Not just any man's wicked mouth. Declan Chandler's.

"Let go," he commanded in an impatient tone, one bordering on panic. "I have to make certain you are—"

"No," she said, pulling him closer, teasing her pebbled nipples against the swells of muscle on his chest. "No, we're not finished."

"But you were . . ." He froze. "You want . . . ? But I . . . how is it . . . bloody possible . . . Everyone thinks . . ."

Francesca hid a smile against his shoulder. It wasn't very often that a man such as he was so completely gobsmacked that he couldn't finish a sentence. "Later," she said. "More. Now."

Apparently lust turned her into a rather monosyllabic creature.

She reached between them, sliding her hands down his impossibly tight abdomen to the impressive member below, delighted to find it still hard.

Hard, and wet. Wet with her own release.

His breath seized when she wrapped her fingers around him. "Don't make me beg," she said huskily.

"Fucking hell, Francesca."

"I know." Drawing back, she pressed her forehead to his, nudging at him with her nose. "I want you. I've always wanted you. Ever since I was a girl, I knew that you were it for me. That you were the man I would have, or none at all. And I mean to have you, make no mistake of that."

A mirthless laugh gasped out of him, choking at the end as she moved her hand in a slight caress. His hips responded, thrusting deeper into her grip before he pulled away.

"Not like this," he wheezed out.

"Then how?"

"The bed." He lifted her off the desk and carried her to the bed, this time with an arm hooked at her shoulders and her knees. She felt small when he held her like this. Small and soft and delicate.

She wouldn't admit she liked it . . . but she didn't hate it.

He placed her gingerly on the bed, and she sank into

her favorite covers that smelled of vanilla and orange blossoms. She stretched, testing her muscles for pain and finding none as he towered over her like a giant tempestuous storm cloud.

"Christ, you're going to ruin me," he whispered.

"Am I?" She opened her arms to him, suddenly chilly and beginning to feel a strange and maidenly apprehension. She needed him against her; then she could do anything.

He joined her, covering her in heat and muscle and masculine need. "Yes. You'll ruin me, and there's nothing I can do to stop it."

This time, he rose above her and stared into her eyes, his gaze searching hers intently as he nudged at her entrance, and then sank into her in one long, slow, endless slide.

This time, the pain was little more than a whisper, followed by something else. An ache, restless and consuming, the ghost of the frenzy she'd felt before.

She took him slowly, feeling as though she'd been shaped for him, by him, and not at all surprised by it.

She belonged to this man.

She always had.

A detached part of her admired his masculine beauty. The slope of his shoulders, the breadth and depth of his chest. The network of veins visible in his powerful arms. It distracted her from any vestiges of pain she would have felt.

"Francesca. Francesca, look at me." A hollow note in his voice drew her eyes, and what she saw in his gaze broke her heart.

She shaped her palm to his jaw, first one, then the

other. And she kissed him, tasting her nectar on his lips.

It was all he needed.

He rode her in long, slow strokes. Each time he filled her, erotic pulses of pleasure unfolded within her like the tendrils of spring ivy.

Awe and astonishment lay like strangers on his features, turning them from savage to utterly seductive.

They said nothing. Barely made any sound but that of their flesh and friction. They communicated in sighs and breaths and the flutter of eyelids.

Francesca focused on the heat of him inside of her, and the warmth of him around her. She felt an intense possession well within, one not unfamiliar. She clutched at it with the same desperation as she clung to him.

She told him so many things without speaking. She told him how deeply and desperately she'd missed him. That she was sorry for the secrets she kept . . . and even sorrier that she couldn't be who he thought she was. Who he truly wanted. But she'd be her best. For him she'd be everything; anything. Anyone. His loss was her greatest tragedy, and his pleasure her greatest achievement.

His life her greatest joy.

She wished he could hear her, or read her, but his eyes were so intent. So full of lust and fire and primitive animal things.

There was tenderness there, too, she thought. Hope, just like he'd said.

Not love. Never that. The gods were not so kind. But hope she could live with.

Hope . . . was everything.

Francesca hadn't known how affected she was by this momentous happening. Not until he leaned down and kissed away a tear.

She ran her cheek against his, savoring the scrape of his shadow beard. A pressure mounted within her, aching and rolling across her bones and dispersing into her blood. It never crested, but she didn't need it to. She wanted to be here. Present. In this moment.

She wanted to stare into his eyes forever, to wonder what color they truly were. She wanted to feel everything, from the hot slide of his cock inside of her to the tickle of the fine hairs of his thighs against hers.

Could this moment never end? Could tomorrow never come?

Just as she had the thought, his movements became faster, more insistent, less careful though she knew he never unleashed the full force of his desire upon her. She could feel him growing against her intimate flesh. Pulsing and pressing against the channel that contained him.

And then he said her name the way dying men pleaded with the gods.

Francesca.

Her name. And not her name.

Warmth spread through her abdomen as his muscles bunched and strained to their capacity, building upon themselves with the excruciating consummation of his release. It lasted for an eternity, or only for seconds, she couldn't be sure, so breathtaking was the moment.

Then he dropped his head beside hers, and stilled

inside of her. This time, when he whispered her name it was framed as a question.

She shook her head and nudged him to settle next to her while she rolled over and doused the light.

He shifted, cradling her close "I—"

She reached up and pressed her fingers to his lips, lips that still carried her intimate essence upon them.

"Tomorrow," she said. They could say all the words that needed saying then.

His mouth tightened as if he would argue, but then they relaxed. "Tomorrow," he agreed.

They lay there and listened to the storm, and eventually his breaths came in deeper increments, and then soft, exhausted snores.

She wasn't going to sleep, though. Not if it meant missing this. An honest, unfettered moment with Chandler.

The tempest died, never turning into rain. Eventually, moonlight pierced the chamber, and she watched it cast him in an ethereal glow. He was a man who belonged to hours such as this. He wore his darkness. He owned it. It was part of his blood.

"I love you," she whispered. That much had never changed. Whether he was Declan Chandler, Chandler Alquist, Lord Drake, or the devil, himself. She loved him.

Still.

Always.

"Whatever souls are made of, yours and mine are the same," she whispered.

In sleep, he'd melted away from the unyielding man into the boy she'd loved.

She murmured her name to him then, revealing her secret to ears that couldn't hear her. She might be brave, fearless even, in some respects. But in this way, she was an ultimate coward.

With her heart.

Don't hate me, she silently pleaded, dashing away another tear before pressing her ear to his heart. Remembering with every bit of her soul the day she'd first heard it beat in the chimney as the world had burned down around her.

Don't hurt me, Declan Chandler. I'm not as strong as they all think.

CHAPTER NINETEEN

Chandler woke to darkness sometime after four AM, choking on the same bloody nightmare he'd always done. His limbs didn't thrash, as some did when they dreamed of death. Nor did he talk or scream or carry on.

No, his nightmare was a paralyzing one. It captured him like a demon and locked him inside his darkest places, making sleep a prison and his body his jailer.

Sleep was an unavoidable torment, and he always dreaded the night.

It was why he never slept with a woman, because he never trusted one enough not to use his paralysis against him.

Just as soon as awareness slammed into him, he'd learned that if he focused on five sensations in his body, it brought his mind around. He did that now. The covers were warm, but not heavy like his. And the room glowed with moonlight.

This struck him as odd. He usually slept in absolute darkness. Absolute silence. So that no one could sneak up on him.

Someone was breathing very close by.

His eyes flew open and the paralysis dissipated instantly as every muscle tensed with combat-readiness just in time to see a siren stretch in the moonlight.

Francesca's arm lifted behind her head in a mermaid pose as the coverlet pooled only over the lower half of her.

Christ, he'd meant to wait for her to fall asleep and then be about his business. He couldn't believe he'd allowed himself to be lulled by the feel of her small body curled into his.

Had she even slept yet? It'd only been a few hours.

Lying on her side, she ballasted her head on her palm as she buried a yawn against her knuckles.

His cock had been at morning attention before he'd become conscious, and now it demanded to be satisfied.

She gazed down at him with direct and open affection that sent curls of ludicrous warmth to the coldest parts of him. "You look like him when you're sleeping," she noted shyly.

His mood darkened, the warmth immediately quelled by a cold stab of panic. "Like whom?"

"Declan. Who else?" Her hand moved to rest idly on his biceps before making a curious path of discovery up toward his shoulder. "Innocent and mischievous all at once, you were, with a healthy dose of melancholy. I remember always thinking I wanted to make you laugh, but I couldn't because you didn't know how."

She waited for him to reply, and when he couldn't

think of anything to say to that, she remarked, "You were dreaming, I think. Just now. You were breathing so hard, I wanted to wake you."

He ignored her casual observation, not wanting to discuss nightmares when he'd woken to a fantasy. "I never should have become Declan. I regret everything that came from my existence at Mont Claire."

Her caress stalled, and she jerked her hand away as if he'd burned her. "Everything?"

"Everything but you." He recaptured her hand and set it back where it was before, encouraging her to finish. No one ever stroked him, not in this way. Without lust or guile. Just . . . because she so obviously enjoyed the feel of his skin.

She resumed, but a troubled crease remained between her brows.

A foreign guilt lanced him, and he turned to face her, adopting her posture by propping his head on his knuckles. "You should have told me your secret."

Her eyes grew round, and her fingers stilled once again. "Which secret?"

He wondered at this. How many were there?

He'd deal with this one first. "Had I known you were a virgin, I could have prepared you. I was such an animal—" Shame clogged his throat, cutting off his words.

To his utter astonishment, a smile lifted her wide mouth and he'd the sense she was relieved. "If I'd told you, you'd probably not have done it at all."

He sighed, uncertain if he could claim the nobility she accused him of possessing. "Likely not," he hedged.

Could he really have turned down what she offered?

He leaned over to kiss her bare shoulder. Only a fool would deny paradise once offered.

He opened his mouth to ask her how she'd fooled the entire ton into thinking her a wanton rakess when she beat him to the punch.

"Did you mean it? Were you truly unhappy at Mont Claire?" she asked.

They'd been the best years of his life, but he still regretted them. "Does that hurt you?"

She adopted a pensive expression, one that gave way to nostalgia as she looked into the past. "It's only that, before the massacre, I have nothing but happy memories of the place. Of the festivals in the spring at the village. The playhouse with the comedies that the university students would stage for us. The scent of fresh bread beckoning me in the morning to wander to the kitchens to watch Hargrave pretend not to read the papers as he ironed them for Father . . ." Her eyes adopted a curious sheen and she cleared it away with a blink and a cough. "I always loved summers, romping in the maze and mucking out the fountain—"

"Hargrave ironing the paper?" he scoffed. "Since when did you ever get up before the crack of noon?" He gave a mirthless chuckle and chucked her chin, his thumb grazing at the indent there. "*Pip* and I mucked out the fountain. You only ever watched."

Her lashes swept down over a guilty look, and he instantly regretted saying so. He charted the curve of her shoulder and drew his hand down the smoothness of her arm until he laced his fingers with hers. "I'd have not dirtied your hands for all the world." He lifted her fingertips to his lips for a kiss, and she watched him do so as if it caused her physical pain.

"I only meant that it was hard to have known such happiness and to see it so utterly and completely destroyed."

She nodded, though she didn't seem quite mollified. "Are we certain everyone else died? It is quite possible someone else could have survived the massacre?"

He shook his head, remembering that he'd hoped the very same. "I got Pippa out, but they shot her in the leg and the poor thing couldn't run. I stashed her in the tree and diverted them back through the forest when they shot me." An ancient well of pain rose within him as the memory of the moment made the scars on his back itch and ache. "There were many more gunshots, even while I lay there thinking I was about to die. I heard them conclude that they'd finished off anyone who'd attempted escape and thrown them back into the blaze."

He'd done his best not to think of poor Pip. After all they'd done to escape the flames, the idea of her being tossed back to them was simply untenable.

"You never witnessed her death. What if . . ." Francesca paused, toying at her hair that was more escaped from her braid than contained in it. "What if she did escape? What if she survived?" The earnest light in her eyes was difficult to see, and so he looked away.

"Then I hope she is far away from here . . . and at peace." So she didn't have to face the shame of what her parents' actions had wrought.

"You were a hero, for saving her," Francesca said. "For holding and comforting her through the ordeal, for making her feel less alone. Do you . . . remember her ever?"

A chuff of laughter escaped him. "I remember that she was stubborn and reckless. She was loud. Unkempt. Wild."

"You don't remember her fondly . . . then." She sounded so glum, he regarded her carefully.

He'd never wanted to do this. To remember. But it seemed she did, and maybe it was time for that. Time for trading war stories with someone who'd been through the fire with him. Literally. They'd been close, Pippa and Francesca, he remembered that.

He wondered if she did all of this for her childhood friend.

Pippa Hargrave. He summoned the girl into his mind's eye. A sturdy thing, on the brink of portly as her older parents denied her nothing. She'd been fair-haired, overindulged, and endlessly opinionated. But she'd smiled brilliantly, often with gaps of missing teeth, whenever he entered a room. As a boy largely unused to his presence being anything but a bother or a burden, he'd liked her for that. She'd laughed at all of his japes, and she'd done anything he asked of her.

She was a favorite of Ferdinand's, which he always found ridiculous because she outweighed and outmatched the sickly boy in almost every respect. He'd always imagined their future, her hoisting little Ferdy around the estates running after a bushel of bastards, as the old earl would have never let them marry. But Pip . . . she was the loyal sort, and just about as robust as anyone.

"I was plenty fond of her," he said honestly. "She

was like the little sister I—I never got to have. I recall that she quarreled just as ardently as she loved. She was . . . fearless until the end, and even then, she was so goddamned brave."

When he focused on Francesca again, tears gathered like gems in her lashes, and he lifted her face, though she wouldn't look at him. "She loved you like a sister, that I remember. She would have been very proud of who you've become, I think."

She just shook her head, swallowing three successive times against his hand. "She loved *you*, you know. To an obsessive degree."

He remembered the last time he'd seen her. The moments before her death. She'd flung her strong arms around him and kissed him.

I love you, she'd whispered.

Dammit. Dammit. Dammit. "If that is the case . . . it is better that she died."

"I insist you stop saying things like that." She pushed at him then, releasing her frustration physically, as he was learning she was wont to do. "What *happened* to you? Why are you like this? You're not culpable in the massacre, and you couldn't have stopped it from happening, so why do you constantly fight such immense guilt? Is it because of Pippa? Because you didn't save her? Because if that's the case I . . . I'll tell you—"

"You are fighting for your legacy, Francesca. To see if it's worth protecting, and that is a noble thing." He forced a frustrated breath through his throat, hating everything about what he couldn't say. "I'm constantly escaping mine. I come from nothing. From lower than nothing. And I am doing my best to . . . to atone. Does that make any sort of sense?"

Her brows pinched together. "What have you possibly done that needs atoning for?"

He reached for her then, wrapping his hand around her nape and pulling her close so his forehead touched hers. "The sins on my shoulders are so heavy, Atlas wouldn't trade me his burden."

She pulled back, impassioned. "*Tell* me," she urged. "*I've* sinned. I've lied . . ." Her eyes moved restlessly in their sockets as she came to some kind of weighty conclusion. "Declan. Perhaps now is the time to trade secrets in the dark. Like we used to."

She sat up, holding a pillow over her lap, like a shield. Thank God. He'd never have been able to pay attention if she'd been cross-legged right in front of him. "We'll tell each other everything. Even if it's painful. I'll start." She cleared her throat against a gather of nerves. "I'll tell you who I really—"

Driven by years of pain and yearning, Chandler rose and swept her up in his arms, pulling her into the cradle of his lap and curling himself around her as if he could provide some sort of belated protection. Shielding her from a world that had already done its worst.

"I'm done with revelations for now, Francesca," he said. "All I want to do is this. Christ, how often I wanted to do this when I was young, just pull you into me and hold on forever. You were so pure. So perfect. And I would spend an entire day just waiting to bathe in your grace. To bask in your beauty."

He smoothed her hair away from her face. Her lovely, angular, elfin features. "And here we are," he marveled. "How did you appear just when I was about to run out of hope? When I felt as though the battles I fought were all for nothing. *Here you are.* A warrior in your own right. A paladin or cleric. Joan of fucking Arc." He drew her closer, tucking her head beneath his chin. "I found you, Francesca. For twenty years, I'd only ever done that in my dreams."

The only dreams he had that weren't nightmares.

"I dreamed of finding you, too," she replied in a voice muffled against his skin. "I looked for you, you know. Serana and I sifted through the ashes of Mont Claire, salvaging what we could. But I was secretly searching for your bones, as if I could have even identified them. But you could not have told me that as a girl." She made a caustic sound, both harsh and soft. "And when I didn't find any trace of you, I wondered if you survived. A part of me has always held out hope."

"Did you?" Her confession heartened him, melted something hard within at the thought of her little-girl hope hanging on him.

She nodded against his neck. "Serana insisted that she witnessed you take a bullet, and it would have taken a miracle for you to survive it."

"And yet, I did." He wondered if he'd ever be able to tell her how he'd done it.

"A miracle," she whispered.

He ran his fingers through her silken strands, untying the ribbon that no longer held the braid. "Listen to me." He cupped her head in both his hands, loving the feel of her. "I'm going to get you out of tomorrow night."

"What? No!" She artlessly scrambled out of his lap,

her motions doing wonderful things to her small, pert breasts.

He swiped for her, but she evaded him, which brought his predatory instinct to the foreground. "Francesca, you've been playing such a dangerous game, and you've been fortunate so far. I mean blind fucking luck. But you have attracted not just Kenway's notice, but his admiration. It is more dangerous to be close to him than to be his enemy."

"I think I've more than demonstrated that I can handle the danger," she said, uncurling from the bed to stand. "We will do it together. It's already decided."

He shook his head vehemently. "I won't be able to do my job if I think you're in peril, especially not now."

She shrugged. "That's your concern. Don't we have this conversation sorted? Use me, Chandler. I have skills you might not."

Oh, he'd no doubt of that. "You are already his victim, Francesca." He unfolded from the bed and went to her, pleading with her to understand. "I refuse to allow you to be his casualty as well."

She swung her right fist and punched him full in the jaw. His head snapped back and an instant temper flared, but he stood his ground, meeting her glare with one of his own.

"The next time you presume to allow or disallow me anything, I'll knock you unconscious," she spat, stomping to the wardrobe to yank a robe from its depths.

Chandler tried not to smile. He rubbed at what most definitely would be a bruise as he admired the back of her. He'd been hit with harder, more well-placed jabs, but hers was more than respectable. And he had a suspicion she'd held back.

That she hadn't truly wanted to hurt him.

A distracting flash of color peeked from beneath her hair covering her shoulder blade, a tattoo it seemed, but of what he couldn't make out.

"Sometimes I don't recognize you at all," he muttered, regarding her with a perplexed sort of humor. "You were such a biddable child . . . one aches for those days."

Her glare went from stormy to tempestuous. "If that's what you want, then I invite you to make use of that door, because I am not her. Do you hear me? I am not—"

"I know." He closed the distance to her in two strides, stopping her from donning the robe by sliding his hands about her waist and pulling her close. "I know. And I'm glad."

At his words, she decided not to struggle, standing beneath his caresses as he smoothed his hands over her like he would an excitable thoroughbred. "You've grown into someone brilliant, bold, and beautiful." He made a sound of disbelief. "Christ. I cannot believe I was in your bed. That you are in my arms. That I am the first man to . . ." He broke off, knowing he revealed too much, but wanting to say everything he could, in case this was his last chance. "It's as though I've walked into a dream, and I'm waiting for it to turn into a nightmare."

Tomorrow, if things went as planned, it would.

The storm of her temper died just as soon as it had

risen, and she regarded him from a guarded, careful gaze. He'd pleased her with his confession, and yet . . . he sensed he'd made her melancholy as well.

Lowering his head, he took the robe from her grasp and dropped it to the floor. "Dream with me awhile longer, Francesca?" He whispered kisses over her sharp cheekbones, eyelids, nose, brows. "Let me have tonight, and tomorrow will be . . . what it will be."

She went to him with no qualms, following him back to bed almost like a contrite child. He spread her beneath the moonlight and proceeded to worship and discover this new woman. With his hands. His mouth. Courting her properly this time. Taking his time and discovering all the curves and hollows of her.

She didn't let him linger on her scars, but she found a few of his, running her hands along his body as if she could memorize every line and groove.

And then, as the dawn licked the sky with silver, their bodies moved together, making new memories in the dark.

Chapter Twenty

In a world where the Crimson Council existed, Francesca never expected to find the records pertaining to the Mont Claire Massacre, and yet, here she was.

Her fingers trembled as she exclaimed her unbridled victory with a very unladylike whoop. The sound echoed off the stone walls of the subterranean records room and frightened a few pigeons that had gathered around the grimy windows above her head. What little light the solitary line of thin portals allowed into the warehouse-sized space was consistently interrupted by the legs of passersby.

"Kindly return to me my five pounds," she called as she hauled a dusty box away from a shelf and dropped it onto a grimy table.

"Bollocks," Chandler answered, closer than she'd expected as his footsteps were muffled by the packed-earth floor and his own brand of light-footed spy magic.

They'd disembarked for the records warehouse early, deciding to pick locks and trespass rather than ask for permission from bureaucrats they couldn't trust.

If they were caught, she had her pistol and Chandler had not one but several official identification papers that would get them out of just about any trouble with the local constables.

In an attempt to make a boring search interesting, they'd wagered over who would find the files first.

And they both hated to lose.

She'd learned this because it wasn't the first wager of the day.

As they'd lingered over coffee in bed that morning, Francesca had suggested that they ride their horses through the London throng rather than take a carriage. She preferred this mode of transportation, and her thoroughbred mare, Godiva, was in dire need of the exercise. Furthermore, should they need to make an escape from the law, from the council, or for any other reason, a horse was better equipped for a swift getaway than a coach.

He'd agreed enthusiastically and, as she dressed, they'd quibbled over the fastest route to take through London to Southwick. He'd insisted the Tower Bridge was likely to be the least populated at this hour, and she stubbornly contended London Bridge would dump them right into the neighborhood of the warehouse.

They'd split up as they shot from the gate of her stables, Chandler seated expertly on a charger named Porthos he'd selected from her fine stock. The sheen of his sandy hair rivaled the brilliance of his arrogant grin as he allowed Porthos to dance on the cobbles, lifting his hand in a salute. "May the best man win!" he called.

"Don't count on it!"

Experiencing some nominal discomfort in her newly unvirginal nether regions, she'd regretted her decision a mere five streets away. Regardless, she'd flown through the city only to find herself frustrated at Derving Square by an upturned cart. Clearing that, she'd encountered the bridge traffic he'd alluded to, and was stuck for a good ten minutes longer than she'd anticipated.

Finally, she'd clopped up to the warehouse, distressed to find Porthos already hitched, the door lock picked, and a handsome-as-sin spy for the crown standing in the threshold wearing a victorious smirk.

"How kind of you, Lady Francesca, to allow me the time to change my suit." He gave her an exaggerated bow over a fresh-pressed vest and jacket he must have donned at his Drake residence a few lanes over from her.

Scowling, Francesca kicked her leg over the saddle and hopped to the ground. Reaching for the billfold she'd tucked into the breast pocket of her riding jacket, she extracted the applicable notes and shoved them at his chest. "We'll rematch on the way home, of course," she panted. Her mood, color, and spirits were high, despite everything.

"As you wish." Once divesting her of the money, he kept her gloved hand and lifted it to his lips before pulling her in for a playful but searing kiss.

Her irrepressible smile frustrated the length of the

kiss, but he was a sport about it as he motioned for her to lead the way into the dank warehouse.

His breath on the back of her neck had been a warm memory of their previous night as he'd followed her closely down the stairs, his entire body a conduit for scandalous flirtation. "Promise you'll protect me if we encounter brigands in here?" he asked in an exaggerated whisper, fondling at the pocket in which she kept her pistol.

"*You* are the only brigand I expect to find in my company." She swatted at him as he investigated the seam of her split riding skirts from behind before pinching gently at her backside. "I insist you stop that, or we'll never get anything done."

"Yes, my lady. " He nibbled at her ear, causing her to hop forward. "You're a peer of this realm, and I a lowly civic servant. I am, of course, yours to command and dispose of at your leisure."

"Oh tosh," she laughed, shooing at him to no avail as his hands continued their delicious wanderings.

"I've always found skirts more convenient," he remarked, shaping his hand to the cup of her bottom. "But I confess I like you in trousers. They display your . . . *ass*ets to great effect."

"Stop being a bother, you cad!" She elbowed him in the chest, and he let out a melodramatic *oof* as his hands fell away from her.

She turned to gaze up at him. Even in the dimness of the warehouse, his eyes sparkled with mischief, and Francesca's heart lurched into her throat.

What fun adventures they might have. What a wonderful coterie of two they made. Generally, after hours in the presence of almost anyone, Francesca longed for the silence of her own company. Even Cecil and Alexander would create a need for space, what with their constant academic musings and infinite emotions. Not so with Chandler. He seemed to have no great need to fill a comfortable silence but if he did, it was endlessly entertaining.

Instead of impatiently hurrying her through her morning ablutions, he'd harassed and "helped" her, which almost led to another bout of lovemaking.

He'd been concerned when she'd shyly expressed her intimate tenderness. Concerned . . . and not a little conceited. And so, when she'd banished him from her dressing room, he'd made himself useful by assisting the groom in readying the horses.

A useful man. Not idle or irate. It was an indulgence she'd not been prepared to enjoy.

But enjoy him, she had.

"Do let's hurry." She tugged at him, pulling him farther into the warehouse stacked with rows upon rows of full and dusty shelves. "The croissant we devoured won't last long, and I'm a terror if not fed at regular intervals."

"One shudders at the thought." He winked and danced away from her swipe at him. "I know a pub around here that makes excellent meat pies."

"Spend a lot of time in the industrial district, do you?" She lifted an eyebrow.

"A bit," he said cryptically before transforming his features into those of an exaggerated Irishman with a severe squint. "If we dine there, you'll have to call me Mr. Thom Tew and put up with me mates from the foundry. We sometimes sneak away and get drunk before the call of the labor whistle."

Thomas Tew, another pirate.

Francesca shook her head at him as he sauntered toward the east side of the warehouse in long, lazy strides. "Five more pounds to whomever finds the documents first," he called over his shoulder. "Or should we raise the stakes?"

The question sobered her a little. Could the stakes be any higher?

Three exhausting hours and a ruined riding habit later, Francesca had stumbled upon a box on a shelf marked UNSOLVED ARSONS. #187 (M) MALDON—MONT CLAIRE.

She opened it with a captured breath, half shocked to find that no ghosts rushed at her from beneath the lid.

Chandler stopped at her shoulder, gazing down into the box as she rummaged about in papers, ash samples, statements from neighbors, and even a list of suspects upon which Kenway never appeared.

She glanced over at him, her gaze snagging on the set of his stubbled jaw. Her skin that bore the abrasions of said stubble prickled with awareness. The insides of her thighs. Her breasts. Her throat. Indeed, she'd had to wear a high-necked lace blouse just to cover a few love marks he'd made with his teeth.

She'd made a few of her own.

Biting down on her lip, she firmly planted herself in the task at hand.

His presence was both a comfort and a distraction. Just knowing he was there beside her to lean on if necessary was such an alien reassurance. One she thought she might just get used to. Chandler at her side. A solid man with uncommon skills and a curious intellect to match her own. Everything was better with him nearby. More dangerous, perhaps. More complicated, but less lonely.

And most definitely more passionate.

When they were through with this, she was going to tell him everything, she decided. She'd whisk him off somewhere remote and exotic. Ride him into senseless oblivion, whisper her secret to him, and then beg his forgiveness.

She had the sense that he wasn't a man prone to clemency, but he *did* understand the need for a good secret . . . and maybe hers wouldn't knock his planet too far out of orbit.

Then why not tell him now?

She'd tried. So often the night before she'd opened her mouth to tell him.

And something had stopped her. *He'd* stopped her mostly by interrupting. She enumerated to herself the many logical reasons to maintain the farce, the chief of which was the unknown human variable.

When people, especially men, were hurt or deceived, they tended to become angry. An angry man was generally an unpredictable creature. Often cruel. And while a part of her was a little afraid of his antagonism, she was more afraid of the consequences thereof. Not emotional, per se—though that was plenty enough to keep her up at night—but legal.

Even lethal.

In the worst-case scenario, he'd turn his back on

her—no—even more devastating than that, he could turn her in to his superiors. The subsequent litany of charges to be heaped on her shoulders would undoubtedly lead to the gallows. She was impersonating a dead countess, after all.

It wasn't that she thought he would wish for her death—though perhaps he'd have reason to—but as much as she desired, admired, and all-out loved this man . . . she didn't know who he'd become well enough to predict what he'd do. Everyone had a moral compass, and his was as of yet undefined.

Which was exciting at times, and also terrifying.

First, she needed to focus on the task at hand, to exonerate or condemn her parents in his eyes . . .

Best get to work.

Francesca whipped through the documents, scanning, dismissing, and handing one over to Chandler when she'd done so to select another. So far, none of this was new information, as through the course of her own investigation, she had talked to the same people, chatted with the investigators, and followed leads to their strange and fruitless ends for what felt like a multitude of years.

And then she saw it. A broken Cavendish seal with her father's tidy scrawl on the outside. Her heart fluttered, then sank as she reached out to retrieve it.

Oh, Papa, she thought. *What did you do?*

Ever observant, Chandler sidled closer, reaching for it. "Is that it?" he demanded. "Let me—"

Francesca swatted his reaching hand away and shushed him, feeling rather than seeing his displeasure at this, though he relented. She opened the missive with trembling fingers and read the words that he claimed had damned them all.

To Whom It May Concern,
I trust this letter will reach the correct hands, as I feel its contents are of the highest relevance.

Some years prior, we, the staff at the Mont Claire estate, took in a stray and starving boy by the name of Declan Chandler and put him to work. He's a good lad, solid of stature, respectful in his interactions, and a dedicated worker, which we all might agree is a missing trait in the youths of today. Decent by nature, is he. This wealth of moral character is inherent, I believe, despite his upbringing or lack thereof.

As he ages, it occurs to me that his future is uncertain, and I gather that many a young man turns to wayward moral turpitude without the guidance of a father.

Fatherhood was a lifelong ardent desire for me, and my only child, Pippa, is my most abiding joy. I have discussed this at length with my wife, Henrietta, and we share a most enthusiastic desire to adopt the boy into our family, so he may enjoy the benefits a proper upbringing can provide.

For the sake of brevity, I will now elucidate my point. I have been unable to obtain any records of Declan Chandler's birth or parentage, and I would respectfully request your help in doing so in that I require certainty that my due diligence can be evidenced when I apply for adoption.

Any assistance in this respect would be very much appreciated.

Sincerest and most respectful regards,
Charles Timothy Hargrave II
Mont Claire Estate, Derbyshire

Francesca read the words again and again, blinking to clear her vision. She rubbed her fingers over the faded script with a heart full to bursting.

Until a laugh bubbled out of her chest, she hadn't realized she was crying.

This letter was so undeniably her father. He claimed brevity in a missive much too long and full of digression. He was both regimented and sentimental, his script perfectly even and neat, his communication a bit untidy.

His heart as massive as the Atlantic.

"Francesca." Chandler's voice was mostly full of concern, though the threat of impatience hovered in the periphery. "Tell me, dammit. What's wrong?"

Pippa is my most abiding joy. She caressed the sentence before handing the letter to him, reluctant to let it go just as much as she was eager for him to read it. To know.

Swamped by emotion, she allowed the tears to flow freely now. She'd seen her mother on the day of the massacre. She'd watched the devotion turn into sacrifice, and nary a day went by that she wasn't grateful for and devastated by it.

But her father had been different. Indulgent but proper. Pleasant but distracted and sometimes aloof, but always devoted. Always. And she'd never gotten to say goodbye. She'd never realized what an extraordinary thing her happy family was until it was taken from her.

And her father, her lovely father, had wanted to offer Declan Chandler a part of that family.

She'd have begged him not to, of course. Because she'd planned to do it herself by way of marriage.

Francesca found herself swathed in shame for even doubting her parents. Of course they'd never been involved in the Crimson Council. Charles Timothy Hargrave the Second would never have allowed such "moral turpitude."

Christ, she missed them.

She looked over at Chandler, whose wolfish eyes devoured the script again and again. She'd thought the kindness of her father would warm him. Would touch his wounded heart while absolving the Hargraves of any wrongdoing in his eyes.

So why did his skin mottle so? The flush splashed from beneath the high collar of his suit. His aristocratic nose flared with increasing breaths and his brow fell heavier over wild, wide eyes.

Little twitches became apparent on his features. She saw in the lips he pulled back from his eyeteeth in the semblance of a snarl. His right eye blinked more violently than the left and a vein she'd never noticed before throbbed at his temple.

It wasn't the reaction she'd expected at all. The opposite, in fact.

Then, quite suddenly, all traces of emotion vanished in a transformation no less than mythical. One moment he was a man, and the next he was a pillar of stone. Cold. Remote.

Unreachable.

The change terrified her more than any display of temper could have.

"I understand why you're angry," she said, attempting to placate him. "Your intelligence was faulty, and that wasted a great deal of time." She stepped closer and reached for him.

He backed away, crushing the letter in his fist. "No. No, it fucking wasn't."

"What? Stop that! Give over that letter. It's all that's left of my—of our childhood." She'd almost said her father.

He thrust it at her and she took it, smoothing the corners.

"That foolish fuck," he said with a flat, droll affect.

"I beg your pardon?" The tether on her temper, short and thin as it was, began to slip. "This man admired you." She shook the paper at him. "He wanted to take you in, to give you a future. What about that is foolish? You were an orphan and he was an endlessly decent man. The best of men, I daresay."

He shook his head, backing away from her, inching toward the door. "We should leave. Now."

"But—" She took another step forward, and he held a hand up against her.

Suddenly she felt like a child again, desperate and unsure. Brash and hurt by his diffidence. "What is wrong?" she pleaded. "I don't understand."

Something in her features must have spoken to him

because his face softened a mere increment. "I know." He let out an eternal breath. "I know."

"Let's go to that pub and get that meal," she ventured. "We can talk about this. You can tell me why you're being so very odd."

He gave his head a curt shake. "I have to go to the Secret Services."

"I'll come with you."

"No."

"No?" she gritted out through ever-clenching teeth. "Have you not yet learned how I react to the word *no*?"

For a moment his eyes turned amber and molten, but that disappeared as he spoke to her with a jaw just as hard and insolent as hers. "Tell me, Francesca, do you have any idea where you are supposed to meet the Crimson Council tonight?"

Her eyes shifted to the side and she crossed her arms, hiding the precious letter from him. "Well . . . not exactly. Kenway said a notice would be sent."

"Wouldn't it behoove us both, then, to have you waiting at your home when it arrives?"

"Yes," she conceded carefully. "But can you not at least share what significance this has—"

"No time for that." He whirled and strode toward the main door. "I'll explain everything when I return the horse."

She rushed after him, taking quick light steps to his heavy long ones. "When will that be?" she asked.

"I cannot say."

"Chandler. Can you not at least—"

"I said *no*, Francesca." The hard ire in his voice

echoed off the walls and battered her with fractals of rejection.

"If you cannot be agreeable, then at least be sensible for once. I will contact you when I can."

Turning, he slammed the door behind him, right in her face.

She stared at the iron ingots in the frame and counted the scratches from untold years of wear as she finished her sentence.

"Can you not at least kiss me goodbye?"

Chapter Twenty-One

It fucking ended tonight. One way or another, this saga was done, and blood would be spilled. Final blood.

Chandler kept a stranglehold on his emotion until he'd put enough distance between him and Francesca. From that goddamned letter.

He wandered at a fast clop through the city, searching for a place for his wrath to land.

When other people ran from danger, Chandler had always found the grit within himself to run toward it. He was the sort of man to douse a raging fire, or to charge someone with a weapon. He was the antithesis of chaos and at his best in a crisis. He didn't flinch, he didn't look away from pain, horror, blood, or suffering. Nothing overwhelmed him, or repulsed him, or disturbed him so much that he could not confront it.

He'd wager he'd seen just about everything and he

found a certain Viking-like freedom in the knowledge that his stars were cursed. That the fates would fuck him every time he reached for happiness, and so the best he could hope for was to never again be shot in the back.

When his enemies claimed him, which was an inevitability, they'd stare the Devil of Dorset in the eyes, and he'd take a fair share back to hell with him.

But for the first time since Mont Claire, he retreated. He ran away. He fled.

His first instinct had been to go to ground. Not because he wanted to hide, but because he needed a place to come apart. The rage injected into his veins could only be released by destruction no less than biblical. He wanted to break something. Someone. No, he wanted to dismantle the entire city, burn the empire to the ground.

And it was from that instinct that he fled, just as much as anything else.

But . . . where to run to? He had more dwellings than most, one for each of his personas. In any one of them he could find a hammer. He could topple things, punch them, dismantle and break them. He could pit his strength against the world and exhaust this need with destructive violence.

He'd start with the mirrors.

Ultimately, he decided against that. Though a temper tantrum of epic proportions would certainly wear him out enough to make him feel somewhat better, it would weaken him. And he could not afford to be weak, not if he was going to save Francesca. To sacrifice himself for her.

It was what they both deserved.

Chandler closed his eyes and summoned her to mind. For all she'd been through, all she'd survived, to reach her age with such vivacious ambition . . . it was no small feat. When so many allowed their tragedies to defeat them, she'd become stronger.

Stronger than him in many ways. Certainly, he was physically more powerful, but even that didn't seem to faze her. She used her grace and skill, her beauty and her brilliance to fell him. And beyond that, she'd managed to do what he never could.

Not just to survive, but to truly live.

To live safe in the knowledge that none of this was her fault.

She might have lost her family, but she surrounded herself with friends just as close. People of rare substance and quality. She'd a title of her own, a fortune, an education, and the enviable status of being both the quarry and the heroine.

She'd done it through sheer strength of character.

And what had he accomplished compared with that? He couldn't even claim an *identity* let alone a life.

Yes, he technically had in his possession many properties, but he'd never had a *home*.

He could claim a few things, however. Like the blood of innumerable innocents on his hands, an accursed soul, and . . .

A responsibility.

To rid the world of an evil so insidious, the people milling about the streets of his city were not even aware that it had infiltrated their government, their economy, and their very lives.

And he would. Tonight.

He'd finally be able to, because he would at least be sure that Francesca would be far away from the Crimson Council. If he was lucky, she'd be home, awaiting a summons that would never come.

He reached into his pocket, retrieving the map that had been left for her in the wee hours of the morning. Intercepting it had almost been too easy. He'd left her to her ablutions and had snooped through a silver tray of cards and invitations, hoping it would be there.

The fates, it would seem, were on his side for once.

Because of him, she'd have no idea where the second ritual would be. And because of its unusual location, she'd have little to no chance of stumbling upon it, even if she searched the entire night.

He'd do what he had to, and it would be over.

But first, he had to rid himself of this reckless rage.

Winding back toward the west boroughs, he found himself at Crosshaven Downs, a posh and pretty spot where the idle rich came to play at all things equestrian. He let Porthos have his head, hunching low over his neck as the gelding galloped like a stallion.

He was not a man prone to running away, and so he let the creature do it for him.

He ran from every ghost haunting the ashes of Mont Claire.

Especially the Hargraves.

Hattie, the simple, endlessly pleasant and untroubled woman who always seemed to have extra food set aside for him.

Charles, who would pat his shoulder every time he

gave him a job to do. Who'd never truly smiled with his stern mouth, but always conveyed amusement with the rest of his face.

The man would have offered to be his father.

With a raw command, Chandler spurred the horse faster, letting the wind whip at him as he ate up the ground.

He ran from the soft, clinging arms of Pippa Hargrave. From her trusting, round face and toothless smile. From her peppermints and her punches and her little-girl love. From the hole in his heart that belonged only to her.

She was his greatest failure. His most profound regret.

Most of all, he ran from his nature, his choices, and his very name.

He ran until the distressed snorts and breaths of the athletic horse beneath him permeated the fog of rage and pain and loss.

Reining in the steed, he walked the horse around the downs for several laps, cooling them both.

The race hadn't exactly the desired effect, but then, he'd not expected it to. If life had taught him anything, it was folly to try to outrun the past.

And impossible to outrun the truth.

The Mont Claire Massacre had been his fault.

Francesca had built part of her pain tolerance from the years and years spent suffering beneath Serana's tending of her hair.

Though her locks had darkened from the silver blond of her youth to a darker gold, she never caught a glimpse of the undergrowth before the Romani woman hustled her into a chair and ground the terrible-looking and foul-smelling paste that stained her hair such a vibrant red into her scalp.

Tonight was to be important, and since Francesca was perhaps the most impatient woman on the planet, she decided that she could busy herself with the necessary evil of personal grooming while she waited for the directions to the next Crimson Council gathering.

Devotion had been a heavy thing to witness. But tonight was desire . . .

At least she wouldn't have to put on an act.

After just one taste of Declan Chandler, her desire had turned from a curious hunger to an insatiable craving. She'd picked the right stag, of course . . . a stag that was still missing, even as the afternoon hour turned late.

"Were you careful, Francesca?" Serana's Eastern European accent had never quite faded, even after all this time in England. Her blazing gold eyes skewered her from the mirror as she pinned her pasted hair tightly to her head with ruthless jabs.

"I'm not certain to what you're referring, but the answer is more than likely no." Francesca busied herself brewing her own concoction of sodium bismuth, vanilla, coconut, and a few other exotic oils that would strip her hair of the smell once the henna dye was washed away.

"I'm asking if you took measures to make certain you and the tiger did not make a child last night." Ever since learning of Declan Chandler's survival, Serana had taken to calling him "the tiger," as she did not like to keep track of his innumerable names.

She'd insisted none of them belonged to him, anyhow.

The woman seemed pleased, though, to hear that she'd been wrong about his death.

Francesca didn't look up as the woman nearly finished toiling behind her, reaching for a scarf to wrap around the muck as it set in the color over a few hours.

"No," Francesca admitted with a rueful twist of her lips. "We were not careful."

"Ah, I see." Though Serana rarely ever made her thoughts known, she was a woman Francesca had always found easy to read. Not that she needed to guess now, as the woman made her judgments perfectly clear by the brutal knots she pulled in the scarf, jerking her head this way and that.

"I will make you tonic," she said crisply. "There will be no child."

"Wait." The word escaped Francesca's lips before she could stop herself. She and Serana stared at each other in the mirror, holding silent court.

Serana reminded her that she'd never wanted a child. That her life was strictly inconducive to motherhood. That every day she lived as Francesca Cavendish was borrowed from a lie, and if the council didn't get her someday, the Crown might.

"I know," Francesca said aloud. "But just . . . wait."

"Where is your tiger, by the by?" The brackets of age around the woman's mouth deepened as she frowned. "You could be called away at any moment by your enemy, and he has left you without a word all because your father once desired to be kind to him? To offer him a home?"

Francesca itched a place where the paste dripped against her scalp, puffing out a beleaguered breath. "It's more than that . . ." It didn't take a genius to realize why he'd escaped her company a few hours ago. He'd learned not only that his entire hypothesis had been incorrect about the Mont Claire Massacre, but that he'd gained and lost a father before he even knew about it.

For a man who'd survived such a litany of such tragedies alone . . . she couldn't imagine what that had meant to him. Of course he would need to sort it all out in his thoughts and his heart. It was a lot to contend with. "It's . . . complicated," she finished lamely.

Serana made an affirmative grunt, giving the scarf a final yank to secure it.

Francesca looked at her reflection. She might have been a maharaja with such a fine turban, save for the fact that she was neither male, a king, nor Indian.

"He'll be there when I need him," Francesca assured, wishing she felt as confident as she sounded.

Serana slid her a sideways look. "I do not think the gods would ever have allowed your father to adopt him," she declared. "He never was meant to be your brother, but your fate."

Francesca opened her mouth to ask her to clarify when a metallic jangle pealed from her bedroom. Holding up a finger to signal that this conversation was not over, she went to the receiver box of her telephone and lifted the earpiece.

"Lady Francesca?" Even through the tinny wires, Lord Ramsay's brogue was unmistakable.

"This is."

"I am calling on behalf of my wife to give ye a firm talking-to," he said without a trace of firmness.

"Stern!" She heard Cecelia call from somewhere in his vicinity. "I said stern, not firm."

His breath was a long-suffering gush against the mouthpiece, and it carried his regret over the miles between them.

"Ye lied," he accused in a matter-of-fact tone.

"You'll have to be specific," Francesca remonstrated, trying to cull the strange compelling urge she had to yell her words into the receiver. Not because she was irritated, but because they really did have to travel a great distance, and she wondered if they needed an extra push.

"The Kenway ritual," he clarified. "It isna at the estate tonight, as ye informed us."

Drat. She'd been caught. "Oh?" she feigned innocence. "Have they moved it? I haven't received the invitation for it as of yet. I think it will come later and we'll have to leave immediately."

"That surprises me, because everyone else has one, including yer lover."

Francesca clutched the phone with hands gone suddenly cold and clammy. "What?" She didn't fight the yelling now. "How do you know?"

"That he has an invitation? Or that he's yer lover?"

Francesca took the earpiece from her ear and made a nasty face at it. "Both," she gritted out. "Either."

"I cautioned him against having you two watched!" Cecelia called from the ether. "But he's quite like you, Frank. Stubborn. His agents saw Chandler go into your house last night . . . and not come out."

Francesca could just see the couple glaring at each other.

"I've had everyone watched," Ramsay admitted with no trace of shame. "Kenway, his household, people I recognized leaving the council soiree last night, names I've gleaned from the council members ye'd already given over to us. They are all being followed. And ye'll thank me for my stubbornness when ye hear what I have to say."

Ramsay took a fortifying breath, and because he was so much like her in nature, Francesca found a place to sit down. If this was unpleasant for the Scot to impart, she wasn't going to like to hear it.

"I did some digging on Chandler Alquist, Lady Francesca," he started reluctantly. "He's not just a spy, he's a ghost. There are no records of him existing anywhere except for when he gained employ. He's assigned to the most dangerous of cases, suicide missions and the like, and has been after the Crimson Council for some time. He's done . . . terrible things, Francesca. Things that would make even a man such as I hesitate."

Francesca let out a deep breath, clutching at the window seat beneath her. "I know," she murmured. "He's told me as much. And isn't it said that one doesn't send a saint to capture a sinner?" She patently refused to believe that he was anything but a good man. "Chandler acknowledges that he's a monster, but he's shown me someone different, Ramsay. He is an agent of justice, and sometimes justice is brutal."

"I doona ken if you understand what I'm saying to

ye," Ramsay interjected carefully. "Chandler isn't a monster. He's the man they send to *kill* the monster. He's death's own emissary from the Crown, and if he's on a job then people end up in the ground."

"You mean to say, he's an assassin?"

"I mean to say he lied to ye, Countess. He was never delivered an invitation to the ritual tonight, but ye were. This morning. My man witnessed it happen, and if ye doona have it, then I suspect Chandler does, and that he's keeping it from ye."

"That rat bastard." Francesca swiped at a vase on the table next to her, sending peonies and other select flora flying as the crystal shattered on the floor. "He means to keep me from my revenge, does he? The high-handed cretin. I'll fucking teach him a thing or two about—"

"About trying to keep those ye care about away from a dangerous situation by being dishonest?" Ramsay cut in, a note of amusement gentling his censure.

Guiltily, she traced the grain of wood on the table top in front of her with a fingertip. "That was different. I don't want Cecelia and Alexandra caught up in this. Francesca is *my* lie. It's my fight."

"We doona want *any* of ye Rogues caught up in this," Ramsay grumped.

"Is this the royal we?"

"Redmayne and I, the duchess, and Cecelia. We'd have ye let Chandler . . . whoever he is . . . deal with this. He obviously wants to keep ye safe, and the man has more than enough expertise. Sending him into the lair of the Crimson Council is akin to dropping an explosive into a room and shutting the door."

"If I'm not there tonight, I think Kenway will suspect why. He has as many eyes in this city as you do, and I'm not naive enough to think I haven't been watched by him, as well." Though she'd been careful not to be tailed through the city that morning. "I think Chandler will be in danger if I do not attend this." Anger and concern warred inside her stomach with such force, Francesca wondered if she might chuck up her lunch. "Do you know where they're holding the ritual?"

The silence on the other end of the line stretched a moment too long.

"Goddammit, Ramsay. If you know something *tell me*."

"Do ye have anything to tell me, Countess?"

Francesca worried at an escaped tendril of hair at the nape of her neck. "Chandler might be the most dangerous spy in the realm, but Kenway has an army of devotees that would throw themselves in front of a bullet for him. Kenway is deranged, Ramsay. He's more sordid than you could have ever even suspected." She spilled all the information about the night prior. About her father, the Cavendishes, the Lord Chancellor, and the rituals. She told him what she knew of their creed and what the council might be planning to do with it.

Once she finished, he said nothing for a moment, and then, "I wish we had more evidence. The kind to put this treacherous—nay, traitorous—council away for good. But as it stands, even if I set up a raid, I'll have little more than several dozen charges of gross public indecency, and no peer of the realm has remained imprisoned for long for an orgy. Not in this day and age."

"Even a seditious orgy?" she wished aloud.

"There'd have to be proof. Testament. And I'm afraid hearsay from ye and Chandler just wouldna be enough. We need something to tie them to the massacre, to the kidnapping of those girls, to the murder of the Lord Chancellor. And, most important, specific plans for an overthrow of the monarchy. Can ye provide me any of that?"

She shook her head, forgetting for a moment that he was unable to see her. "The Lord Chancellor's bones are fodder for the dogs by now, I'm afraid, and Kenway is much too clever to keep documents."

"And he obviously has agents in the government." Ramsay expelled another of his long, hissing breaths, and Francesca could all but see him pinching the bridge of his nose. "This is even bigger than we all thought."

"I know," she said, worrying at her lip with her teeth. "Tell me where Chandler is. Tell me what you know about tonight."

"I doona think I should." He hesitated again, and Francesca surged to her feet. "I have a sense of duty to protect ye."

"Don't let the fact that I'm a woman fool you, Ramsay, I am *just* as passionate and possessive as you are. Chandler is *mine*. I've loved him for decades, and my love is no less fierce than yours. You desire to see a monster? You want to see an agent of death? Look no further than me, you sanctimonious son of a bitch.

I'd never think to keep you from Cecelia if she was in a similar position. So help me, Ramsay, if you keep me from him by some misguided notion that I'm the weaker sex and in need of protection from my own decisions, it'll be *you* I come after next."

This time, the silence on the other side of the phone was more astonished than hesitant, and she could hear the muffled sounds of Cecelia's voice.

He drew a long intake of breath, holding it for a beat. "I've gathered a small amount of information from the men ye've already turned in to us. I have a few names. When pressed, they might have let spill that there was talk of holding one of the rituals in the catacombs off Isambard Tunnel in the Underground."

Trying not to choke on her guile, her desperation, and maybe a little of her hurt, Francesca nodded for a while before realizing he couldn't see her.

"I'm . . . obliged to you," she forced herself to say.

"Och," he replied with his own brand of curt fondness. "And let me tell ye, Lady Francesca, woman or no, ye're as fierce and formidable as any general. I'd follow ye into battle anytime."

"Well . . ." If that didn't take the tempest out of her sails. "Thank you." This time, the sentiment was more genuine and easier to express. "How does tonight sound?"

"Fair enough . . . Francesca?"

"Yes, Ramsay?"

"I'm going to help ye get yer man and get out of there."

"But how—?"

The line went dead, and Francesca stared at it for several furious moments before slamming it back on the receiver.

She swept aside the shards of glass as she went to prepare for the evening.

"Where are you going?" Serana asked.

"To rescue Chandler," she said darkly. "So I can murder him, myself."

Chapter Twenty-Two

Objectively, it was the perfect place for a cultish ritual, Chandler thought, a forgotten underground chamber with access to the newer Tube stations branching out in three different directions. From what he'd read in the blueprints, it had been dug and buttressed as a hub from the Thames in 1863, but a drunk and wayward architect hadn't delved enough into the earth and so it spent perhaps a month of the year submerged in knee-deep water.

In the summer, however, when the river was low, it remained dry and the raised walkways that might have been train platforms rose from the groundwater. The grooves plowed for the tracks made perfect trenches beneath which Chandler and his two fellow operatives Benjamin Dashiell and Theo Howard would station themselves.

Logistically, it left everything to be desired for a

police raid, as three different tunnels converged into the unfinished space. This not only left nowhere for a force to hide, but allowed plenty of means to escape as smaller passages branched from almost every tunnel, some of them nothing more than ancient walkways or Jacobite escape paths dating back to the Tudor era.

With the *unsolicited* help of Lord Ramsay, Chandler and the Secret Services had hatched a plan. Three operatives would be sent in with three low-grade, fairly harmless explosive devices, and place them in each tunnel. When the raids began, they would be detonated in little more than a percussive nightmare and billows of smoke, corralling the cultists and signaling the police to surround and isolate the gathering in a sweeping arrest the likes of which hadn't been seen since the Inquisition.

During the day, trains would shake the very ceilings of this place, but at half eleven at night, the Underground was nearly deserted by all but vermin.

Vermin that wasn't limited to rats and roaches.

Signs of danger made from no official office had been posted on the gates to dissuade any lurkers in the tunnels from becoming curious.

And to guide the cultists in the right direction.

The gates had been latched, but none of them locked, as Kenway was too clever to block his own escape.

Chandler and his contingent of two agents swooped in from the north tunnel, drawn by the sounds of low, rhythmic humming and a lone drum. There was no chamber music tonight. Nothing that would draw attention from the main passages.

The festivities had only just begun.

And the Crimson Council would be finished before the night was out.

There weren't any footmen this time, though piles of cold food and drink lined a table against the far south wall where it was obvious excavators had simply stopped their work in the middle of it. Depravity did work up an appetite, and these were not people who were used to suffering a desire left unfulfilled for long.

Confident that their movements were little more than shadows in the dark, Chandler, Dashiell, and Howard slithered about like indefinable serpents in a pit, setting the charges to detonate on command. They took cover behind a wall of brick that might have once been laid in the hope of becoming an underground vendor for the likes of candied nuts or newspapers.

The humming of the devotees was louder here, a refrain that sounded exotic, Indian perhaps.

Dashiell, a veteran in his late forties with a grievance against variables and an unflappable nature, pulled his watch from a vest pocket. He was careful not to catch a glimmer from the numerous candles flickering from the platform upon which maybe forty souls groaned and groped at each other with increasing fervency.

"Ramsay and the Chief Inspector should be in place within a quarter hour," he whispered through an impressive mustache, confident they wouldn't be heard over the humming some several yards away. "I suspect that'll give this . . . gathering a bloody good start." He scrunched his eyes to peer at the goings-on with no little interest. "I've been at this a long time," he breathed. "And I've never seen the like."

Howard, a fair-haired man who was barely old

enough to grow a beard, stared with round, unblinking eyes.

Chandler questioned the intelligence of bringing him, but the spy had a special skill with explosives.

"What punters, eh?" He nudged Chandler in the ribs. "I mean, I wouldn't mind being invited to the odd orgy someday, but this . . . it's diabolical."

Idly, Chandler grunted as he glared. Something held the cultists back. They writhed together, kissed and fondled, all the while keeping up their incessant, throaty chant. But nothing went further, as if their lust was on a leash, waiting to be released by the command of a master.

His lip curled in disgust.

If one provides the weak-willed and small-minded a trifle they've been denied, something they hunger for, they'll put on their own chains and call it freedom.

His father had told him that once, a lifetime ago.

Dashiell shook his head. "Only the toffs would do something like this. It's all that inbreeding, says I."

Howard nodded, sagely. "Makes one wonder how many bastards are gotten at such things, and passed off as nobility."

Unable to stand the wait, Chandler rubbed at the back of his itching neck. "Something's off," he muttered.

Howard sent him a quizzical look. "This whole bloody affair is daffy."

"Kenway isn't here yet. Could someone have warned him?"

Dashiell shook his head, ducking back down to sweep a look through the darkness of the trenches, as if he could see anything. "Not even the bobbies know what they're getting into."

Still, it didn't feel right. "Let's split for our respective tunnels, just in case. No one in or out."

"What about Kenway? What if he's just . . . tardy?" Dashiell queried. "We could scare him off if he sees us on his way in."

"I . . . don't think so." Kenway was never late, unless it was by design.

A troubling thought lanced his blood with ice. What if, by some impossible construct, Kenway was one step ahead of him? What if he'd been drawn away so that the fucking bastard could get at Francesca?

He'd left her protected, and it was not like she was helpless.

But still . . .

"Sure thing, boss." Howard touched two fingers to his forehead in a subdued salute. "I'll stay at this tunnel and . . . uh . . . monitor the . . . er . . . festivities."

Chandler shared a look with Dashiell before he hunkered into the trench and angled north. He'd have to cut up, over, and back to avoid risking a dash over the dais. Anyone with a careful eye might see a shadow and investigate.

As he was about to turn a corner, he noticed an opening in the stone wall big enough for a man to fit through if he turned sideways. Frowning, he passed it. It would be difficult to cover both exits, but it could be done.

Three yards up the trench, he spotted another passage. And another a few after that.

Bloody. Fucking. Hell. These hadn't been on the

blueprints. How many were there? And where did they lead?

Who did they hide?

He'd barely thought the question when the answer presented itself.

Or, rather, himself.

Across the way, Kenway appeared as if he'd stepped out of the very stone. He was followed by seven stags.

Chandler had imprisoned one, Marcus Fettlesham, before he'd taken the lad's place as a stag at the previous night's spectacle.

Who, he wondered, had replaced him?

Chandler knew what many did not . . . Luther Kenway had always *preferred* stags over does, which was why his interest in Francesca was so confounding. She wasn't possessed of a voluptuous physique. Indeed, her slim body's attributes were stunning in their strength and symmetry, but neither was she mannish.

No, she was all woman.

None of it made any sense.

A smile toyed with the corner of his mouth. With neither he nor Francesca in attendance, a wrench had been thrown into the evening. He imagined Kenway was scrambling to explain the absence of his main attraction. Maye he'd lose a bit of face with his followers, before he lost everything.

God, he couldn't wait to watch the man choke on his own guile.

The crowd parted for him as he strode in his lion mask to what they'd formed as the top of the dais. Women broke from the crowd, padding to trunks beneath the food table to extract cushions, blankets, and pillows to strew about the hall.

Chandler looked down at his own watch. Ten minutes. Plenty of time for Kenway to say something treasonous in the earshot of the other agents.

The earl raised his hands as though he were Moses parting the sea, and the humming ceased. "Tonight, we pay homage to desire," he said. "The second precept of freedom. Tonight, nothing is forbidden you, as it shall be when the walls of our oppressors will crumble, and we will govern the empire by right of might. Power will not be born into, but seized. And to the powerful, nothing will be denied."

Chandler curled his fist, pumping it with a little motion of victory. There it was, enough to damn him in the eyes of the law.

Kenway held out his arm to another split in the wall. "Come forth, vixen, and I shall do you the honor of serving as your proxy, as well as any of these eager stags."

No vixen mask emerged from the darkness.

But a dragon did.

The swell of victory shriveled as Chandler swallowed his heart.

The woman in sheer red robes floated down the path Kenway had previously taken. Though her dragon mask was made after the same fashion as the others, it didn't at all belong. Teeth bared and eyes wide, it threatened the seductive tone of the entire gathering with its ferocity.

Still the devotees worshiped her, as if this deviation was a lark.

She passed him at one point, and he ducked lower into the trench, beneath where the candlelight didn't reach.

His growing fury didn't need visual affirmation of just who glided up the path. He didn't need to see the tattoo on her back, nor the nearly nude form he'd become so intimately acquainted with the previous night.

He recognized the grace of her stride, the set of her shoulders, the strength of her purpose.

Francesca.

It took everything he had not to snarl her name as insolent rage welled within him.

How dare she defy him? How dare she profane herself with the filth of this place? Had she no sense of self-preservation? Did she delight in putting herself in this kind of danger?

Alone. And without weapons.

For fuck's sake, he could see everything from the sharpness of her shoulder blades to the cleft in her ass.

And so could his men.

Five minutes. Five minutes and the might of the Scotland Yard would descend on this place.

Chandler's mind raced with alternatives as she approached the dais, an uneasiness hitching the confidence out of her stride.

"Where is my chosen stag?" she demanded in a strong voice.

Chandler would have given his eyeteeth to see Kenway's reaction.

He'd always hated strong women.

"He deemed himself unworthy," the earl said. "*I* will service you in his stead."

The stags descended in lines of three and encircled her, closing in as if to crowd her toward Kenway.

She stood her ground. "But I didn't select you. What do you mean he was not worthy? What did you do to him?"

Kenway put a hand to his own in the parody of a wounded heart. "Why, nothing, my dear. He simply . . . vanished. Now come."

When she didn't move, the two men nearest to her drew up beside her. Too close. One of them looked as if he would push her forward.

Murder shredded Chandler's self-control and sent him reaching for his asp.

If they put a fucking hand on her he'd—

"What do you mean, vanished?" she insisted.

Kenway put up a staying hand to the stags, his robes cascading behind him as he stepped toward her. His lion head cocked to the side in a doglike assessment. "Do you know this stag of yours, Countess?" he asked.

No one could see her face, but her angst was apparent. "I think you know I do," she said, her voice containing more daggers than she'd ever strapped to her body.

"Let me put your mind at ease, my dear, he is unharmed." Kenway reached out and touched a tendril of her hair, gently examining it in his hand.

Red filtered Chandler's vision, spilling liquid, molten rage through his veins.

"You will *come* to me, Countess." The command was intentionally wicked, and Francesca jerked away from him.

The stag on her left seized her elbow, shoving her forward.

Chandler leapt out of the dark, clearing the platform and sprinting toward the dais.

He'd broken the hand that touched her before the first cultist had time to scream. With a roar, he picked the man up and hurled him into the dark. The crack his body made on the unused rails was a beautiful sound.

The six other stags surrounded him, locking Francesca into their circle with him.

She yanked off her mask and hurled it at one of them before whirling back to face Chandler, panic and relief warring with wrath in her eyes.

He retrieved his asp from his belt and readied himself. He was going to beat to death every one of the men who'd threatened her and see the foolish woman to safety.

Then he'd deal with Kenway once and for all.

Chapter Twenty-Three

Francesca wanted to stand back and watch Chandler work. It was almost a thing of beauty, to witness the grace and speed at which he could inflict pain.

Any blows that landed on him seemed to glance off the shield of his near-demonic rage.

The last time she'd seen him, he'd been a cold mountain of ice. Bleak. Remote. Unfeeling.

Now he was a volcano.

His motions were controlled, his determination absolute. He hit for maximum damage and economy of movement. Like a machine calibrated for violence.

Bones crunched, flesh split, blood flew.

And she had to do something to help.

Francesca ached for her pistol, but when she'd seen her costume for the night, she'd been chagrined to notice there was nowhere to put it.

That had been by Kenway's design, she thought. He wanted them all not just naked, but bare. Defenseless. Vulnerable.

However, just because she had no weapons didn't mean she was helpless.

As the stags focused on Chandler, she took advantage of their underestimation of her as a woman to turn for Kenway. He scurried to the south, away from the tunnels, followed by some of his people, to whom he paid no heed.

Men like him always saved themselves first.

No doubt he planned to escape to another of the portals that led from this cavern. They'd been built to drain water, she imagined, and if Kenway followed them, he would end up exactly where he belonged.

The sewers.

She needed to stop him before he escaped.

When she lunged after him, a burly man rose up from the panicking cultists and made as if to stop her. She drew her arm back to gather power and drove the flat of her hand into his nose, feeling the bone give way beneath the blow.

He collapsed instantly, and she turned back to where Kenway had last been seen.

Chaos had erupted, and two other men in suits had joined the fray, lawmen, it seemed, trained to capture and kill.

They shouted commands as they fought to regain control over the anarchy.

In the distance, whistles pealed, and footsteps echoed like cannon blasts on the granite.

The police!

People were scurrying everywhere, some frantic beasts, others pale-faced and terrified, having divested their masks as they made for the various tunnels.

She couldn't worry about any of them. She had to get to Kenway. He'd almost disappeared.

Thunderous sounds drove her to her knees. Not cannon blasts, exactly, but deafening in the echoes of the underground. She covered her ears with a cry of distress that was lost in the din.

Strong hands lifted her, and she turned to strike out before she looked to find that Chandler had swept her from the floor and was conducting her—half running, half dragging—toward one of the very tunnels that were now filled with smoke from whatever charges they'd set.

"Kenway." She pointed to where he'd slithered out, coughing against the smoke.

"Fuck Kenway," he snarled. "I'm getting you out of here." He shoved a handkerchief over her nose and, for the second time in their lives, led her through acrid smoke to safety.

The ringing in her ears disoriented her enough to make her stumble, and so Chandler picked her up and carried her through a distressing maze of catacombs. Every time he took a turn, he stomped out a candle that seemed to have been purposely left to illuminate a personal escape route.

He'd always been so endlessly clever.

Eventually, he paused where an ancient-looking passage gave way to a larger, more modern one.

Gas lamps replaced the candles at the far end of

what she assumed was the way to an active Underground station that had been locked and gated for the evening.

Which brought up a problem. She was still wearing the sheer robes. Gathering some of her wits, she squirmed to be let down. "Wait. Where are you taking me?"

"Home, where do you think?"

She was able to go slack enough to squirm to the ground, but there was no escaping his viselike grip. "But Kenway. We have to go back. What if he escapes?"

He turned on her, his expression one she'd never seen before. "You were not supposed to be here," he thundered before forging ahead, still dragging her in his wake.

"Wait," She tugged against his grip.

"I cannot imagine what possessed you," he puzzled furiously, as if to himself. "How did you even find out?"

"I said stop!" She dug her heels in. "I can't go out there. Not like this!"

He whirled on her, his teeth bared in a snarl as if he were a beast who would bite her, no doubt ready to thoroughly dress her down.

But there was no need. She was already mostly naked.

And she could tell the exact moment that fact reached through his single-minded anger and arrested his notice. The fury never drained from his eyes, but it transformed into something else. Something equally as violent and ultimately more perilous.

What she read in his gaze caused her to step back.

Had she not retreated, she might have been safe. She might not have activated the primal, predatory instinct inside of him.

But she had.

He lunged, knocking aside the hands she'd held up to ward him off as he gripped the back of her neck and pulled her in for a punishing kiss.

Francesca trembled as his arms locked her against his inflamed body, one hand behind her head, threading into her hair, and the other ripping at the single cord that kept the diaphanous robe secured.

The thought occurred to her somewhere in the back of her mind that she should stop him. That there was a raid going on in the distance, and they might be discovered. She wanted to know why he hadn't informed her of his plans. To demand where he'd been all day.

And why he'd lied to her.

But as his mouth devoured her with almost violent ardor, he kissed the questions out of her head and she felt helpless to do much but allow him to meld her body to his in wordless demand.

Sometimes, submission was the best strategy.

The moment she became pliant, his kiss didn't gentle so much as it altered. He made wet, delicious promises against her mouth with animal sounds. His heart pounded in his chest like a sledgehammer against her breasts. His body was hot and hard even through his clothes, and she felt a frenzy in him that was barely human.

He needed to claim her. And she needed to let him.

He growled as she began to kiss him back, his hand curling in her hair, pulling her head back and imprisoning it there.

He broke the seal of their mouths, his eyes appearing demon black in the near-darkness.

He was a man who owned the dark. Who wore it on his skin and wrapped his soul in it. And Francesca knew in that moment she was going to meet his darkness; he was about to pour some of it into her.

She had it coming.

He lowered his head to run his mouth down her neck, using his teeth in little scrapes that made her gasp and jerk.

They had so much to say to each other. So much anger to analyze and enmity to examine, but first . . . this. None of it would matter until this was satisfied. Until she no longer drowned in a pool of her own longing.

A pleading sound she never would claim as her own escaped her throat and snapped whatever tenuous tether he'd had on his self-control.

Much as he'd done the other night, Chandler lifted her, wrapped her limbs around his waist, and staggered forward a few paces until he could press her against the cold stone wall.

His arm around her back shielded her from as much of the grit as he was able, even as his body ground against her.

Without preamble, he reached between them with his free hand and wrenched his trousers open. His knuckles brushed against her sex as he did this, and even that insignificant touch electrified her, releasing a flood of moisture in readiness.

She wrapped her arms around his straining shoulders, her nails biting into his long, predatory muscles as the blunt head of his cock drove into her with such force, her body gave a feeble resistance.

She arched toward him, needing to have him, to take him all, creating incredible friction.

A low, desperate noise rose to the stones, echoing back at them with ephemeral fractals of pleasure and pain. She couldn't tell which of them originated the sound.

And it didn't matter as he began to move.

Before he drilled her against the wall, his hand rose to cup the back of her head, protecting it from the stone.

It touched her, his tenderness in the midst of this turbulent encounter.

His strokes were long, brutal, and lovely. She cinched her ankles behind his lean hips and took him. Took from him. All the lust and loss, the pleasure and pain. She drank it in like a delicacy meeting the mindless need in his movements with matching strokes.

Something else lurked beneath his fury. An almost reverent incredulity. A raw awareness that reminded her of someone lost in a dream, fully aware that he could wake at any moment.

So she kissed him, hoping to ground him in the moment. To assure him that she was here. With him. That she wasn't going anywhere.

Groaning, he hiked her higher up the wall, repositioning his hips so his thick shaft would angle inside of her in such a way her breaths became pants of exquisite torture, then vulgar demands.

His sex was like a bolt of lightning, suffusing her with electric sensation that scraped her nerves raw and laid her soul bare. Even as she all but climbed the wall to escape what she knew was going to be a life-altering climax, he never changed his demanding pace. He plunged inside of her with single-minded efficient grace.

Then, oh God *then*, he broke their kiss to lick his finger and plunge his hand between their bodies.

The moment his thumb brushed her clitoris, the entirety of her world combusted into shards of crippling pleasure. The pleasure moved past awe inspiring to incomprehensible. Unrelenting. Overwhelming.

Vicious.

His bark of mirth was almost cruel in its victory as the pleasure became so intense it spilled over into pain.

Only then did his movements lose their grace, taking on a jerking violence before he locked into shuddering tremors.

His teeth scored the tender skin where her shoulder met her neck, pulling the pleasure out of her sex and diffusing it into the rest of her body.

They locked together for an unparalleled moment of suffusion. It became unclear which movement belonged to which body, so clearly could she feel every twitch and pulse of his pleasure.

Finally, Francesca collapsed against him, wrapping her long limbs around the bulk of him as slowly, incrementally the rest of the world returned. The cold of the rock against her back, the heat of his shaft still inside of her. The scruff of his jaw locked against hers.

Her muscles uncoiled and her fear seemed to drain away, replaced by a sense of peace. Of calm. Of rightness and gratitude.

She ran her nails through the shorter, softer hair at the nape of his neck, enjoying the little sensations of aftershocks thrilling through her belly.

After several quiet moments she realized his experience was nothing like hers. He remained taut. Shuddering. His hands biting into her thighs as he held her aloft with trembling, unsteady fingers.

Troubled, she ran the flat of her palms over his back, wishing she could reach the straining muscle beneath the suit.

"Chandler?" Her whisper of his name was overloud in the cavern. "What is it? Are you—"

His withdraw from her was immediate and stunning. His hands were barely gentle as he let her feet touch the ground, and he turned away immediately to set himself to rights and refasten his trousers.

Not having that option, Francesca stood there, naked, staring at him in wide-eyed confusion.

Bending, he retrieved her garment, such as it was, and shoved it in her direction. His features were distorted with emotions she couldn't even begin to fathom.

She clutched the garment to her as he plunged a hand into his hair and pulled, his expression still tormented.

Francesca had the sense that even though she was

undressed, the man before her had never been so naked. So exposed.

"Chandler," she ventured, still struggling to reclaim her breath.

"He's *not* to touch you again. Do you understand me?" He swiped a hand back toward the darkness, his voice breaking against the stones. "That fucking demon goes nowhere near you. Never. *Never* again. Do you fucking hear me, Francesca?"

Those eyes were still black with rage and . . . terribly familiar.

Both physically and emotionally raw, Francesca wrestled her temper, feeling as though she would lose at any moment. Now wasn't the time, a part of her knew that. She'd never seen him like this. This angry. This out of control.

Murderous.

"You do not command me." She was proud that her voice remained somewhat level as she said, "I will give you a chance to explain yourself before I tell you to go hang and let the devil take you straight to hell."

The sound he made was so full of pain, it could have been a sob, but he was not weeping. "I'm already there, goddammit." He bit his knuckle and strode several paces away, as if he couldn't bring himself to touch her, and also couldn't stop himself from doing so. "I was born into it and no matter how hard I try there is no escape for me."

She stepped forward. "Chandler."

He shook his head. "Now that we're . . . that this is . . . It's fucking incestuous, his desire for you, and I think he knows it. I don't know how but he does."

She flinched, then gaped. "You mean . . . Kenway?"

"Yes," he snarled. "Luther fucking Kenway, the king of the ninth level of hell." He whirled to her, the raw agony contorting his features into something altogether unrecognizable.

"My father."

CHAPTER TWENTY-FOUR

Hours later, Francesca lay on her belly, stretched next to Chandler as he ran rough fingertips over her bare back still slick with the sweat of their sex.

They'd still not discussed his revelation.

In fact, they'd said very little to each other as he'd wrapped his jacket around her and carried her up into the night. He'd commandeered a police carriage, set her inside, and took her home. All the while furiously, inscrutably silent.

It had taken one more bout of frenzied lovemaking to settle him. And now, they lounged naked in a puddle of tousled blankets, gathering both their breath and their thoughts.

His finger worked in a familiar pattern at her spine, tracing the symbol eternally etched there.

"So fierce," he murmured, pressing his lips to what she knew was the dragon, a white animal with red accents in the scales and claws. "I see you identify with the dragon, so why depict the tiger, I wonder?"

She stretched in a full-body arch, shuddering a bit before she turned to face him. He watched this intently, allowing her the space to do so. When she settled back in, he brushed her hair away from her back, revealing more of the portrait and resuming his idle caresses.

"I spent some time in Hong Kong after finishing school," she answered, loving the warmth of him next to her, relishing a story she could tell with no secrets attached to it.

"To unlearn everything you were taught there, I imagine."

"To train." She nudged him with her shoulder and smiled at the fond teasing in his voice. "I met an old man begging in the street, who asked me if I would hear a story he was supposed to tell me in return for some coin, and so I paid him."

"He was *supposed* to tell you?" Chandler cocked a quizzical brow.

"It's probably the most mystical thing that ever happened to me, before you, I mean."

"How so?"

"Serana used to say that I was a dragon and you were a tiger."

"She did?" His eyes had lost the darkness she'd seen in the catacombs, and had become whiskey and moss once again. They shone with interest as he propped his head in his hand. "I never knew that. How does this story of the dragon and the tiger end, I wonder?"

"It doesn't."

His fingers stilled at her answer, and he couldn't seem to meet her gaze, so she continued.

"In the story, the tiger is a being of ferocious energy. He is hard, brute strength and raw power. His attacks are straightforward, aggressive, and unrelenting, all claws and teeth. The dragon, she is smaller than the tiger, so she must understand movement. She must be defensive and circular. Soft but indomitable. She is the representation of all creatures, and is the keeper of secrets and treasure. She must have agility, flexibility, and cunning."

"You *are* a dragon," he said, pressing a kiss to her shoulder.

"The Chinese man said that many believe the tiger and dragon must be locked in eternal battle. The tiger like stone and the dragon like water."

"Really?" His gaze sharpened. "Stone and water?" He repeated this as if it were significant, and she was pleased that he followed.

"This battle between them, many believe, balances everything. Light and dark, east and west, good and evil . . . order and chaos."

"Male and female?" he suggested with a wicked tone.

"Precisely." She pushed back on her elbows to regard him. "The man said he doesn't believe that the tiger and dragon are fated to battle eternally. Instead of fighting, they might be falling, spinning, perhaps . . . becoming."

"Becoming what?"

"They are spirits so vastly different, and yet so

wildly similar that their destiny is intricately linked. He said the battle is won when they find a way to come together and create wholeness. Then the hard and the soft find a place in the universe to live in harmony."

He stared at the tattoo for a long moment, his gaze pensive before he said, "I think this man was trying to sleep with you."

She made a sound of mock outrage and shoved at him. He chuckled and fell back dramatically.

Rolling away, she took the sheet with her to pluck a knife from a silver tray on her nightstand and skewer an apple from the repast of cheese, fruit, wine, and cold meats she'd rung for earlier.

Interested, he rooted closer to her, accepting the wine she handed him and taking a careful sip. Arranging a wealth of pillows so he could both recline and drink, he sat back to watch her with heavy lids as he rested his hand in her lap. He looked like some bacchanalian god, replete and reclining.

She'd have donned a robe and worshiped *him*, of that she had no doubt. A body such as his begged a devotee, and what they did to each other was something like a religion.

Or a blasphemy.

"In all seriousness, I appreciate the analogy. What it means to you, what you think of me . . ." He seemed to lose what he wanted to say next in a furrow of abstraction as his gaze turned inward for a moment.

Burning to hear his thoughts, and to ask him a thousand questions, Francesca summoned her lacking stores of patience and busied herself by peeling the flesh off the apple.

His faint rumble of amusement gave her pause. She looked up to find him scrutinizing her intently.

She tucked a lock of hair behind her ear. "What?"

He lifted his hand behind his head to cup his own neck, and the movement did something distracting to the muscles in his arms. "You just reminded me of something I'd quite forgotten."

"Something good?"

The bracket on one side of his mouth deepened as a memory lifted it. "Something . . . rather sweet."

He reached for the peel hanging from her apple, examining it in the lamplight before he ate it.

She made a disgusted sound. "You just ate the peel by itself?"

He lifted his shoulder. "It's the best part."

She made a face and then prompted, "Tell me the memory. Am I in it?"

He swallowed, his gaze swinging back to hers. "I always had terrible nightmares as a boy . . . I still do sometimes. At Mont Claire, I used to sleep in that room behind the boiler for warmth, and Pip, she would hear me cry out and flail in my dreams. Ears like a hawk, that one."

She stilled, a slice of apple halfway to her mouth when she noted the lamp cast something like fondness on his features.

"Pip'd sneak something from the larder and come down to wake me up," he continued. "I'd wake with all the gentility of a hibernating bear, because the nightmares would steal me away from myself and—" He swallowed and didn't finish the thought. "Well . . . she stayed with me, through it all. And I never told her I appreciated that. I didn't want to go back to sleep. I . . . didn't want to be alone. She might have sensed that, I think."

Yes. She had.

Francesca returned her slice to the small plate. She couldn't have swallowed past the lump of emotion in her throat.

He didn't seem to notice her reaction to his story, so lost was he in the memory.

"One time," he continued, "she brought more than one knife, and she gave it to me. We played at being buccaneers, and she told me something as she ruthlessly stabbed my apple, peeling it much like you've just done. She said, *I'm going to steal your heart one day, me hearty, and ye'll never get it back.*"

He was quiet for a moment, long fingers digging into the covers as he visibly battled emotions both bitter and sweet. "I thought—I thought she meant it as a threat at the time. I was a boy, it was all blood and battle for me then, and she was just the kind of little savage that would rip a heart out and lock it in a box."

The thought made him chuckle, and had her swallowing convulsive emotions.

Then his smile fell. "I should have been kinder to her. Looking back with a man's eyes . . . I think she meant to do exactly that. I think she wanted to steal my heart and keep it. That . . . she might have considered it a treasure."

Francesca cleared the emotion out of her throat and looked down so he couldn't see her heart in her eyes. She had a feeling if he truly looked at her in that moment—he'd know.

Would that be so bad?

"Do you think she could have?" she whispered. "Stolen your heart, I mean."

"Hard to imagine it, she bothered me so much." He gave a wry chuckle and took another sip and was quiet for a few breaths. "I guess we'll never know." His voice hardened. "My father took that from us."

Quite suddenly, he folded at the waist as though he'd been punched, startling her as he sat up and threw his legs over the opposite side of the bed.

Francesca stared at the scars in his back. Little holes left by the pellets of a shotgun at long range. One whose trigger might as well have been pulled by his own father.

"God, how can you even look at me?" he agonized. "I'm the bloody reason your entire family is dead."

"No." She abandoned the knife and crawled across the bed to him, wishing she could close the distance she felt growing. "No, no, you can't think that." She pressed her cheek against his back, locking her arms around the breadth of his shoulders and smoothing the mounds of his chest.

She could hear his heart. God . . . was it real? The rhythm she'd thought was forever lost to her pounded at his back with suppressed emotion.

"I wondered why the letter from Hargrave piqued you so . . ." She readied herself to broach this subject, hoping he finally would. "You were . . . hiding from your father at Mont Claire, weren't you? And the letter, however innocently meant, revealed you to him."

He nodded, his jaw clenched too tightly for speech for a moment. "Mont Claire was burned to the ground for the sole reason that it sheltered Luther Kenway's last remaining son and heir. He murdered everyone only to send me a message. To tell me nowhere was safe from him. He was—" His voice broke for a moment, and he grappled with his composure before finishing. "He was calling me home."

"I'm glad you didn't go." She pulled back, but his hands caught hers, as if he wasn't ready for her to pull away from the embrace.

"We still don't know the certain reasons for the attack," she soothed, pressing her body closer to him, settling her breasts against his back and her chin against his shoulder. "The Cavendishes were a part of the Crimson Council. Did you know that Lady Cavendish was once courted by your father?"

He shook his head. "I didn't. When I was a boy, I was ridiculously ignorant of anything like that."

She went on, eager to assuage his guilt and pain. "I've subsequently found out that the Earl of Mont Claire was Kenway's fourth cousin, and the countess chose him over Kenway rather publicly. That must have rankled a man like your father to no small degree. He could have been taking revenge on Mont Claire on her behalf."

"I must have known, somehow, that our families were linked. I must have been to Mont Claire before, though I don't remember when," he said.

"Chandler." She hesitated. The question hovering on her lips kicked her heart faster. "I read a great deal about Kenway when I investigated him. I combed through reports and found one on . . . Kenway's countess. Your mother? It reported that she . . . drowned her three children."

His jaw worked to the side for a moment, and he turned his face from the light.

"She did."

A hard pebble of grief landed in her middle, and she steeled herself for this conversation. "I always remembered their names," she ventured. "William, Arabella, and—"

"Luther." He said the word as if it tasted of ash and filth on his tongue. "Luther Beaufort de Clanforth-Kenway."

The magnitude of this knocked the wind from her. "De-clan-forth," she echoed, her heart aching. "De-clan."

He nodded.

"You . . . didn't drown?"

He made a gruff, caustic noise. "No, no, I did. I remember it well. I fought the water in my nightmares." He put a hand to his chest and filled his lungs, his wide ribs expanding as if he had to prove to himself that he was still able to inhale. "I still do."

"It's why your mother died in the asylum."

"Yes." His chin returned to touch his shoulder, brushing against her fingertips as if searching for solace. "She was a fragile woman, my mother. Kenway liked to toy with her, to torture her with his cruelty, without even touching her." He gave a suspicious sniff. "I remember she thought she was saving us from him. She said as much before she . . . pushed me under."

"Holy God," she whispered. "How did you . . . How are you still . . . ?"

"My father found my mother, I was told. He grappled her away as the servants pulled my . . . the children out of the tub and dragged her somewhere else, I'm not certain where. I wasn't conscious."

She could tell the story agonized him. His muscles twitched and his fingers were restless. Cold sweat bloomed on his skin, and his breaths were slightly uneven.

Crushed by the horror of it all, Francesca could only hold him as his secrets spilled forth, hoping they purged something in the telling.

"Two of his . . . well, I think they were henchmen . . . found me. They pressed the water from my lungs. I don't know how. And after I coughed up everything, I was spirited outside. I remember that. Maybe they weren't part of the council, or maybe they'd just been struck with a fit of conscience on that day. I'll never know. But they bundled me up, wet clothes and everything, put me in his carriage, and told the driver to take me somewhere safe. Somewhere else."

"How did you end up at Mont Claire?"

"The carriage stopped at the priory for the night, and the driver made noises about taking me home. So I ran."

"Bronwell Priory?" she gasped. "That's miles away from Mont Claire."

He lifted his shoulder against her chin. "I just remember running, my legs and lungs burning. My wet clothes filthy and cold. So fucking cold . . . everything hurt . . ."

"*Stop.*" The word tore from Francesca in a low, raw wail. Her tears flowed freely now, dripping from her chin onto his shoulder. "Stop, I cannot bear to hear more. The thought of your suffering. Of the nightmares. God, Chandler, they made you clean out the fountain at Mont Claire." She let him go so she could cover her eyes, as if that would blind her from the memories, from the images of that little boy staggering up to the manor house. "I would wonder why you were so pale. Why you dreaded the water so . . . why you bathed in the lake instead of the tub . . ." Her sobs came harder now, flowing from some fathomless well she was unaware she'd had. "Oh God, oh no," she chanted, the prayer one of desperate dread. "I'm so sorry."

Chandler turned at the waist and dragged her into his lap, crooning soft and comforting things into her hair as she cried.

Francesca was distraught, but also embarrassed. She never cried. Never. Not during all the hard times. Not when Serana had blessed the ashes of Mont Claire, of her parents and her friends. Not when she'd had to bury her best friend's rapist at finishing school. Not when she broke her wrist in Argentina or when she was beat down in training by men who were bigger, stronger, and meaner than she was. She'd fought more tears in the last two weeks than she had in the last two decades.

And now, the storm of her grief for him turned into a flood, and she sobbed twenty years of sorrow against his chest. Sometimes, when she could manage it, she would hiccup a soggy apology. "I'm sorry. God, I'm sorry." And she was. She was so fucking sorry. Sorry that he'd suffered so. Sorry that he was the one soothing her when it was him in need of comfort. Sorry that—

"I love you," he said against her hair.

She snapped her mouth closed, lifting her head away from the wet mess she'd made of his chest.

He dragged his knuckles down her cheek, his expression as peaceful and tender as she'd ever seen. His eyes glowed with a light she dared not identify, and it searched her face with a reverence she found both humbling and terrifying.

She blinked up at him, and he answered her unspoken question.

"I love you," he repeated, as if she hadn't heard. As if he couldn't believe it, himself. "I think I was halfway in love with you before I even realized I was falling."

Francesca's tears turned to terror and she scrambled from his lap. "You—you can't say that to me. Not right now."

He searched his empty arms as if they befuddled him. "Why not?"

"Because . . ." She swallowed an instant confession, any sort of courage abandoning her. "You *don't.* You don't love me. You love who you *think* I should be. Who I was as a child. You are annoyed with me more often than not and—"

"I love you," he repeated in an infuriatingly calm voice.

"I'm telling you. You don't *know* me. Not really," she insisted, turning to look for a robe, for something that would make her feel less naked. She'd left one on the back of the chair this morning and now it was gone. Damn her staff for being so efficient. "Think about what you're saying. You keep telling me what not to do.

You insist I must be other than I am. I've seen love, and that isn't it."

He was behind her in an instant, turning her to face him. "You misunderstand me, Francesca. I love who you are, but I insist you stop risking your life, that is all. I want a future with you, so you have to stop putting yourself in danger." He gathered her close, burying his face into her hair. "You are mine, Francesca. My woman. My dragon. I . . . love you."

Bloody hell, she was going to start weeping again. "But—"

"I love you, dammit, now stop arguing." He pulled back, his command tempered by a soft light shining on his features and a determined set to his hard jaw. "You're the hope I have for happiness. The light at the end of this dark tunnel. Can't you see that? I am irate when you put yourself in danger because you *have* to be there at the end, or it was all worth nothing. I can't lose you, Francesca." His fingers tightened on her, a fervent—no, desperate—emotion pushing to the forefront of his gaze. "I won't survive it a second time."

Francesca.

She froze as still as the ice needled through her. Was now the time to be honest? And if she was, would he be glad to hear it? Or would she be the woman to kill Francesca all over again? He'd hate her for that. And maybe it would . . . cause him greater pain. What was the kindest thing to do?

What was the right thing?

He brushed at her cheek, now dry and itchy from the salt of so many tears. "Do you remember what I said that night in my carriage, back before you knew who I was?"

She searched her memory. "That I'd ruin you?"

"I knew you would. You would ruin Chandler Alquist and Declan Chandler and Thom Tew, and Lord Drake, Edward Thatch, all of them. I knew, somehow, that you would forge someone new. Someone real. That you would scramble about the sun and stars until I could no longer find them in the night sky without your help. You would make me care about something other than myself. Other than my revenge. That you would become someone to die for. Would give me something to live for. I think I knew, even at the first kiss . . ." He looked at her lips as if seeing her for the first time.

Francesca stared at him, unable to move. Unable to breathe. Her nostrils flared and her eyes pooled, but she couldn't seem to bring herself to say anything.

After a long moment, he seemed to read the torment in her eyes and let her go. "You . . . don't feel the same way."

The confusion and uncertainty in his voice broke her of her paralysis, and she clutched at him.

"Of course I love you, you bloody dolt." She shook him a little for emphasis. "I loved you the moment you wobbled onto the Mont Claire estate and I *never* stopped. I loved you as a boy, and as my hero, and as a ghost. I loved you even when I was angry enough to *murder* you. Chandler, there's been no one else for me in the entire world but you. Why do you think I remained a virgin until I was nearly thirty? To touch someone else seemed like a betrayal, so I—"

His lips were on her before she could finish, and

his hands were everywhere. He crowded her back to the bed where they fell together in a heap of limbs and love.

Francesca forgot about any truth but this. Chandler loved her, and she loved him. The rest would be sorted out later, when they had a moment to breathe and grieve and tell truths when their love wasn't so new. So vulnerable. When other truths were not so painful and Kenway and the council had been dealt with.

For now, a dragon would guard her secrets and his heart.

Because she'd finally stolen it, and wasn't ready for the chance that he could take it back.

Chapter Twenty-Five

A sound Chandler had never heard before pulled him out of a deep and blessedly dreamless sleep.

"What the devil—"

It jangled his nerves. It . . . jangled, like a little bell repeatedly pealing.

He leapt out of bed and was reaching for a weapon when Francesca's plaintive moan broke him of his panic.

"Telephone." She pressed her hands to her ears. "Off with its head."

"How do you have a telephone?" he demanded, blindly making his way to the corner where it was located. "I thought they were only used for business and government."

"That's why I have a telephone," she said, as if that were any answer at all.

Chandler picked up the receiver, rubbing his shin

where he'd kicked the edge of some furniture in the dark.

"We have the fucking devil, Lady Francesca," growled a familiar Scottish brogue through the tinny circle at his ear. "We have Kenway in a cell and, if I have anything to say about it, he willna see the light of day again."

Chandler closed his eyes, a torrent of relief and darker, more complicated emotions swamping him in a cascade of strange sensations. He'd known he had much to answer for once morning came. That by abandoning the raid with Francesca, he'd risked Kenway going to ground. He risked the priorities of the raid, and that wasn't the decision he'd have made in the past. But if it came down to who he'd rather get his hands on, his father or Francesca . . .

He peered at her across the room, watching the glow of the city slant across the pristine white of her bed, turning her into a tangle of pink flesh and red hair. The woman who'd brought color back to his life.

Somehow, she'd become more important than his vengeance.

"Countess . . ." An uncharacteristic hesitation crept into Ramsay's voice at the silence. "He's making some incredible claims . . . I ken this is an indelicate question, but is Chandler with ye?"

"I'm right here," he rumbled.

"Christ, man." Ramsay almost sounded relieved that it was he and not Francesca on the line. It didn't even seem to faze him to find him in her residence at—he glanced at the mantel clock—half past three AM. "Kenway is either a maniacal genius or a raving lunatic."

"Both," Chandler grunted, rubbing an exhausted hand over his face.

He'd have thought the news would rouse him, but it served to only deflate him. Not with melancholy, but with a deep, soul-weary reprieve. It was as though a war had ended, and the idea of it was a bit disorienting.

"He says . . . well, he insists, really, that ye're Luther Kenway the Second, his son and heir. Does he speak the truth?"

Francesca made another plaintive noise and stretched like a cat before rolling over to grope for the lamp. Chandler didn't want the light. He didn't want any of this. He merely wanted to be allowed to crawl back in the white clouds of her sheets, pull her close, and sleep until noon.

"Yes," he sighed.

A slew of rather guttural Gaelic curses had him pulling the receiver from his ear as Francesca finally lit the lamp and blinked over at him. She looked as bleary as he felt. Bleary and beautiful. The tousled tangles of her hair created a halo of scarlet around her face and shoulders, reminding him that she was no angel, and he preferred it that way.

"Is it Ramsay?" she asked.

He nodded.

"Did he apprehend Kenway?"

Another nod.

Ramsay let out a wicked breath. "With a father like that, no wonder ye never claimed yer nobility."

The man's words thrust a pang through his middle. He'd expected censure, not understanding. "There's nothing noble about that man," he said darkly. "The world is better off without him."

"Of that I have no doubt. But first . . ."

"Was anyone hurt tonight? Dashiell and Howard, are they all right?"

"One officer was stabbed, by Kenway, if ye'd believe it." Ramsay seemed less than perturbed by this.

"Bloody fucking—"

"Och, it was only in the hand. He'll live, with a commendation no less."

"I should have caught the bastard myself. It's only that . . ." Chandler trailed off, feeling a complicated form of remorse for how little guilt it caused him that he'd come for her first.

"Doona be too hard on yerself. No man could have kept his head were his woman in danger like that. Least of all me."

Chandler shook his head, wondering if he was dreaming. Was the Lord Chief Justice, high justice of one of the highest queen's benches, calling him on Francesca Cavendish's newfangled telephone in her bedroom? Absolving him of almost treasonous dereliction of his duties for the Secret Services, all because he was in love. How did the bloody Scot know of his feelings in the first place?

Chandler remembered the ferocity with which Lord Ramsay fought for Cecelia. He'd abandoned his post on the queen's bench and swept her into hiding. And then he'd enlisted Chandler's aid to save her life and that of those seven young girls.

If anyone understood Chandler's own motivations, it was Ramsay.

"I could have stashed her and come back." He'd simply been too angry. Too afraid to let her out of his sight. Some sort of primitive need to claim her had overtaken all sense of reason.

It was dangerous what she did to him.

What she made him capable of.

"Bah." Chandler imagined Ramsay waving his words away. "We are none of us blameless. Francesca could have stayed home and allowed us to do our jobs. I could have not told her where the ritual was going to be, knowing full well she'd go after Kenway. After ye. In my defense, she's a dragon when provoked, and her need to avenge ye moved me. Alas, that is what affection does to us fallible humans."

"Alas." Chandler shared a short rumble of amusement with Ramsay before releasing a long, troubled breath. "What will happen to him?"

"He'll hang," Ramsay said gently. "I'm sorry."

"Don't be, he deserves it." Chandler lowered himself into the chair behind him, suddenly feeling twice his age. "I'll report to the Secret Services in the morning for a debrief and—"

"Chandler . . ." Ramsay interrupted. "I doona even ken what to call ye. That isna yer name."

"It can be for now."

"We have enough to charge yer father for high treason, but there is the Mont Claire Massacre to put to rest. The kidnapping of children and the . . . murder of the Lord Chancellor among others.

"I understand."

"Aye. Ye see . . ." A quiet uncertainty leached into

Ramsay's voice, as if he didn't relish what he had to say next. "We arrested others but have little to keep them on, and I fear the reach of the council is longer than we feared. In order to dismantle it, Kenway must denounce it, himself. He should confess his horseshit to his followers and publicly state that he was a traitor and a conspirator against the Crown."

"Good fucking luck," Chandler muttered.

"He's agreed to do so, but only . . . if he may speak with ye first."

Chandler's insides turned into bricks. He'd known he'd have to face his own personal demon, but his entire being railed against it. "I-I'll be there in the morning."

"He wants to speak with ye now."

"He's in the room?" Chandler surged to his feet and Francesca sat higher, suddenly looking alarmed.

"Next room."

He swallowed a refusal, locking eyes with the woman he loved. The concern and compassion he found there calmed him somewhat. He drank in the sight of her, desperately clinging to the miracle that was her existence. Just her presence gave him strength. Gave him life and hope and peace. His Francesca.

"Very well," he agreed.

"Son." The one word spoken in a voice as oily as the muck at the bottom of the Thames caused his blood to curdle.

"You don't deserve to call me that," he snarled.

"No, it's best, I think, that we do not use words of kinship. We were always disappointments to each other." The bastard spoke as if he weren't in chains. As if he were a man celebrating a victory rather than suffering a defeat.

If Chandler had been standing over him, he'd have struck him. Cut out his venomous tongue.

"What do you want?"

"You'll be an earl soon," came the reply. "And I want to make certain the Kenway line is untainted by common blood."

It was the last thing he'd expected the earl to say. "What do you mean?"

"Are you looking at the Countess of Mont Claire right now?"

He was. He was staring deep into the verdant depths of her eyes, and he saw a glimmer of something there, something that lanced him with a dread no less than biblical. He felt a cold fear flushing the warmth of their lovemaking from his veins.

"You don't have to say, I know she's there." Kenway suddenly sounded very young and relentlessly eager, like a youth about to receive his first kiss. "What a lovely woman she is," he crooned. "So supple and skilled. Ruthless, like us. Brilliant, wouldn't you say? And beautiful. Those long, lean legs that seem to go on forever—"

"I'm hanging up now, you fuc—"

"Those legs are not so smooth, my son. If you venture lower than what's between them, you'll find a scar on the left calf, just below the knee . . . a scar my men put there twenty years ago as the both of you ran from them into the woods."

Chandler dropped the receiver as if it burned him.

The chill of fear solidified to ice. Hardened in his veins and in the very fibers that knit his soul together.

"What did Ramsay say?" she asked anxiously. "Was that your—"

Chandler lunged forward, ripping the coverlet off her still-naked form.

Startled, she instinctively bent her leg up and crossed it over her body to cover her nakedness . . .

Displaying a shallow, faded scar to ultimate effect.

"Chandler! What the devil are you doing?"

A bleak, icy rage colored the night with an azure hue. Not red, not like murder. It was hotter than that, blue like the flames that burned at the highest temperature. Like the deepest parts of hell that even the souls of the damned couldn't reach.

The chamber saved for the devil, himself.

He seized her calf, bending closer, letting his thumb test the knitted flesh. Someone had stitched it long ago, when the bullet had grazed it while they both ran for their lives.

He let it go as if the flesh had burned him, nearly flinging the offending appendage away from him. "*Pippa.*" Her name was an accusation. A curse. Nay, a profanity. How could she fucking *dare*?

She rose to her knees on the bed, and he stared at her nubile form with more assessment than appreciation. Pippa fucking Hargrave? The short, chubby little blonde with the round cheeks and the talent for driving him mad. She'd turned a tragedy into a personal triumph, and had stolen the legacy of an entire bloodline. And for what?

"I can explain," she whispered, reaching for him.

He reared away from her, turning to search the room for his trousers. "There is no excuse in the world good enough for what you've done."

"I know!" She astonished him by agreeing. "I wanted to tell you from the beginning, but I—I didn't know it was you at first, and then . . . I wasn't sure whether or not you would turn me in to the Secret Services."

He snatched his trousers from the floor at the foot of the bed and shoved his legs into them. "You were afraid that you'd, what, lose her title? Her fortune?" he demanded as he fumbled with the fastenings. "That's so fucking diabolical."

She pulled the sheet to her breasts as if it could shield her from his words. "How can you think that? I was afraid I'd lose her revenge. *Our* revenge. I was afraid I could lose my life! I did this for you most of all—"

He whirled and stabbed the air with his finger in her direction. "Don't you fucking *dare* say that."

"Why? It's the truth." She kept having to turn as he stalked around the bedroom, gathering his shirt, his shoes, his cravat. "You were dead, Chandler. Everyone was dead and your father stood in line to inherit everything. I couldn't allow that. I didn't think I'd hurt anyone by keeping it from him, so I reshaped my body with training and discipline, I dyed my hair, and . . ."

"And you fucking took Francesca's fucking life?" He punched his arms into his shirt.

At that, her features lost some of their fear and replaced it with obstinacy. "No, I didn't. Tuttle took her life, that bloody American, right in front of me. He slit her throat while I was still holding her hand. I have to live with that. I have to see that when I close my eyes.

You don't." She crawled from the bed and wrapped the sheet around her. "Yes, I claimed Francesca's identity, but only to go after the council."

"And look what a disaster you made of that," he said with a snide curl of his lips, doing up the cuff at his wrists.

This time she recoiled. "What the devil does that mean?"

"I told you to stay away from this. How many times did I tell you that you're not a goddamned spy?" he demanded. "When people like you get involved, innocents get hurt. Just like they did tonight. A fucking officer was stabbed and more of the council escaped than were caught."

Her hands went to her mouth. "Is he . . . did he live?"

"No thanks to you."

"It isn't fair to lay that at my feet!" she hissed, her advance impeded by the long sheet she began to gather into her arms to keep off the ground. "I would have been a help to you if you hadn't left me out. You shouldn't have taken my invitation. You should have informed me of the raid. You should have trusted me!"

"Trusted you?" he scoffed. "God, I can't even look at you!" He retrieved his shoes and stalked to the door.

She chased him, dragging the sheet like a wedding train until she blocked his exit by throwing her body against the door. "Chandler. Chandler, listen to me." Her pose was one of submission, supplication, and he'd be lying to himself if he didn't admit the ice over his heart didn't crack just a little at the pain and desperation in her eyes. "I love you. I love you and you love me. I know you do."

He shook his head, searching for that love and finding nothing but a yawning well of numbness and humiliation. His father was listening to this. He hadn't disconnected the fucking line. That reality was the last straw.

"Neither of us knows anything about the other, that's blatantly obvious now."

She swallowed and pressed on. "That isn't true. I never was like Francesca, not then and not now. This entire time we've been together, you've been with *me*. You've spent time with me. We've laughed and worked together. We fought and we—made love—"

"We fucked, that's all it was."

Her head wrenched to the side as if he'd slapped her, but she took a deep breath and summoned that will he'd admired so much.

"I know tonight didn't go how either of us would have wanted. But . . . Chandler, we have our revenge, despite everything. You said that you were half in love before you knew you were falling. And you fell for *me*. I am who I am right now. Francesca is just the name I go by. It is the woman who lives in this body you fell in love with, and that is not a lie. Please. Come and sit with me. Give me a chance to—"

Chandler shook his head and held up his hand, silencing her effectively. "It was her *memory* I was in love with. I see that now."

"What?" She shook her head, denying his words.

"Now that she's truly gone, I feel nothing. I suppose I should thank you for that." Now he was the deceitful one. It was all there somewhere, locked in a vault down deep in the blackness of his soul. A vast chasm of pain and loss and dark, dark despair. He'd feel it, eventually. When everything didn't seem so very bleak, so very far away. He'd take her betrayal out of that vault and examine it. Before he threw it away.

"Nothing?" she echoed in a pained whisper. "After everything we shared, the sheer magnitude of it . . . how can it be so easily reduced to nothing?"

He shrugged as if there was nothing to be done. "I'm not even that angry anymore, which tells me everything I need to know."

Her eyebrows slammed down, temper flaring in her emerald gaze, a green he didn't remember or recognize, not even from their shared childhood. "I don't know what right you have to be angry in the first place," she said vehemently. "You lied about your father, your name, and your very origins. And I understand why you would. We both had reasons to hide who we really were . . . but I forgave you your falsehood. Why am I held to a different standard?"

It was everything he could do not to punch a fist through the door. Mostly because the truth of it flared a new, defensive ire. Rather than giving in to the urge, he backed away. "It wasn't your forgiveness I wanted, Pippa. It was *hers*." He pointed out the window, as if Francesca's ghost lingered there in the wisps of the draperies. "And you stole that from me. Stole *her* from me. Again!"

She was a bundle of energy and emotion behind him, and he knew he had to escape her. Escape this house and this bedroom, and the impediment between them that could never be usurped.

"I understand your emotion, Chandler, you're entitled

to that. But I don't understand your hypocrisy. How can you, the man with no name or identity, stand and call me a liar for claiming the identity of someone I loved? For helping to avenge her and Ferdinand both!"

Seeing his chance to escape, he turned to the door and yanked it open. "I warned you I was a monster. You should have listened, and I shouldn't have been so blind."

He slammed out of her room, but she opened the door not a second later.

"You were never a monster," she called after him, her voice chasing his retreat down the marble stairs. "Do you hear me? You were not a monster, not until tonight."

Chapter Twenty-Six

"'Tis done. Though I doona ken whether to offer my condolences or my congratulations."

Ramsay's gently delivered pronouncement stirred nothing inside of Chandler.

It should have. The newly appointed Lord Chancellor was, after all, conveying the news that Kenway's death sentence had been carried out.

Chandler was now the ninth Earl of Devlin. A disgraced lord. King of the ashes.

Earl of emptiness.

Disgusted by his own melancholy, Chandler couldn't bring himself to face the man he'd come to know and respect over the past two months of pure, unmitigated hell. So he simply nodded his head curtly to signal that he'd marked the words. He remained at the window of his study, looking down over Harigate Square, from one of his father's—no—one of *his* many West End properties.

One he'd never lived in as a child.

"I was surprised not to see ye at the . . . event," Ramsay admitted. "Ye attended every session of the trial, staring at him or, rather, staring *through* him. I thought ye'd want to see him along to hell."

"He'd have wanted me to watch him die," Chandler explained dispassionately. "I wouldn't dream of granting him the satisfaction."

"I ken that." After a hesitant silence, Ramsay asked, "So . . . what now?"

Chandler tossed a droll glance over his shoulder. "What do you mean, what now?"

"What will ye do next?" Ramsay gave the impression his question was laden with more meaning than mere idle curiosity.

Chandler knew they were skirting the subject they'd studiously avoided these past weeks while they worked together to put the Crimson Council to death forever.

Francesca.

His eyes immediately locked onto the black oak tree in his garden, its foliage ablaze with the vibrant scarlet of autumn. He couldn't pass that tree and not think of her.

Not burn for one more taste . . .

He'd always had a well of darkness in his chest. A fathomless bit of emptiness he knew made him incomplete. Other men with this same void sought to fill it with vice or power. Drink or danger. Chandler had attempted all of these at one time or another and had learned early on the futility of it all.

As petite as she was . . . Francesca had filled that emptiness for a while. Filled his life and his heart to overflowing, in fact. With the threat of happiness. With hope.

Until Pippa had ripped her out, leaving an unfathomable chasm in her absence. Some bottomless, swirling, arctic abyss that seemed as if it would yawn open and swallow him whole.

He rather wished it would hurry.

He stared at his ghostly reflection in the window. His skin had lost any hint of sun; his eyes were bruised for want of sleep. His muscles ached all the time. He'd lost maybe a stone. A shade gazed back at him. A husk crafted around naught but sinew, bone, and blood with a heart that no longer beat. It merely ticked away the minutes of his increasingly unrecognizable life.

And for what? So he could spend the rest of his days tortured by loss?

By *her* loss.

"Will ye go to her?" Ramsay murmured the question. "Francesca."

At the mention of her name, something within him stirred to life. A dormant and hungry beast. Prowling the cage of his ribs, roaring with possessive hunger. Growling in tormented captivity.

Something like a tiger.

Would he go to her? His heart leapt and his stomach twisted.

"Would you?" he asked Ramsay. Or maybe the ghost in the window.

"Pardon?"

Finally, Chandler spun to face the Viking-sized Scot who leaned on the high back of one of his chairs, testing its mettle. "My first instinct was to mistrust her. To not believe her. And she convinced even me, possibly the most credulous man alive. After such a cracking wallop of a lie, would you go to her?"

Ramsay shrugged. "I did. I have."

That stopped him. "What?"

"Cecelia kept her identity as the Scarlet Lady from me well into our acquaintance," the man recalled. "And aye, I was angry upon first discovering her deceit, but in the end I realized the faults of her secrets were not only hers, but my own. I didna make the truth a safe thing to tell, and in doing so I perpetuated her dishonesty."

"This is different," Chandler insisted, feeling itchy and restless, as one often did in the presence of the truth.

"How so?"

"Because . . . you can be certain of Cecelia's intentions now that the truth is out. Whereas I have no measure of this woman. I do not know if her intentions are selfish or simply for survival."

Ramsay scratched at his jaw, looking as if a slew of words tumbled into his mouth and he could neither swallow them nor spit them out. "Forgive my asking, but what exactly about her actions causes ye to question her?"

"You must be joking. I knew her as a child, yes, but look at what she's done." He threw his arms out, opening them to encompass all of his doubt. "She claims she took upon herself Francesca's identity for the purpose of justice. But would she have done so if Francesca was born a peasant rather than a countess? Sure, she investigated the deaths of her family, but she's also enjoyed a fortune and a place in society that never belonged to her. She knew how I felt about Francesca. She knew because I bared my fucking soul to her. I never would have had I thought she was anyone else." He raked trembling hands through his hair, wondering why his reasoning suddenly felt thin. Why his anger seemed to be pointing in the wrong direction.

"Furthermore, she claimed to love me as Francesca. And I can't stop wondering, would she ever have revealed her true identity to me if my father hadn't exposed her? Or would I have walked around a blind fool for the rest of our lives?"

Ramsay chewed on that question for a moment before he answered. "Tell me this, would ye have been a happy fool?"

"Don't be ridiculous." He swatted the question away.

"I'm lethally serious. If ye'd never known the woman's secret, would ye have claimed her as your own? Would ye have happily loved her for the rest of yer days?"

A yearning rose within him with such ferocious potency, he had to lean against the desk lest his knees give out. "I never would have even looked at another woman."

Ramsay visibly tried, and failed, to keep a smirk from twisting his lips. "Then . . . did ye ever consider that ye're being a bigger fool right now than she could ever make of ye? Ye love *her*, not the memory of a poor girl some twenty years dead."

A well of ire seized him, and Chandler had to turn away to keep from striking the Scot. "You speak of what you do not know."

"Perhaps," Ramsay replied with a newfound sobriety. "But I'll tell ye what I *do* know. Ye'll never find a more honest and honorable soul than Francesca. She's like a sister to my wife, and I've heard every conceivable story, and a few I cannot fathom. She's stubborn, argumentative, crass, bossy, and a pain in my arse most days, but damned if she wouldna rip her own heart out and hand it to those she cares about if they asked it of her. She buried the bodies of Alexandra's enemies, and she's protected both Cecelia and my daughter with her very life. She went to *war* for the mere memory of ye, Chandler, and I doona ken if I've seen any man so courageous, selfless, or resolved as she. So ye intimating she might have intended to take the identity of a murdered countess to enjoy her luxury makes me want to laugh, or maybe weep at yer sheer stupidity."

Chandler whirled, his fists clenched and his rage sparking beneath his skin.

But when he saw the equal parts fervency and understanding in Ramsay's hard features, he realized who truly deserved his anger.

Himself.

Ramsay shook his head as if the entire business were a damned shame. "There are few people in this world that I tolerate, and even fewer I can claim to care about," he concluded. "But the woman has something that's almost impossible for me to give. My respect."

The hairs lifted on Chandler's flesh, vibrating in the presence of such truth. The last walls around his heart threw up their fortifications against the onslaught as his own truth rose to the surface. "She could destroy me, Ramsay," he breathed.

"She could save what's left of ye, and ye know it." With that, he plunked his hat on his head and reached for the door, pausing to say one last thing. "Love has made fools of ye both."

"How so?" Chandler queried, suddenly alert. Concerned.

Alive.

"It's making her do something I'd never have guessed in all my days on this earth." He sighed, pausing for dramatic effect, the bastard.

"What?" Chandler demanded. "What is she going to do?"

"She's running away."

CHAPTER TWENTY-SEVEN

It was time for her to leave. Past time, Francesca supposed, but she'd waited long enough. For consequences. For a miracle.

For a word.

Leaves crunched loud enough to sound like bones beneath her boots as she climbed the stone steps that had once been the entrance to Mont Claire Manor. No stately home waited on the other end of the archway, only the crumbling skeleton blackened by long-ago smoke.

Autumn was always a bit melancholy, but none so much as this. At least not in many years. In the frozen cold of the November day, her breaths created a mist that she parted as she walked over what was once pristine marble. Grit champed beneath her footfalls now, the inlays of artisans of the past covered with nigh twenty years of dirt as the place had been exposed to the elements for want of a roof.

The Crimson Council had certainly loved to set fire to fine houses. First Mont Claire, and then Cecelia's manor in town.

They wouldn't be doing that anymore, now that they didn't exist.

She'd not come back here before. Not since that fateful day, and she didn't want to now.

But it seemed apropos to say goodbye, and the graveyard in which she'd set stones for her mother and father and even the Cavendish crypts felt empty.

No, all their ashes were here: Ferdinand, Francesca, her parents, the staff she'd been fond of and the few that she hadn't. Their dust was here, and their memories, too.

Francesca relived so many of those memories as she strolled through what was once the kitchens, promising herself she'd only visit the good memories.

The stove remained, of course, and she ran her finger through the grime of it before wandering down the halls past white stone pillars that held up nothing but the sky.

Enough of the grounds had been reclaimed by ivy and other flora, she felt like she might have been walking into a relic of a bygone age, not merely one from her own past.

A past she needed to leave behind. Permanently, if she was to do anything else with the life she had left.

After Chandler had stormed out of her life some months ago, Francesca had barely spent a day alone. Alexandra and Cecelia were constantly at her side, in her house, inviting her to functions and doing their best to distract and divert her. The love and care and concern of her friends was more abiding and all-consuming than she'd ever realized.

She loved them so dearly.

And they were driving her barking mad. Bonkers. Because they reminded her how sad she was. How pathetic and alone. Seeing their happiness illuminated how empty her life would be now that she didn't have vengeance to fill it.

Now that she didn't have someone with which to share it.

No, best she moved on for a while. She'd go back to the Carpathians maybe, in the east. Get away from the noise, stink, and glitter of the city and lose herself to a place both primal and private.

And maybe find herself, too. Whoever she was now.

For days after their falling-out, she'd waited for Chandler. When he never came, she waited for the officials. To be stripped of everything. Or arrested.

It was likely she deserved it. A sin committed with good intentions was still a sin, and a lie was still a lie.

Chandler proved himself a good man, she thought. Or maybe he was just that indifferent to her, now. She couldn't be sure. He could take everything she claimed, after all. It was technically his. Because of his father's machinations, he was her heir. Well, the Mont Claire heir. He *could* be an earl twice over.

Suppose she just . . . gave it to him? She could renounce her title and claim to the Mont Claire lands. She didn't want to be mistress of the ashes. There was no reason for it anymore.

She'd closely watched the very public, very accelerated trial of Luther Kenway, hoping for a glimpse of

Chandler. And she'd done so a few times in the courtroom, though he apparently still couldn't bring himself to look at her.

She'd watched him, regardless. Drank in the sight of him like the condemned might search for a glimpse of the sky, or the faintest hint of kindness.

After Kenway was hanged, Chandler had, indeed, claimed his title as Earl of Devlin. Cecelia had revealed that he didn't take up residence at the London home, however, and Francesca understood why immediately.

He didn't want to live with ghosts.

She found herself in the Mont Claire library, staring out a window that had no glass, looking down the hill toward the hedge maze that was no longer. Her childhood refuge.

Refuge.

The word drew her to the chimney, the stone hearth still relatively in one piece. She heard the frightened voices of children, a boy and a girl, echo from bricks inside. Memories, of course.

She had to duck, now, beneath the mantel she'd once thought as tall as her father. Standing in the chimney, she could barely lift her arms. How small they'd both been back then. How frightened and brave.

How insignificant she felt now.

Here was the first place she'd ever heard Chandler's beating heart, where it soothed and comforted her. Newly orphaned, traumatized, and terrified.

And still . . . regardless of all the pain she'd felt over the years, it didn't come close to touching his.

The first time everything had been taken from him, it had been with water.

The second had been fire.

She didn't blame him for his distance, for his antipathy toward her . . . because the third time he'd had his hopes taken from him, it had been with little better than breath.

She'd given him hope and love and the tender starts of trust, only to crush it.

"I'm sorry," she whispered to no one. To everyone. To the children who had once been right here.

The whinny of a horse preceded the galloping crunch of frozen grass beneath trotting hooves. That would be Ivan. She should go. Her goodbyes didn't have to be protracted. She'd said she wouldn't linger, and she shouldn't be late for the train.

But when she would have left, something kept her here. A soft little brush at her heart, the tug she'd felt whenever Francesca had taken her hand as a child.

A gentle pull encouraging her back from doing something reckless or foolish.

Stay. The whisper echoed through her memory. *Just a few moments longer.*

She stayed, humming a little song she'd loved from the nursery as she wrote all their names with her fingertip in the soot of the chimney. FRANCESCA, FERDINAND, PIPPA, and . . .

She paused. Certainly not Luther; not Declan, either.

CHANDLER. He'd always be Chandler to her.

The sound of boots on the gritty marble filtered through what was now a very short chimney, perhaps only twice as tall as her, the second and third stories of Mont Claire having collapsed in the fire.

She took a bracing breath, wishing for longer. "I'm

sorry I dawdled, Ivan," she sighed. "I'm just . . . saying goodbye."

Impulsively, she drew a heart around Chandler's name, and ducked back out of the fireplace, batting the soot from her dark traveling kit.

"Where are you going?"

She froze, her lungs seizing in her chest and her heart diving out of its cage in her ribs to land in her stomach.

There he stood, the Earl of Devlin.

His hair was longer, a bit more fashionable perhaps, and he was leaner, too, as if he'd not been eating.

He still radiated primal, masculine energy, and his form was fit as ever, draped in an extraordinary suit the shade of grey that brought out striations of gold in his darker locks.

Shadows lurked in the hollows of his cheeks, and smudges darkened the skin beneath his eyes. Eyes that pierced her like the point of a rapier, pinning her where she stood.

"What are you doing here?" she asked, suddenly breathing as if she'd run a league.

He just looked at her, his eyes raking down her body in such an inscrutable way she couldn't tell if he was undressing her or sizing her for a coffin.

"H-have you ever been back?" she asked, desperate to fill the silence, to make him say something. Anything. "This is the first time . . ." She trailed off as his eyes left hers to touch the stones, searching the shadows created by the gloom of the overcast sky. "I couldn't, before. But it felt as though I should say goodbye."

His gaze returned to her, lingering on the smudges of soot at her bodice and hem. For the first time in forever she felt self-conscious, wishing she didn't look so windswept, soiled, and dowdy when he appeared so fine.

Was he angry to find her there? Or had he come after her? Dammit, why didn't he *say* something? Do something. Kiss her. Throttle her. Murder her, she didn't care at this point.

He just stood there, his hands fisted at his sides, and let his cruel silence unravel what little composure she had.

Apropos of nothing, she blurted. "It's yours. Mont Claire. Legally, I mean. You're the heir to the title and holdings and fortune and I want you to have it. I'm—I'm going away, maybe for good. But before I do, I want you to understand something about this place . . . about me."

She took off her riding hat so she could see him better, or perhaps to be respectful, as one did at church. "Pippa . . . she died the moment you were shot . . . No. No, that's not entirely true, and I've promised to tell only the truth from here on out." She began to pace a little a few steps this way and two steps back.

"The *only* thing about Pippa that survived that day was her love for you. I became Francesca not only because *you* loved her but because I loved her, too. I've lived longer as Francesca than I ever did as Pippa, and after a great deal of consideration, I've come to the conclusion that I'm not sorry—that is—I'm sorry you were hurt," she hurried to amend. "But I'm not sorry for what I did. It was my responsibility to my friend. And I know . . . that both of us loved you. Francesca and . . . and I." She tugged at the cuffs of her sleeves. "And, well . . . I love you still, and it doesn't matter to me if you know that because my love feels like it might be maintained not only by my heart, but also by hers. Her memory."

She pressed a few fingers to her brow, below which her nose was beginning to burn with the threat of tears. God, his very presence laid her bare, raw, stripped her of everything, even her pride. "What I'm trying to say is we loved you, and each other. If there's nothing else, there's that. I never lied about that—"

Suddenly he was in front of her, his gentle finger pressed against her lips to silence her.

"I did," he said simply, his voice hoarse and raw, as if he rarely had reason to use it anymore. "I lied."

"What?" she asked from behind the pressure of his finger.

He removed it, his hand falling back to his side. "I always thought my love was a precarious thing meant for a fragile girl. That being a hero meant saving the damsel and proving my worth to her. I thought . . . love was honesty and purity and all the things you and I never had. I believed that trust, once broken, could never be regained and then . . . I remembered something."

Francesca waited. Hesitated. Wondering if he was being cruel, or just saying goodbye.

Wondering if she had a reason to hope.

He looked down the green expanse of the estate as though he was looking toward the past. "The day I arrived here at Mont Claire, you and Francesca were having tea in the garden. I remembered her face, so perfect and clean. She looked at me with . . . disgust. Not compassion, not kindness, not even pity. She saw a filthy, soiled, freezing beggar and recoiled from him."

"Well, she was young and well brought up," she rushed to defend. "She changed her mind about you, obviously."

He seemed to lose a battle with himself, lifting his hand to touch her mouth again, this time with his thumb. It caressed the sensitive outline of her lower lip as his features finally melted into something she couldn't define; it was so beautiful. It went beyond tenderness, to an aching, longing adoration that threatened to turn her into a puddle.

"*You* ran to me, your hem already dingy from where you'd been chasing frogs earlier. You took me by the hand and pulled me inside. Fed me your tea, and then dragged me to the kitchens, where you commanded your parents to feed me and take me in. You bullied a footman into giving me his son's trousers and then you bullied me into bed."

She'd rather forgotten that. Not the first sight of him, but everything after.

His other hand joined the first, cupping her face as if it were a delicate thing. A treasure.

"When I look back now, you're all I can remember," he said. "That girl in the fireplace, clinging to me. She ran by my side. She took a bullet in the leg, meant for me. She always tried to save me, even if it was just from the dark. She set aside an extra peppermint from her father's pockets, or an extra hour of work by laboring at my side, knowing I despised the fountain. That the water made me miserable.

"She spent her entire life trying to avenge my memory, and theirs." He gestured to the ruins around them. "And . . . when I thought I'd found my damsel again, she tried to save me from her loss a second time."

Her breath hitched as her heart began beating once again.

"I never stopped to consider how much a secret like that must have weighed year after year. How oppressive and frightening it would be."

The weight of it pressed on her now, pressed her throat shut against any reply.

His eyes, full of his heart, glimmered down at her. "*That* is love . . . I know that now."

Did he? Was it possible that he finally saw, that he understood the depth of her devotion? She curled her fingers around his wrists, keeping them there. Wanting to reply but not being able to. Not yet.

He seemed to understand. "It took me too long to do this, I know. I . . . I was humiliated by my father and he used you to do it. I couldn't come to terms with that until he died, and then after . . . I couldn't imagine that you'd want to give me another chance. I've been setting my house in order, and finishing what we started. And the entire time, I wanted you there with me. I realized you were right, that you have been by my side from the very beginning, and when it was my turn, I failed you."

She shook her head, wanting to say that she wasn't angry. That she was so happy he'd come to this conclusion, but it had taken so long. Almost too long. He'd almost missed her.

"And then Ramsay told me you were leaving . . ."

She nodded. How did she tell him? How did she say that she couldn't abide in the same city, the same country with him and not be at his side?

His eyes became pools of sentiment, his face softening. "I haven't stopped thinking of that girl, the one who clung to me in the fireplace . . . I . . . have a proposition for her. For Pippa, for Francesca, for whoever she wants to call herself. I'll be whoever she wants me to be. Whoever she fell in love with. Because it is impossible to be worthy of such a woman, but I can try. All I know is that if I am a spy, a scoundrel, or an earl, none of it matters. I am no one if I am not hers. And I have nothing, if she is not mine."

Francesca surged forward and collapsed into his arms, not sobbing this time, but simply breathing. Taking in deep lungsful of his wonderful scent, and releasing months of pent-up misery.

He petted her hair with one hand, smoothing his other down her back. "I'm sorry. I'm so fucking sorry. I was a stupid, angry, blind fool—"

Still unable to say all the words that leapt to her lips, Francesca she did what she always did in these desperate situations. She drove her mouth against his.

The kiss opened her heart and her soul, released pain and fear and sadness and torment like a flock of dark and awful birds to dissipate to the sky. He tasted good, like forgiveness and pleasure and soft things neither of them had allowed themselves.

Like home.

Finally, after they did their level best to devour each other, she pulled back, finding her words.

"I . . . I did hate keeping anything from you," she said, shaping her hand to his jaw. "You are the only person alive who can shame me. Somehow my love for you gave you that power, and I'll confess I was a coward, unable to give you the truth to whip me with."

She dragged a deep breath into her nose and blew it out in a puff of cold steam against his coat. "I cannot take back what I did . . . the lie I told . . ."

"Neither can I," he said soberly.

"Is it possible we can love each other enough to trust?" she asked—the last question weighing on her heart.

He looked pensive for a moment, before his eyes alighted on hers. "Trust mirrors life, I'm coming to understand. Some get to build on pristine new ground, and others . . . have to sift through ruins and rubble. Our path might be more fraught with the later, but if anyone has the grit to do it, it is us. Wouldn't you agree?"

She looked at the ruins of her childhood home, her heart swelling to encompass her entire chest, beginning to crowd out the fear that this wasn't real.

"Tell me you want to," Chandler said, pressing a kiss to her forehead, her brows, her fragile eyelids, her temples, before working lower between his words. "Tell me we can build a new life together on top of the ruins of the old. Tell me it's not impossible. What can I offer to entice you to share your life with me? I'm a very wealthy man now, you know."

Before he could claim her mouth again, she gave him a halfhearted shove. "I would live in the roots of a tree with you, you know I would. But you can tell me one last thing."

He seemed to brace himself.

"What do I call you during this life together?" she asked. "Surely you don't go by Luther. And you never seemed to quite take to Declan."

His eyes brightened, and a smirk pulled one side of his mouth higher. "Oh, didn't you hear? I officially changed my name to Chandler. Chandler Beaufort de Clanforth-Kenway, the ninth Earl of Devlin."

"You didn't!"

"I did."

"Why? What significance does that name have to you? I never knew."

"Chandler was your and Francesca's favorite pony in the stable, if you remember. He died before either of you saw ten."

"Yes, but . . . surely you told us your name before then."

He shook his head. "While you were feeding me, you and Francesca were both chattering so much, and you mentioned the horse in passing. I fell asleep before really having to explain myself to anyone. And when I woke the next day, I sort of just . . . made up a name when I was asked."

"How . . . utterly unromantic," she teased, kissing him tentatively, then with more confidence.

"I took the name Chandler officially because I was always Chandler to you. Declan Chandler or Chandler Alquist, you knew me by that name."

She nodded, changing her mind instantly about the

romance of the gesture. "I've lived as Francesca longer than anyone else. A part of me wants to keep her, to live the life she never was able to, and marry the boy we both loved. Would you be amenable to that?"

His dark brows climbed high on his forehead as he cast her a scandalized look. "Francesca Cavendish, did you just propose to me?"

"I believe I did," she said, rather dazedly. "Wait. No." She lowered to one knee. Taking his hand in hers, she turned it over and kissed it over his scar. "Chandler Beaufort de Clanforth-Kenway. Will you make me the happiest woman in the world and marry me?"

"I would say yes but . . ." He placed a rather scandalized hand over his chest "Where's the ring?"

Before she could retaliate, he pulled her up and lifted her into his arms, kissing the wits right out of her. Once they were both breathless again, he pressed his forehead to hers.

"Is this what life with you is going to be like? You always one leap ahead of me and me trying to clean up the chaos?"

"Probably."

"Good. I think that anything else for us would be boring, don't you?"

"We can't have that." She pressed her ear to his chest, sliding her hands inside his coat and around his middle as she listened to his heart.

Their smiles collapsed as they looked out over the place that had forged them in fire.

"What would you like to do with Mont Claire?" he asked. "Do you want to rebuild?"

Francesca listened to the birdsong and watched a bunny disappear into the bramble that was once a well-manicured maze. The ivy-choked fountain still mirrored the sky, and the arborvitae lined the edge of the abandoned drive.

Was this home?

She looked at Ferdinand's tree and could have sworn she saw a little leg swinging there. Her heart ached, but not with the pain it once had.

"There's a big world out there, a great deal of which I still haven't explored," she said. "So many places that hold no memories or sadness, nothing but potential."

"Where would we go?" he asked.

"I would like to take a dogsled and touch the northern lights one day, and to race Arabians over the golden sands of the desert. I want to visit pirate wrecks in Antigua and volcanoes of Hawaii." She looked at him. "What about you?"

His expression was carefully blank, and then a look of wonder stole some of the cynical age from his bones. "I never really thought in terms of the future, but all that sounds like an extraordinary life we might have."

"So . . . we will sell this place, then, so we never have to look back, and let it finance a great many of our adventures."

He nodded, bending over to select a silver rock from the fireplace and slipping it into his pocket.

She tilted her head "A memento?"

"A keepsake." He pulled her to his side and led her toward the hallway they'd once used as an escape. "I love you, Francesca. But I want a reminder of Pippa, of that wild, willful little girl who promised me she'd steal my heart someday."

"You're never getting it back, me hearty," she said in her terrible pirate accent.

"Good. It's yours. Forever."

Don't miss the other books in **Kerrigan Byrne**'s
The Devil You Know series!

How to Love a Duke in Ten Days
All Scot and Bothered

Available from St. Martin's Paperbacks